Love Happens

Love Happens

Trenia D. Coleman

Library of Congress Control Number: 2006910181
ISBN: Hardcover   978-1-4257-4383-3
               Softcover   978-1-4257-4382-6

To order additional copies of this book, contact:
Xlibris Corporation
1-888-795-4274
www.Xlibris.com
Orders@Xlibris.com
36296

CONTENTS

Acknowledgments

I first have to give thanks to God Almighty for blessing me with this incredible gift. I continue to pray that I do everything in your name.

A special thanks to my wonderful husband, Chris, who has always supported me. A big thank-you to my husband and children, Gabriel and Brianna, for their patience in allowing me to write this novel. To my dear friend, Shirlene Zimmerman, for your honesty, support, and friendship. To my grandmother, Edith Cornelius, of Dubberly, Louisiana, for your never-ending love. To my mother and father, Betty Mitchell and Jesse Hill, also of Dubberly, Louisiana, for giving me the love and necessary tools to be successful in life. A special thanks to Ohio author, Vanessa Miller, for inspiring me to write my first novel.

This book is dedicated to my best friend who succumbed to Sickle Cell Anemia on March 18, 2000—Curlie Sharie Rambo of Ringgold, Louisiana.

—until we meet again . . .

INTRODUCTION

I t had been six months since Serena had broken up with Rocky. She felt like she'd gotten a new lease on life and vowed to enjoy each day as if it were her last. Tara had been asking her to go home with her to Georgia for months; but with Serena's work schedule and her relationship with Rocky, she could never find the right time to take off. Tara was going home for Memorial Day and invited Serena as she always did. This time Serena agreed to accompany her friend to Georgia, but never did she dream in a million years that she'd run into Antonio Walker. He was an absolutely gorgeous man she'd had an instant attraction to. Little did she know the gorgeous man turned out to be Tara's half brother. As they got to know each other during her visit, Serena also got to know Tony's girlfriend a little all too well. The attraction between Tony and Serena was not something that could be easily hidden, not even from Melissa. As Melissa tried to hold on to her relationship with Tony, she began to realize that Tony never loved her, not the way she loved him anyway, and was forced to use drastic measures to keep him. Serena knew Tony was unavailable; and as she tried to admonish herself for lusting after this handsome stranger, she realized that she had fallen in love.

LOVE HAPPENS

T hinking back to that spring night in May still sent chills throughout Serena's body. She thought it could only happen in the movies; she could not believe that it would happen to her—not until she met Antonio Walker. It was indeed, love at first sight.

It was late May, and Serena was excited about the upcoming Memorial Day weekend. She'd been working around the clock and completely worked through the last two weekends while stationed at Fort Sam Houston, Texas. Being in the medical field was very demanding, but being a leader in charge of soldiers in the United States Army had its advantages. So this weekend, she was going to do absolutely nothing but enjoy having four consecutive days off, and she knew just how to get her weekend off to a great start.

Serena enjoyed being stationed in San Antonio, the great historical city known for its River Walk, and being located in close proximity of the state's capital. She frequented Austin to go on shopping sprees with her friends or going to her favorite seafood restaurant Pappadeaux Seafood Kitchen. She and Tara had been friends for two years since being stationed in Texas. They had a lot in common and hit if off from their first meeting. Tara was also in the army and worked in the medical field. Both were single, enjoyed dating, shopping, traveling, and sports.

Tara was five feet two, smooth brown with large almond-shaped eyes. She wore a bob, and her boobs were her main attraction. She had lived in Georgia all her life until she joined the military two years ago. Fort Sam Houston was her first duty station. Her uncle had been in the army, and she liked to look at people in uniforms. Since going to college wasn't her number one priority, she enlisted into the USA for four years. Serena and Tara met at the gym during a basketball game. The girls bumped into each other the next day at the hospital's cafeteria on seafood Thursday, and they shared a table. This was when they discovered their fondness of Pappadeaux. Although most of Serena's closest friends had been males all of her life, she and Tara had no problems maintaining their friendship.

Serena's father, brother, and uncle had all been in the USA. Her father and uncle had both been in Vietnam. Serena had some college, but her heart seemed to have the desire to serve her country and follow in her father's footsteps. She joined the United States Army Reserves during her senior year in high school and planned to make a career of it.

Serena was about five feet three and had smooth creamy caramel skin. She was very athletically built and had been a tomboy growing up. Her attraction had been her flawlessly sculpted legs and her hourglass body. She had been blessed with a small upper body to include a twenty-four-inch waist, which was the sexual precursor for the introduction of her true blessing. Serena had always had a large butt, and it seemed as though no one else in her family had such a large attachment. She must've gotten mixed genes, and this was what was created; she always joked about it with her mother.

As Serena entered her favorite nail salon, she picked up a magazine and sat in the waiting area until Yongmi was ready for her. Yongmi was from Korea and spoke very good English. Serena loved Yongmi's attention to detail when doing her pedicures and manicures. She'd been desperate a few times when Yongmi was out and regretted it, so now she is known as Yongmi's client, and that's the way she wanted to keep it.

Well, it's Thursday, and the first sergeant had called an early formation, and they were released earlier than normal. Not having any plans, Serena decided to pamper herself by getting her nails done and thought maybe she'd catch a movie before matinee ended. Serena was sitting at the table letting her nails dry under the fluorescent light when her phone rang. She looked into her bag and tried to get a glimpse of the caller ID without ruining her nails but was unsuccessful. Serena wondered who could possibly be calling her. *Oh well,* she thought, *they'll call back if it was important.*

Serena was out of the salon in ten minutes and decided to drive by the theater to see what was playing. As she put her car in drive, her phone rang again, and she'd completely forgotten about the call she missed when she was in the nail salon. "Hello," Serena said as she caught the phone on the third ring. It was Tara, and she was headed home to Georgia. Once she found out Serena had no plans, she begged her to go with her. Tara had told Serena plenty of times that she wanted her to go home with her to meet her family. This would be a great weekend to travel home for Tara since she wouldn't have to report to work until Wednesday. Serena had always wanted to go with her, but their work schedules had always been the problem, but with this four-day weekend, only those who had twenty-four-hour duty were on call. Tara had attempted to make the drive home by herself several times, but fifteen hours was a bit much for one person. Instead of going home to Georgia, she'd visit friends in Shreveport. Serena contemplated the offer as Tara assured her that they would have tons of fun. "Well, it's not like I have plans that I can't break; sure, I'll go. When are you leaving?"

Looking at Texas in My Rearview Mirror

Since her breakup six months ago with her boyfriend of two years, she spent most of her time at the gym playing basketball. She had turned down a full-ride scholarship to a two-year college in Texas to join the United States Army. It was one decision she regretted; but at this point, there was no turning back. She always felt all things happened for a reason, and you had to make the best of any situation you were faced with.

Serena made Tara promise they'd be back on Sunday to recoup and have a whole day at home before going to work on Tuesday. Tara told Serena she'd stop by to pick her up after she gassed up her car. "What do you mean you're headed out now?" Serena asked.

"No, actually I was going to come over and beg you to go with me in person but thought I'd call first. How long will it take you to pack a bag?" Tara asked.

"Give me an hour to throw some things together and lock up the house." Serena had bought her first house at the age of twenty-two. It was a long and painful process since she was single. Being a black female didn't help her situation either, but it was all worth it in the end. It was a modest three-bedroom brick home not far from the base. She was very proud of her house and took very good care of it inside and out.

Tara was filling up her tank when she called her mom to let her know she'd be on the road by five thirty and that she was bringing Serena with her. It was a fifteen-hour drive; and when one wasn't asleep, they chatted away. It would be Friday at nine in the morning when the girls would hit Fairburn, which was located right outside of Atlanta. Tara had spoken with her mom and sister several times during their trip, and they'd decided to have a Friday-night fish fry.

By the time the girls arrived, the sun shone brightly; and they were exhausted. Tara had driven the first eight hours, which put them in Louisiana. Serena took over driving in her old stomping grounds—Grambling, Louisiana. Serena had attended a semester at Grambling State University after taking a break after high school. It felt good to be back in the area. There was nothing like watching the sunrise in the good ol' South. As the girls got closer to Fairburn, Tara knew she would have to take the wheel to get to her parents' home. Fifteen minutes after taking the wheel, Tara pulled in her parents' driveway. As she crept quietly up the graveled driveway, she came to a halt and smiled as she looked around at her old neighborhood. Tara's family had twenty acres of land, and her relatives were spread out all over the land. Before Tara could put the car in gear good, the front door burst open; and her baby sister Tonya was running full speed headed straight for her. Tara and Tonya hugged and giggled, showering each other with compliments. Tonya's hug was one that said, "Sister, it's good to have you home." It was good to see sisters so happy to see each other. Serena never had any sisters, and she often called her close friends sister. Having a sister was something she had always longed for. Before Serena could finish her thought, Tonya was headed for her as Tara attempted to tell her who Serena was.

"I am so happy to finally meet you," Tonya told Serena.

"Likewise, I've heard so many wonderful stories about you," Serena said approvingly.

"Are you girls gonna stand there and giggle all morning, or do you think you might be able to give an old man some love too?" Tara immediately started laughing; and before she spoke another word, Serena knew exactly who was speaking before she turned around. She saw Mr. Danston standing on the porch with his arms folded. He was a handsome middle-aged man who looked like he could've played football back in his day. Tara and Serena turned and headed to the porch as Tonya ran ahead of them. Tara had forewarned her about her father who had a keen sense of humor and was always laughing. Serena knew immediately where Tara had gotten her outlook on life. As the girls approached the porch, Mr. Danston gave Tara a big bear hug and a kiss and called her baby girl. Without missing a beat, he reached over and pulled Serena in for a warm hug as well.

"Miss Serena, welcome to my humble abode; please come in and make yourself at home." He led the girls inside and began asking them about their trip. Five minutes later, Mrs. Danston emerged from the back room dressed in her hospital uniform.

"Hey, baby." She walked toward Tara as they met for yet another hug and kiss. Tara's mom made her promise not to let another two years pass before she came home again, and Tara obliged. Tara turned to look at Serena as Mrs. Danston headed over. The soldier in Serena forced her to extend her hand to greet her, but Mrs. Danston ignored the gesture and offered her a warm hug instead.

"It is so good to meet you. I'm glad you girls made it here safely." Serena knew immediately she was looking at the woman Tara would look like in another twenty years. The resemblance was so strong that they could have passed for sisters.

"There are some bagels and cream cheese in the kitchen. I've got to get to work before I'm late. Tonya, don't forget you need to have your chores done before Beverly comes for the sleepover," she yelled toward the back of the house. Tonya was going to sleepover at Beverly's house tomorrow.

Tonya responded, "Yes, ma'am, I will."

"I'll see you girls this afternoon," she said over her shoulder and headed for the door. Mr. Danston was already headed out the door behind her with her bags.

Wow, what an introduction, Serena thought. She already felt like part of the family. "Your family is awesome," she exclaimed, turning to Tara.

"Yeah, they're all right; let me show you around," Tara offered.

The girls took a tour of the four-bedroom home that had recently been remodeled and now was a five-bedroom home with a sunroom that sat on nearly two acres. As Serena looked at the family portrait, she saw a picture of Tara when she was a baby and also saw the resemblance Tonya and Tara shared. Tara had her mom's smile but her father's eyes and, of course, his sense of humor. Tara had mentioned her older half brother who lived in Columbus, Georgia. There were no pictures of Tony, but she felt she would have the same rapport with him as she'd had with the rest of the family. Mr. Danston had Tony from a previous marriage and was fortunate enough to play a part in his life because Tony and his mom lived nearby. This allowed Mr. Danston to be there for his son as much as he needed to, and the girls were able to grow up with their big brother watching out for them.

It was nine o'clock when the girls decided to take advantage of the bagels and cream cheese. Mr. Danston had left shortly after his wife. He was a truck driver and had to take his truck in for a service, so the girls would have the house to themselves. As they finished up in the kitchen, they headed back outside to Tara's Honda Civic to grab their bags.

Since they'd been on the road all night, they both were a little tired, so they agreed to get a nap before the fish fry. Mrs. Danston had left a small grocery list on the refrigerator and money to cover the expenses. After reviewing the list, Tara made plans as to how they'd spend their day in town.

ONCE-IN-A-LIFETIME CHANCE MEETING

The girls awoke to the phone ringing, but neither of them made an effort to answer it. There was a knock at the door, and Tonya stuck her head in and asked Tara if she could go by Rite Aid and pick up their grandmother's prescription.

"Yeah, find out what time she needs it and tell her I'll bring it over." After the girls washed up, they headed into town to grab a bite to eat from McDonald's. The girls ran into a couple of Tara's classmates from high school. They joined the girls while they ate McDonald's fish fillet sandwiches and garden salads. Sheila and Carmen had invited the girls to go to the movies that evening.

Since it was only twelve o'clock, the girls decided to wash Tara's car. It still had bugs on the front and smelled of roadkill from traveling on the highway overnight. The girls believed in working out, taking care of their residences, and keeping their cars clean. Serena loved having the freedom to wash her car at will in her own yard and not have to frequent the local car washes. Washing her cars often took up to an hour each, and she believed in taking her time and doing a good job cleaning the inside and out. Serena loved the idea of pulling the cars into her two-car garage after washing them in hopes of preserving the clean look. She and Tara were finishing up drying her car when her phone rang. It was Tonya calling saying Big Mama wanted her to call her right away. Tara tossed Serena the ArmorAll to do the two tires on her side as she reached into the car to get her mom's grocery list. She probably wanted something from Piggly Wiggly as Tara searched for a pen. She dialed her grandmother up as she took a seat in the car. "Hey, Big Mama, how are you?" Whatever news Tara received from her Big Mama, it was definitely good news; and she was eager to hear what was going on. Tara talked for a few more minutes and got off the phone and was beaming.

"Hey, girl, what's going on?" Serena asked.

"My brother, Tony, is coming in this evening from Columbus! I have not seen him in almost three years. Tara and Tony had sent each other pictures over the years, but that wasn't like seeing someone in person."

She was so excited that Serena felt happy too and couldn't wait to meet Tony. The girls soon left the car wash and were on their way to Rite Aid and the local grocery store to pick up the items for the fish fry.

On their way from town, Tara took Serena on an abbreviated tour of Fairburn; and Serena fell in love with it instantly. "Oh, this reminds me so much of home." Home for Serena was Tulsa, Oklahoma. Both the girls had a love for southern living.

Serena's mom would always say, "There's nothing like southern living." Watching the moon and the stars and the sun set and rise was a powerful reflection of God's power, and something Serena learned to appreciate at an early age.

During the drive, Tara filled Serena in on how she first met her half brother. She described how close they were coming up and how her mom accepted him as her own. Tony lived with his mom not far from Fairburn until he moved away to Columbus a few years after high school. They kept in touch but didn't see each other as often, with him being a firefighter and her being in the military.

Pulling into the driveway, Tara got quiet when she spotted a blue truck parked under the carport. "That's Tony's truck," she shrieked. "I can't believe he beat me here." She was so excited she threw the car in park and almost ran into the house. Serena was a few steps behind her in a slow jog, feeling the excitement too. They knocked on the door, and Tara barely had the patience to wait for the door to open. Her face was lit up like a kid at Christmas, until a young lady opened the door to Tara's surprise. She introduced herself as Melissa, Tony's girlfriend. Tara introduced herself and Serena and began looking for Tony. "Oh, he's in the back helping his grandmother," offered Melissa. After speaking, Serena took a seat and began watching the basketball game that was on the television in the living room. Tara went to the back to take her grandmother her medication. It sounded as if they were moving furniture around.

Serena and Melissa made small talk about the weather. Serena having a background in sports was excited to catch an NBA game in the first half. The Miami Heat was going up against the Chicago Bulls. She loved both teams, but she especially loved to watch Shaquille O'Neal. Terry Jones had a pretty decent game also, but Shaq was her man.

Having gone to school at Grambling while he was at Louisiana State University was a wonderful experience. She'd watched him play several times and was fascinated by the way he ruled the court on offense and defense. He was the ultimate player. When she first arrived at Fort Sam Houston still in a training status, she was helping buff floors and offices in a building on the base and had to enter one of the occupied offices there. As she was moving some items around, the sergeant came in, and they struck up a conversation. Both of them loved basketball, and there on his wall was a picture of Shaq. She asked him why he had a picture of Shaq on his wall. Little did she know that he was Shaquille O'Neal's stepfather. She did not believe him at first because of the difference in the last names; but after telling her things only a close friend or family would know about Shaq, she knew that what Sergeant Harris had told her was indeed the truth. They both got a big laugh out of the whole ordeal especially when she offered a challenge to Shaq through his father.

Serena had almost forgotten where she was when Melissa was staring in her direction as if she was waiting on her to say something. "I'm sorry, did you say something?" Serena asked.

"Oh yeah, I was just wondering where you were from."

"Originally I'm from Oklahoma, but I'm stationed in Texas." Melissa immediately looked surprised but never explained why.

"Well, actually Tara and I are stationed together in San Antonio."

That was the first of many intrusive questions, some of which she didn't answer truthfully. She was happy to see Tara emerge from the back with Big Mama following. They held hands as Tara led her over to Serena. They shared a warm embrace, and Big Mama invited them to stay over while she finished preparing a snack. She and Tara agreed that they could snack on a little something since they already had lunch at McDonald's. *Washing the car worked up an appetite,* Serena thought as they accepted the invitation. Serena asked to use the bathroom, and she was led into the bathroom up front. Again, she heard furniture being moved and figured it was Tara's brother again. Before she came out of the bathroom, she heard the doorbell ring and soon heard several male voices laughing and talking loudly. When she made it back to the living room, there was an audience; and she was the main attraction. She was standing there facing three young men, and she immediately focused on the one in the middle. The one who stood out the most was about 5'11, 175 pounds, beautiful brown eyes, medium brown complexion, very nice hair, and teeth as white as snow, and oh, the smile was breathtaking. She didn't know why she focused on him, but she couldn't take her eyes off of him, and he seemed to be intrigued by her entrance as well. She was completely taken aback by her reaction to him. She wondered if anyone else noticed, and she hoped she wasn't making a spectacle of herself. Tara quickly introduced her to their friends from high school who were Tony's classmates. She told them that they were stationed together in San Antonio. Then she introduced her to Tony who was standing between his two friends. Her mouth hung open, and she felt so silly. The entire time she had been salivating over this fine young man right in front of Melissa, and it was Tony the whole time. "Oh," she said, very surprised, "you're Tara's brother. It's very good to finally meet you." She shook his hand. Upon shaking his hand, a warm feeling erupted within; and her heart actually skipped a beat. She had heard of this happening before but never to her. Her heartbeat was pounding so loudly that she just knew everyone else could hear it too. It played like a drum in her ears, and all she could do was stare into Tony's face. She tried to control herself; she realized they were still holding hands. She was too embarrassed, so she tried to recover by saying, "Tara's told me a lot about you." *Did I already say that,* Serena thought. This was becoming a bit awkward, not to mention embarrassing.

Tony smiled and said, "I hope it was all good," with a look that she couldn't read but made her nervous.

She was sure glad when Melissa stood up to join the introductions. Tony turned to his friends, Derek and Vincent. "This is Melissa." From the look on her face, she was expecting a more informative intro. Not hearing the word "fiancée" made Serena feel light inside. *Maybe they are just friends,* she thought to herself. *Why does he have to be*

Tara's brother, and more importantly, why does he have to belong to Melissa?
He doesn't look anything like Tara or her sister; I guess being a half brother
only makes sense. Her mind was still reeling over the shock of meeting
Tony that she was startled to hear Tara call her name. She wondered
if Tara had to repeat her name.

It was time to eat—maybe this was the break she needed to
pull herself together. As they all sat throughout the kitchen and
spilled into the living room, she got to know a little more about
Derek and Vincent. They decided to stay and eat some of Big
Mama's famous meat pies after all. Derek, Vincent, and Tony had
played on the football team together during high school and were
inseparable. Derek and Tara had gone to her senior prom together
and dated on and off for several months after high school. Serena
really enjoyed the meat pies and wondered what Big Mama put
in them. They were delicious, and it took no time for the group
to demolish them.

As Serena listened to the old friends catch up, she enjoyed
listening to Tony speak. His voice was very distinguished, and she
loved the drawl on his southern accent. The entire time sitting
around the table, Serena found her hands shaking and clammy. She
tried to steal looks at Tony as much as naturally possible like when
he was talking, but she didn't want to draw attention to herself. She
was completely embarrassed by her demeanor and hoped no one
noticed how out of place she felt. She even caught Melissa looking
in her direction from time to time.

"So, Serena, how did you and Tara become such good friends?"
Vincent asked.

"Well, actually we have a lot in common. We both love sports,
and we have a lot of the same habits. Well, one day we were at the
gym, and there was a pot of about $250 on the best two-man team
that could make the most three-point shots. Well, Tara now tells
me that she'd seen me play before, but I'd never met her or seen
her in action on the court. So we signed up for the contest. We
were the only two females on any of the teams, so naturally the
guys dismissed us as noncompetitors and gave us no respect. I soon
found out that your sister," she said, looking at Tony, almost losing
focus, "was just as competitive as I was. So to make a long story
short, we won the contest and the $250; and we split the money.
We then got props everywhere we went. That following weekend,

we met up at the mall and went shopping. From that moment on, we've been like sisters and play basketball every weekend unless one of us has duty."

They were all fascinated by her story. "So you girls got game, huh," asked Derek. They all knew Tara could play ball but seemed surprised that Serena had skills too. Sensing their hesitation in accepting the story she had told, Tara spoke up, "Yeah, Serena had a full ride to a college in Texas but decided to go active duty instead." They were all in awe while they processed what Tara said.

Melissa, seemingly wanting to break the spell, asked, "So what made you turn down the scholarship?" A look of surprise spread across Serena's face, and everyone listened as if she was going to divulge some deep, dark secret.

"I actually had a lot of reasons for wanting to go into the army full-time, but I don't want to bore you. I can say that I regret the decision sometimes, and the only thing that keeps me from being so down on myself about it is that I have been playing basketball for the post team since joining the army. We travel to compete against a lot of college teams, and it's almost as exhilarating as the life I would have lead in college. So I am thankful for the opportunity to be able to participate in the sport and work full-time too."

From the look on Melissa's face, Serena didn't think she was expecting that kind of answer. She knew from Melissa's expression that she wasn't finished questioning her though. The guys were going on about how cool it must've been to be in Serena's position at the time, and she simply said, "Well, you know everything happens for a reason, and I do believe that I made the right decision."

Tony was quiet and seemed to be concentrating on something intently. *Serena seems to be very sincere, and she has a wonderful outlook on life,* he thought to himself. "Yeah, my girl has it going on," Tara said out of the blue. "She has two cars and a new home; she's very talented, and she's doing all this by her damn self."

"What are you talking about?" Vincent asked.

"Serena is all that, and that's why she's my girl." The two girls exchanged glances and smiled. Tara knew she had been through a bad breakup with her boyfriend of two years, and they'd just broken up recently. He seemed to have a problem with her independence, and that led to the surfacing of other insecurities, and they drifted apart. This was Tara's way of letting her know that who she was or what she had should have never been a threat to any man—if he was a real man.

Melissa was at it again. "So what kind of cars do you drive?" she pried.

"Oh, I have a hooptie and a Nissan Maxima," Serena said with a curious frown on her face.

Melissa continued, more intrigued. "So what kind of car is your hooptie?"

"It's a '78 Chevrolet Monte Carlo," she said, a little annoyed. Before she could finish her sentence, the boys started laughing and joking. "That's not a hooptie, girl, that's a classic," said Vincent and Derek, and Tony agreed. She was beginning to feel like she was under a microscope, and Tara once again picked up on it and suggested they play a game of spades. The group was all for a card game. Vincent's phone rang, and he stepped outside to take the call. Serena was thankful for a reason to look at Tony from across the table since he'd asked her to be his partner. Stunned by his offer, she looked surprised when he asked her instead of Melissa. As if he could read her mind, "Oh, Melissa doesn't play cards," he explained as he glanced over in her direction. It took everything in her not to look as she accepted his offer, but she sensed there was some tension between the two. Tara partnered up with Derek. Tara and Derek had history, and it was obvious he was still interested in her by his comments. Tara later explained that she and Derek could never be more than friends, but she still liked his company. When Vincent returned, he started up a conversation with Melissa. Once Tony heard Melissa engaging in a conversation and laughing with Vincent, he seemed to relax a little.

After a couple of games of spades, Derek and Tara had had enough. They'd lost both games to Tony and Serena who dominated both games from start to finish. Derek and Vincent told the group that there was a dance on Saturday night at the VIP and extended an invitation to the group.

"Yeah, we just might do that," said Tara, speaking for both of them. It was three o'clock, and the girls had to go and take the grocery items home in time for the fish fry.

"Oh, is it the typical southern Friday-night fish fry?" Tony joked.

"You know it is; why don't you come over and join us. Daddy would be happy to see you. He's picking up a load in the morning and won't be back until sometime on Sunday."

Tony glanced at Melissa and said, "Yeah, that sounds good; we might stop by later."

"Well, make sure you come by before nine o'clock. Serena and I are going to the movies with Carmen and Sheila."

"Oh," Tony seemed interested but said no more. Derek and Vincent were headed to Augusta to play basketball and said their good-byes to everyone.

"We'll see you tomorrow at the dance," Tara said, and she waved good-bye.

As the girls hugged Big Mama good-bye, Tara asked Big Mama to come to the fish fry too if she was feeling up to it. Big Mama had started having problems with her legs. Tony had rearranged her furniture in her bedroom to make getting to the bathroom easier and the door more accessible. "I'll have to see; but if I can't make it, make sure you send a plate by Tony." Serena seemed surprised by her statement as if she knew that Tony would definitely be coming.

The girls said their good-byes as Tony walked them to the car. "So what movie are you going to see?" he asked while standing in front of Tara's car with his hands in his pockets, holding Serena's gaze longer than he should have, especially if Melissa was his girlfriend. As Serena got into the car, she said good-bye to Tony. He gave her one of those smiles and said, "I'll see you tonight." Not sure what he meant, Serena looked a little stunned as she slid into the front seat of Tara's Honda. Tony finished talking to Tara and turned to go back into the house. "Boy, I'll see you later," Tara said with a smile.

Watching Tony walk away was very pleasing to Serena's eyes. He was wearing some faded Levi's, and he wore them very well.

As soon as the doors closed, Tara said, "Tony really likes you Serena. He couldn't keep his eyes off of you." Serena contemplated the statement for a while before responding. Finally, she said, "Well, he certainly does have his act together. I think he's really nice too, but quiet."

"Girl, Tony is nowhere near quiet. I think he was just taking in all that was being said about you and checking you out the whole time." She exaggerated the word "whole." Serena could feel Tony's eyes on her, but she also felt Melissa's eyes, so she tried not to focus on Tony too much.

"Tara, what is up with Melissa? She was giving me the third degree as if she felt that was acceptable."

"Well, from what I can tell, that is her norm. She was so curious about you and what you had. She seemed to want to discredit you so Tony wouldn't be interested or something."

"Yeah, or something," Serena said. "Why didn't you tell me your brother was so fine?" She screamed. "I have never reacted to any man like that before. He is so fine, his teeth are white like pearls, and they're so straight, and his smile . . ." She let her words trail off. "Please don't let your brother come over tonight," Serena begged. The girls laughed together uncontrollably as they pulled out onto the highway.

Serena let herself drift in thought. *So Tara thought Tony was interested in me.*

It was five thirty when the girls made it back to Tara's parents' home. There were cars everywhere. They were lined up and down each side of the road. "Wow, this fish fry must really be a big event," Serena asked, and she stared in amazement.

"Yeah, you know when you say free food down South, that means bring your entire family to eat and your friends too." The girls laughed, but Serena thought Tara couldn't be too far off target. As the girls parked the car, they were greeted by several of Tara's cousins, then uncles, then aunts, and the list went on and on. Two of her cousins assisted them with taking the groceries inside. They already had the fire going and dominoes on one side of the yard and cards on the other. The music was blaring and it already felt like a party and it was just getting started. Serena felt the excitement and really felt like part of the family. They went inside and immediately washed up and helped Mrs. Danston with the green salad, punch, and iced tea. Once prepared, Serena placed the salad in the refrigerator to keep it cool until the fish was ready to serve. Mr. Danston had taken the seasonings they'd bought at the store out of the bags before the girls made it in the house. When they finished prepping things in the kitchen, he was calling for Tonya to bring out the foil trays to put the cooked fish on. Tara and Serena went out to mingle with her family and make small talk with Mr. Danston. "Dad, you know Tony's here for the weekend."

Mr. Danston was surprised. "Oh yeah, when is he coming over?" he asked.

"He's supposed to be coming over tonight for the fish fry."

"Oh, that's good 'cause you know I have to pick up a load tomorrow. If I'd known he was here, he could've been over here helping me with all this fish," he said with a chuckle.

Beverly arrived while we were chatting with Mr. Danston, and she and Tonya headed for the basketball court. Tara looked at Serena, and soon they were at the court too. They played two on two with the two ninth graders and showed them a few tricks.

It was seven o'clock when Tony and Melissa pulled up. Melissa had been in a funky mood all afternoon, and Tony didn't feel like making peace, but he at least wanted to be cordial. Big Mama decided to stay home and Tony promised he'd bring her a plate. As Tony and Melissa walked toward Mr. Danston, he spotted Tara and Serena on the court with Tonya and her friend. He immediately smiled to himself watching Serena handle the ball. She was very attractive, almost too attractive to be out on a basketball court. He liked watching her on the court playing around with the younger girls. She definitely had skills. Melissa spotted Mr. Danston and walked over to greet him, and Tony followed, trying to pull his attention away from the court. He warmly embraced his father and asked him how he was doing.

"Everything here is fine; how's everything with your mom?"

"She's doing well in Savannah and comes to Columbus every chance she gets to help with the house." Both of them started laughing.

"Do you need help with anything before I go inside to speak to Barbara?" Tony asked.

"Yeah, just grab another foil container on your way out. I'll need to pull this fish out in a few minutes," he told Tony.

As he greeted Barbara, he introduced Melissa to her as his friend. While he searched for the container, Melissa took a seat at the table and offered to help Mrs. Danston.

"Thank you, that's kind of you, but Tara and Serena have prepped everything, and I'm just cleaning up a bit," she said. "Where'd they disappear to anyway?" Mrs. Danston asked.

"Oh, they're out on the basketball court with Tonya," Tony said.

Melissa was surprised to hear Tony state that so matter-of-factly. She wasn't sure he'd noticed them when he walked up. Of course, she noticed them right away. As Tony headed out the door, Mrs. Danston asked Melissa to pass her the plastic utensils and paper plates out of the pantry. Tony walked over to the court after he'd dropped the pan off with his dad. Serena was taking a break on the sideline when he walked up behind her. She turned when she heard someone approaching and was pleasantly surprised to see Tony. He watched her face light up as she smiled, with a few beads of sweat on her forehead.

Um, she looks good even when she's working out, Tony thought as she spoke.

"Hey there, when did you get here?" she asked, feeling a little more comfortable one-on-one.

"Hey, lady, we just pulled up about ten minutes ago." They sat in silence and watched the girls shoot around. Tara joined the two after realizing what time it was.

"Serena, do you still want to hit the movies? It's already seven forty-five, and the show starts at nine fifteen."

"Yeah, you know I'm all for a movie even if it's the twilight show." They both laughed because Tara knew Serena was a movie buff and would be at a show at midnight by herself if she really wanted to see the movie.

"Okay, well, Serena and I need to go shower and change. We should leave no later than eight fifty."

Serena agreed. "That is plenty of time," Serena said.

"Yeah, I'm going to grab some food and take it back by Big Mama's so she can eat before it gets too late." Just as he finished his sentence, Melissa walked up. Having heard part of the conversation, Melissa was curious to know what she had missed.

Tara and Serena would meet Sheila and Carmen at the nine fifteen show at East Side shopping center. As they walked toward the house, Tara said, "I'll call the girls to let them know we're on schedule." Tonya and Beverly had rented two movies, and Tara was sure they would be up all night.

As the girls got dressed, their excitement was hardly bearable. This was Tyler Perry's first motion picture film, and it had been out one week and had already received extraordinary reviews. The girls were supposed to see the movie the first night it opened, but Serena had duty at the last minute, and Tara didn't want to see it without her. Tara always wore skirts and low-cut blouses to show off her bountiful upper body. She was truly blessed in that area, and she knew it. Serena had to give it to her she knew how to work it. She was a little self-conscious about her bottom half, so she avoided jeans. Serena on the other hand was tiny but cut up top with a twenty-four-inch waist and thirty-eight-inch hips. She had been termed as a shorty with an "apple bottom." Serena didn't particularly care for that description, but she'd heard it more than once and knew it was an accurate description. Tara had on a beautiful khaki skirt with a soft pink blouse with her hair tied up in a ponytail. Serena wore her favorite pair of low-rise jeans and a white sleeveless top with her favorite tan sandals. Serena had arms like Angela Bassett and sometimes had to cut back on her upper-body workouts when her arms began to look too masculine. Serena and Tara said good-bye to the family, and they left for the movies. Serena drifted off and ended up on Tony. He looked so good earlier today walking away in his Levi's and baby blue polo shirt. He had a very muscular back and arms and seemed to be in very good shape. It had to be from years of working out or credited to his current job as a firefighter. Her thoughts then jumped to his showing up at the basketball court unaccompanied.

Maybe I'm reading too much into it, but it was hard not to, she thought.

"Earth to, Serena," she could hear Tara say as if she had said it more than once.

"Yes, I'm—"

Tara interrupted her before she could finish her sentence. "I know you were thinking about Tony. I asked if you wanted to do anything special tomorrow. We've got the whole day to do whatever we want to since the party doesn't start until nine o'clock."

"No, I'm just here to do whatever it is you want to do. I am having such a great time with your family and friends, so whatever you want to do is fine with me."

"Okay, well, we'll play it by ear and not make any concrete plans."

"Sounds good to me," Serena said as she smiled.

The girls were waiting inside the theater when Serena and Tara pulled up at ten after nine. They'd already purchased the tickets, popcorn, and soda. As the girls headed in, Serena excused herself to go to the ladies' room before they went inside. Once alone, her thoughts drifted back to Tony. *Why can't I stop thinking about this man I just met?* She was really getting freaked out by the invasion of constant thoughts of Tony even in the bathroom. It wasn't like he was single, and she was certain of his desire to be involved with her. This was a first for her, and she wished she had had more time to talk with him. Suddenly the stall door next to her banged shut and startled her out of deep thoughts. She was still sitting on the toilet in a daze and instantly felt guilty and wondered if she had been thinking out loud and then wondered how long she had been in the bathroom. She glanced down and noticed black sandals with rhinestones. *Cute shoes,* she thought. When she walked out of the bathroom, she looked down to make sure everything was in order before she met up with the girls again. She looked at her watch, and it was nine fourteen, and the movie would be starting in one minute, so she quickened her step.

Oh, I must've gone to sleep on the toilet. How could I have been in the bathroom that long? she wondered. As she rounded the corner, someone stepped out of the men's restroom in front of her. She ran directly into him, and all they could do to keep from falling over was to hold on to each other. At that moment, Serena could clearly see that she was about two inches from Tony's face. He stared down into her eyes without saying anything at first. It felt as though minutes had passed before either one of them uttered a word. Finally, Serena said, "Oh, I'm so sorry. Please forgive me for not paying attention to where I was going. Obviously, I was in another world." She laughed. After processing Serena's apology, Tony smiled and said, "No need to apologize; I'd like to think we're here in each other's arms for a reason." He smiled even harder, but this time a hint of mischief was present. Tony's eyes bored into Serena's, not taking a chance of losing the moment; neither one could bring themselves to look away. Her thoughts were rushing around inside her head, but nothing came out. She wanted to ask him what he was doing there and so many other things when Melissa emerged from the women's bathroom, and she was wearing the cute black shoes. As Serena looked down at Melissa's feet, she knew she had been the other person in the stall. She walked up to them as if she wanted to interrupt whatever was brewing. Serena spoke as she released her grip on Tony. Melissa gave a sneer and a short hi and asked Tony if he was ready to go in. Serena said, "Yeah, I guess I'd better be going. Tara's waiting for me."

Tony spoke up, "Actually, Serena, Tara and the girls went inside and said to look for them in row 16."

"Oh, okay," Serena said. "Well, nice seeing you both again." And she started for the door.

"I think we're going to the same movie, so we'll walk in with you to make sure you link up with them." Melissa stopped in her tracks and looked at her boyfriend in amazement. She wondered just how much she'd missed during her bathroom break. She watched as Tony walked in the door behind Serena, and she followed. She did not like what she saw one bit and felt she needed to put some distance between them.

On their way to row 16, the lights dimmed; and Serena, still adjusting to the darkness, passed the row. Since Tony was accustomed to frequenting this theater, he knew exactly where row 16 was located. When he realized Serena had gone too far, he reached out without thinking and gently pulled her back toward him. Serena was clearly not paying attention to the seating. She was so enthralled by the thought of running into Tony the way she did. How coincidental? She was so embarrassed when Tony reached for her. "Thanks, looks like you've saved me once again," she said, smiling up at Tony with Melissa standing nearby.

"It's about time you got here; did you get lost?" Tara was joking.

"Sorry for the delay. I kinda got sidetracked," she said as she took her seat next to Tara. Serena wondered what would happen next when Melissa took off for a seat several rows ahead of them. Tony and Melissa seemed to be in an intense discussion as they took their seats.

As the movie started, Serena decided to put her thoughts on something else, anything else but Tony. She came to enjoy the movie and have a good time with her friends.

Tony couldn't stop thinking about Serena. She had been on his mind since walking into the living room at his grandmother's house. He had never been so captivated by anyone, especially someone he'd probably never see again after this weekend. He felt as if he was running out of time, and he had to get to her to be in her presence. She made him feel like a teenager again. Not many people have had that influence on him, not even Melissa. Melissa was a nice girl who made herself available. She was young and independent. That's what first attracted Tony to her. He wasn't looking to get serious or start a relationship when he met her, and that hadn't changed. The last time he'd told her how he felt, they got into a big argument about it, and now the subject doesn't come up anymore. Tony wanted this trip to be unaccompanied so that he could clear his head and spend some quality time with his family—not be under a microscope 24/7. He knew it was going to turn out this way, but Melissa got someone else to work her shift at the last minute, and here they were. He had no idea his sister was going to be in town or bring Serena, but she did, and now he felt like Melissa was watching his every move. Tony tried to put Serena out of his mind as Melissa asked him to get her popcorn before the movie started. After she tapped him on the arm and seemed to be talking very slowly, it occurred to him that she had been talking to him while he was in deep thought. He left for the snack bar still in somewhat of a daze.

Serena noticed Tony standing up as he headed up the aisle. She sat very still and held her breath as he headed straight for them. He stopped briefly to ask them if he could get them anything from the snack bar. Serena heard the question but was speechless. She could only manage to stare as she was so focused on his voluptuous lips. He leaned toward her as he was speaking so as not to disturb the other moviegoers. He didn't take his eyes off of Serena until he'd gotten a response from the others. Serena swallowed hard and had to restrain herself from reaching out to touch his face. As Tony walked away, Tara whispered, "Looks like my brother really has it bad for you." Focusing on the movie again, Serena smiled at Tara and returned her attention back to the screen to watch more previews. Serena was a very private person and didn't talk about personal things in front of people she wasn't sure she could trust.

As Tony reached the counter, he thought about his face to face with Serena. That was too close for comfort. He was so close to her as she looked up into his eyes. There is definitely chemistry there, and he practically had to pull himself away from her before he embarrassed himself. He reached for a napkin and asked the cashier for a pen as he began to write. The movie was about to start when Tony approached Serena and whispered something in her ear and placed a note in her hand. She was startled by his closeness once again, but she was even more stunned by the message he'd left with her. His breath was hot on her neck, and she could feel his body heat beginning to stir her insides. Serena's heart skipped a beat. She could hardly wait to see what was on the napkin Tony had so discreetly placed in her hand.

There was a lot of laughter during the movie. Serena found herself laughing and crying during some of the more emotional scenes in the movie. Tyler Perry's work had always had that effect on Serena, but tonight was more emotional than most nights. *I guess I have Tony to thank for that,* she thought to herself. The girls all enjoyed the movie and decided to split up. Carmen and Sheila were headed to a party, and Serena and Tara agreed to call it a night.

On the drive home, the girls were going on and on about the movie. They decided to stop by the twenty-four-hour Food Lion and pick up their favorite ice cream. Once home, they showered and enjoyed their ice cream while listening to some music down low. Tara's parents were asleep, and the girls were still up in the front watching movies. It was one o'clock now, and Serena had almost forgotten about the note Tony had given her. Melissa had made sure Tony got nowhere near her after the show. "Oh my god, where is it?" she screamed and began to look for her pants. She'd stuck the note in her front pocket and forgot to read it.

"What is going on, and what are you looking for?" Tara asked.

"I almost forgot your brother gave me a note in the movies."

"He did what? He's smooth because he got that one in without my knowing." The girls laughed as Serena opened the napkin and read Tony's writing.

It read, "I'll call you tonight." Serena smiled as she read it over and over again and noticed how neatly he had written the words. She was shocked that he would do something so bold as she turned to Tara. "How is he going to call me at this hour? He doesn't have my cell phone number," she exclaimed.

"Tony is smart," Tara said. "He knows that Tonya has a separate line and that he won't be disturbing my parents." There was an instant look of relief on Serena's face. "Tony's trying to lose Melissa so he can spend time with you," Tara said. "But I think ol' girl is suspicious now. She should know Tony by now. That boy's going to do what he wants to, and right now that is to be with you."

"Girl, are you serious? How's he going to lose her? He brought her home with him." Serena thought, *Well, if it's meant to be, it will be.* "I am definitely feeling your brother, but I don't want to cause any problems in paradise."

"Serena, please, Melissa is too clingy for Tony. A man or any woman for that matter needs some time for themselves every now and then." The girls looked at each other and smiled.

"Yeah, I hear you. Well, I'm really attracted to him too. I can't help it. Tara, you know me better than to chase after any man or go on and on about a man I've just met."

"Serena, you know what my brother needs?" Tara asked. "He needs a strong black woman to keep him straight, and I know you are up to the task." She smiled at her friend. The phone rang at one forty-five, as if Tony had heard their conversation.

Tara exited the room to check up on the girls out front while Serena spoke with Tony on the phone. Serena was thankful for the privacy as she reached for the phone. "Hello," she said in a hushed voice so as not to disturb anyone. Tony on the other end was startled at the sound of the sexy voice speaking through the receiver. He wondered if he had the right number. He waited, and she repeated it, "Hello . . . Tony?" There was hesitation, but then she'd spoken his name, and he was relieved. "Hey, lady, were you asleep?" he asked.

"No, but I was beginning to think it was a wrong number and was about to hang up."

"Oh, I'm sorry, I've just never heard your voice on the telephone before, and it didn't sound like you at first." Serena laughed but didn't push; besides, she was still smiling at the fact that Tony called her lady. She didn't know why he chose to call her that, but she loved hearing it.

"It was good seeing you tonight; you made my evening," he said.

"Yeah, it was good seeing you too. It was so unexpected but refreshing." They both started laughing thinking about their run-in. "So where's Melissa?" Serena asked. She knew it would put a damper on the mood, but she had to know where his head was. "Oh, she's asleep, and I am sitting out on the porch enjoying the moon," he offered without a hint of deception. Serena was surprised and immediately put at ease after hearing his answer. The question and his answer only made things more exciting. After making small talk, Tony and Serena both began to yawn. After all, it was three o'clock, and they'd been on the phone for over an hour laughing and talking about their childhoods. "I'd better let you go so you can get your beauty rest," he said. "I hope to see you later on, at the dance maybe?"

Was this his way of asking me out? Serena thought as she pondered a response. "Okay, I hope to see you there." They both said good night and ended the conversation.

By the time Tara returned to the room, Serena had drifted off. She smiled at her friend as she slept in peace. Tara hopped in the bed beside her and turned off the lights.

BLAST FROM THE PAST

I t was ten o'clock Saturday morning when the girls decided to get up. The house was quiet as if everyone was gone, or *Are they still asleep?* Serena wondered. Serena rolled over to find Tara gone too. She hurried to the bathroom to wash up and headed for the kitchen. As she entered the hallway, she could hear distant voices but couldn't make out what was being said or who was talking. No one was in the kitchen, the girls were gone from the living room sleeper, and the front door was open. The sun shone brightly, and she welcomed the nice, gentle breeze coming in from the outside. As she stepped outside, she heard unmistakably Tony's voice speaking low accompanied by laughter. It was too late to turn back as Tara said, "Good morning, sleeping beauty," to Serena. "Oh, good morning," she said as she walked out onto the porch. "I could've sworn—" She stopped in midsentence and stared at Tony sitting across from Tara, sipping on what appeared to be coffee. There was a Krispy Kreme donut box sitting on the table between the two of them. He stood immediately and said, "Good morning, lady," to Serena as he went over to greet her with a gentle kiss on the cheek. Serena was startled but accepted the kiss as it was meant to be and said, "Good morning yourself," with a warm smile. Her mind was spinning, and she wondered what she'd missed and how long he'd been there and more importantly, where was Melissa? Tony, sensed the tensed expression on Serena's face. "I just thought you might like some Krispy Kreme donuts since you only have Dunkin' Donuts back in Texas. I wasn't sure how you took your coffee, so I grabbed cream and sugar," he said with a forgive-me-for-not-calling-you look. Serena, picking up on it as she took a seat between the two of them, said, "Thanks, that was awful sweet of you. I love surprises!"

After making sure the girls were taken care of, he said, "Well, I'd better be going. I have to get the other donuts over to Big Mama's." He turned to look at Serena and said, "I'll see you later." Tara was looking on in amazement from Tony to Serena. "Okay, thanks again," she said as he turned to leave. Her heart began to feel a flutter as she watched him walk away. Tara was still staring at her when Tony had driven away. Serena watched Tony's truck until it was out of sight and then turned her attention to her friend who was sitting beside her still staring at her in disbelief.

"What is going on with you two? What just happened here?"

Serena laughed out loud. "I don't know."

"Did you two plan this, or was it really my brother's plan with a touch of spontaneity?"

"It was really a surprise for me. We talked about a lot of things last night, and Krispy Kreme did come up; I had no idea he was planning to surprise me with it this morning. Wow, that was really nice," Serena repeated.

"Okay, you had no idea. Well, he showed up this morning about thirty minutes ago with a dozen of mixed donuts. The girls and I were just about to start breakfast when we heard him knocking at the door. So we all ate donuts, and he and I had coffee while the girls drank milk. Now they're out playing basketball, and I'm sitting here looking at your glow and wondering what you've done to my brother. I've never known him to be such a gentleman catering to someone's needs in such a manner. This is mind boggling."

Serena's smile widened as she processed what Tara was saying. "What a way to start out your day; it's almost as good as breakfast in bed," Serena exclaimed. As the girls sat outside and enjoyed their breakfast, they developed a menu for dinner they would prepare for Mr. and Mrs. Danston. They both had to work; and since the girls had no plans until that night, they would treat Tara's parents to a night of romance. It would be perfect because Tonya and Beverly would be headed to Bev's house around three o'clock. Tara decided to make her famous chicken and rice casserole topped with cheese, garlic bread, and green beans. Serena offered to make her favorite 7Up pound cake, which was her family's recipe, and she totally enjoyed whipping them up. The girls would have to go to the grocery store and pick up a few items, so they planned to drop Bev and Tonya off on the way back. After conducting an inventory of the cupboards, the girls determined that they had everything they needed for the main meal except the garlic bread; and Serena needed to get butter, cake flour, vanilla flavor, and a can of 7Up for the cake.

After the girls straightened things up around the house, Tonya and Bev made a phone call to her house and packed their bags. Tara was prepping the chicken to go in the oven while Serena was looking for the recipe in her PDA. Although she'd made it numerous times, she always felt comfortable with having it nearby just in case. As she sat in the room thumbing thru files, she began to think about how wonderful Tony had been that morning. She hadn't asked for any of it but was sure thankful Tony had been so thoughtful. She was glad she got a chance to see him first thing this morning. Now she wondered if she'd really see him at the dance tonight. *He managed to get to me this morning, but had he forgotten he had brought Melissa home with him this weekend? Well, that's something I can't worry about right now. I am going to enjoy my time in Georgia regardless of what happens with this crush I have on Tony.* Serena found what she was looking for and went out to join Tara in the kitchen. "Okay, it's one thirty; if we leave now, we can make it to the grocery store and stop in at Coleman's and get a bottle of wine for tonight and still be back by three o'clock, no later than three thirty. Mama's due home at five o'clock, so that will give you plenty of time to get the cake started." The girls agreed on the plan, and soon the four were headed into town.

Thinking back to the look on Serena's face when she laid eyes upon him was exhilarating in and of itself. She was thoroughly surprised and seemed to appreciate the gesture of delivering her favorite donuts for breakfast. Tony smiled to himself and thought of how beautiful Serena looked upon waking up. He had noticed that she wore very little, if any, makeup; and he liked it. He knew that once he got back to his grandmother's, Melissa would try to find a way to keep him from going to the party. He was determined to go, and the guys were going to be there too. It'd be almost like old times. He hoped Sheila and Carmen wouldn't show up. They were Tara's friends, but he had his reasons for not trusting the friendship.

When he arrived, Melissa was sitting out on the porch with his grandmother in her favorite swing. Tony had already mentioned to

Melissa that he was going to pick up donuts for breakfast. It looked like they were already sipping on their coffee when he walked up to deliver the donuts. He kissed his grandmother and took a seat in the rocker next to the swing. They sat in silence and enjoyed the sun and the peacefulness of the South and most of all the Krispy Kreme donuts.

MY OLD LOVE

Tara and Serena chatted about what they were wearing to the dance that night while Tonya and Beverly contemplated going to the mall later. Serena never mentioned whether or not she was concerned about Tony and Melissa showing up for the dance, but Tara knew it was on her mind. The girls pulled into the parking lot at Food Lion, and all had a list of items to get. On the way over, Tonya and Bev decided to make nachos and brownies for later. Once inside, they split up and agreed to meet up at the register in ten minutes. Since Tara only had a few items to get, she was at the register waiting when someone came up from behind and covered her eyes saying, "Guess who?" The voice sounded familiar, but it had been a while since she'd heard it. Whoever it was had nice male hands, and there was no wedding ring on his left hand. Tara had not had a steady relationship in three years. She had been dating but no one seriously. As Serena rounded the corner with her basket, she saw Tara standing by the express line. She also noticed the handsome tall stranger standing behind her laughing while he was entertaining himself with the guess-who game. As she approached, she could tell Tara was not sure of whom she was playing this game with, so she made her presence known to Tara and the handsome stranger. He looked familiar, but Serena knew no one from Georgia except the people she'd met earlier that day. "Hi, I'm Serena, and you are?"

"Oh, I'm an old friend of Tara's; we actually went to middle school together." As Tara listened to the hints, she was thinking hard about who this person could be—he was at least six feet tall and had very nice arms.

Who could this possibly be from middle school? She was racking her brain. *There was only one guy I was interested in middle school, but he was*

39

too occupied fighting off the girls and playing sports to have time for me. Nah, she tried to convince herself, *it couldn't be him. The last time I saw him, he was not much taller than me.* She decided to take a stab at his identity and said, "Well, the only person I had any interest in during those years was the star of the basketball team."

"Go on," he said. It suddenly occurred to Tara that this could actually be Terry from Stone Mountain High School. "Well, the person I'm thinking of is Terry Jones who actually moved away to Florida and got a full ride to Miami State." As she gave a name to the handsome stranger, he released her, and she turned around to see the Terry Jones she'd known as a teenager but was now a full-grown man, and boy, was he beautiful. They embraced as Tara let out a scream and wrapped her arms around his handsome strong neck.

"What are you doing here?" she asked.

"I should be asking you the same thing. What brings you home?" he asked.

"Well, it's been a few years, and being stationed in San Antonio has kept me busy."

"Oh, you're in the military. That's great. I'm sorry, go ahead."

"Well, I'd been trying to get here for the last several months, and finally my friend"—she turned her attention to Serena—"and I got our schedules to coincide, and we decided to come down for Memorial Day."

Terry turned to Serena and shook her hand. "Nice to meet you," they both said.

"Now, what are you doing here? I thought you were in Florida."

"I am actually still in Florida and am now playing with the Miami Heat."

The two of them started laughing.

"Yeah, I know, my baby sister keeps me in the loop on all the NBA happenings. It must be amazing to be out there on the court with Shaq."

"Yeah, it's awesome, and I wouldn't trade it for anything in the world."

"I knew you would make it big; congratulations on all of your success."

"Yeah, maybe you and your friend, Serena, can fly down to one of my games. I'll get you some really great seats. I'm just in town to do a ribbon-cutting ceremony at the new boys and girls' club in Stone Mountain."

"Wow, that's very admirable; how did you get selected for that?"

"Since I had been a member of the club since I was a boy and because of what I do for a living now, the city is actually naming the center after me," he said, sounding modest.

"Well, congratulations are in order again. I'm very proud of you," Tara said. "That must be very flattering to see something named after yourself."

"I think that is truly remarkable to be able to give back to the community," Serena chimed in.

"Yeah, I'd do anything for the club. I mean, how could I say no?" He smiled. "So, changing the subject, how long are you in town for?" he asked Tara.

"We'll be here until sometime tomorrow."

He reached into his wallet and pulled out a business card. "Here, take my card and give me a call if you get a chance to later on today."

"Sure," Tara said, taking the card. "It was great seeing you again."

"Yeah, you too," he said with a laugh as he walked away.

Tara noticed that the Terry she'd known had grown into an extraordinary man who stood about six feet four inches tall. The girls finally joined them at the register. As Tonya ran up to Tara, she asked, "Was that Terry Jones talking to you?" She knew her sister ate, drank, and slept basketball. "Yeah, that was Terry Jones all right." The girls were going crazy, and Tara somehow managed to get everything on the belt to the cashier and paid for their items. As the three of them talked about the star they had just seen, Tara still seemed to be stunned and was moving toward the car. When they got in the car, Tara just sat there not moving and not saying anything. "Tara, are you okay?" Serena asked. She didn't answer at first. Tonya spoke up from the back, "Do you want me to drive us to Bev's?" Finally, she spoke up, "Yeah, that might not be a bad idea." Tara and Tonya switched places, and Tonya was overjoyed that she got to drive her sister's car. She had been driving for just over a year, and it was normally her dad's old truck. So this was a change of pace for her, and she didn't want to mess it up. She eased out into traffic while Serena looked on, trying to help in any way. She couldn't help but think about her friend in the backseat. The girls listened to the radio on the way to Beverly's, but Serena couldn't take her mind off of Tara who still seemed to be dazed and had not uttered a word. Tonya pulled into Bev's driveway, and the two girls got out and went to the back to get their bags out of the trunk. Serena got out also to help the girls with their bags. Tonya hugged Serena, and Bev followed suit. "Hopefully, I'll see you tomorrow before you leave," said Tonya. Tara had gotten out of the car with the girls' bag of groceries and came around to hug the girls too. "You feeling better?" Tonya asked. "Yeah, I'm all right. You girls have a good time tonight and be safe," she said. She then took her seat behind the wheel and looked reassuringly at Serena. Serena looked over at her friend and said, "You wanna talk?" "Maybe later," Tara said. Tara waved good-bye to the girls and backed out of the driveway.

As Tony sat in front of the television set and watched the local news, he sat and stared in amazement when the sportscaster showed a segment where they were interviewing Terry Jones of the Miami Heat. Tony had not seen Terry nor thought of him since he left Fairburn after his senior year. He was surprised to hear that Terry was in town until Tuesday. His thoughts drifted off back to the day when Tara was betrayed by him, and he instantly felt his pulse quicken. Tony no longer held Terry solely responsible for what happened to Tara; but had he not tried to take advantage of his sister during her freshman year, her reputation would not have been tarnished.

Beverly's parents had a really nice brick home with a four-car garage, which sat on at least five acres of land. There was a bridge beside the house leading to a lake. On the opposite side of the house was a full basketball court, which sat next to the pool house and pool. *They were doing quite well for themselves,* Serena thought as they drove away. Now that Tara was coming around, Serena was able to see the beauty of Stone Mountain. Tara began to point out different places to Serena, and Serena was pleased to have her friend back. The girls enjoyed the scenic trip home.

Pulling away from the Food Lion, Terry looked in his rearview mirror and saw Tara crossing the street. She looked as good as she did in middle school as he smiled at the thought. He and Tara had been really good friends before they decided to cross the line. They both played basketball, and Tara enjoyed softball while Terry ran the hundred-meter hurdles in track. Before that night, he felt that he and Tara would be dating throughout high school because of their great relationship. Things were going well until the incident with Sheila happened. He pondered over the pain and agony his mistake put Tara through. Terry knew it would have been detrimental to Tara and Sheila's friendship to divulge the information he was holding on to. He had not heard anything about Sheila in years and figured she'd moved away from the area. Tara's a strong and independent grown woman now, and he was beginning to wonder whether or not bringing up the past would be welcomed or a disaster. *Surely, Sheila still had no control over the situation,* he thought as he drove away.

It was three forty-five when the girls pulled into Tara's driveway. "A little behind schedule, but the chicken should be almost ready to come out of the oven. By the time you prepare the cake, I'll be out of your way," Tara told Serena. Tara's father was out on his riding lawn mower and waved at the girls. The girls pulled out the groceries and made their way inside the house. Serena started prepping the cake immediately. They wanted everything to be perfect before Mrs. Danston got home. Tara chopped up the chicken while the rice was cooking and excused herself. Serena figured Tara was getting prepared for the dance, so she took control over the kitchen, and soon her cake was baking in the oven. She knocked on the bedroom door before she entered out of courtesy, but she got no answer. "Tara," Serena called out to her friend, "where are you?"

"I'll be out in a minute," she yelled from the closet.

Serena began to gather her things together for that night. For the first time since this morning, her thoughts had not been full of Tony; and she thought maybe the initial infatuation phase was dying out. This pleased Serena, and she turned on the music while she headed for the shower.

It was after basketball practice when Tony decided to do what any brother would do and confronted Terry about the rumor going on about Tara. After speaking with Terry, to Tony's surprise, Terry had a complicated and somewhat far-fetched story to tell, which was hard for Tony to believe the first time he'd heard it. But after he started observing the person involved, he knew Terry was telling the truth. This incident was very damaging to Tara as a teenager, but Tony felt the truth would have been too traumatic for Tara to bear. So Tony was there for her as much as he could be while she was dealing with it all, and soon that year was behind them, and Tara was almost herself again.

Tara was still sitting on the bed with a shoe box opened with letters and pictures spilled out over the bed when Serena came out of the bathroom. "Hey, Tara, what's going on?"

"Oh, just going back down memory lane," she said as she shared her pictures with Serena. Serena sat beside Tara and began looking at old pictures of Terry and Tara and of Tara, Sheila, and Carmen. Tara laughed and said, "We were the three musketeers—absolutely inseparable. When I wasn't with Terry, I was always with the girls." There was a picture of a much younger Tony posing for the picture, shooting a basketball. He wore an Afro and appeared to be a little heavier. There was a second picture of Tony. This one was a school picture, and Serena was fascinated to see that he'd possessed that beautiful smile even in his earlier years. There was also a group photo of the three musketeers: Terry, Tony, and Vincent. When Tara realized Serena had recognized Tony's pictures, she laughed. "Tony would kill me if he knew you'd seen these." Looking at the photo, she said, "You know, Tony never really liked Sheila. He was okay with Carmen, but he couldn't stand Sheila."

"Why didn't he like her?"

"Probably because she thought she was all that, and he disliked people who thought more of themselves than they actually were." There were several pictures of Tara and Terry at a school dance and at a basketball game and other snapshots probably taken around school. The two of them looked happy, and Serena decided not to ask questions but to let Tara tell her what she wanted to tell her and when she felt like talking. "He was my first love, and I was absolutely crazy about him, but so were all the other girls at my school, which made it difficult for us. We had been dating about six months, and I decided to lose my virginity to him. He wasn't a virgin, but I was, so it was very special to me. At that time, a lot of girls were 'saving themselves' for marriage or that perfect relationship; but I felt that Terry was the one I wanted to share that part of my life with. So to spare you the gory details, a few days after we made love, there was a letter floating around the school describing the incident; and it made me sound like a whore and that I was doing the whole school. You know I've always had more male friends than anything, and that of course made it worse. Naturally, everyone assumed I was sleeping with all the guys I was hanging with, and it was a very painful year for me. Needless to say, we broke up over it. He actually doubted my story about only being with him, and I was pissed because who else could have started such a nasty rumor. It took me the whole summer after that school year to get myself together, and I recovered quite well. I was thankful Stone Mountain Ninth Grade Center was only for one year and that we transferred out the next year. So I left a lot of what happened that year behind me. Just seeing him again today, I got down on myself and wondered why I decided to lose my virginity to him in the first place. I was way too young, and I guess I thought I would lose him if I didn't agree to have sex with him. I chalked that up to a bad judgment call and a learning experience. It still didn't take away the fact that I was deeply scarred as a result of having an intimate relationship with him. Terry denied starting this whole mess from day one, and his story never changed. To this day, I still do not know who started the whole thing. I gave up trying to find out because it was beginning to take over my life. I'm sorry I shut you out, but the shock of seeing him brought back all of those old insecurities and along with that the pain and trauma. I had to get myself together first. There was no way I could've talked about this around Tonya. She looks up to me and has no idea I lost my virginity in middle school. Now that she is about the same age I was when I lost my virginity, I've always encouraged her to practice abstinence until she graduated from high school or until she knew without a doubt that she'd met Mr. Right and they were going to be married. So I felt like I had to protect her in that situation, and I'll always be protective of her. I do not want anything remotely close to happen to her."

"Well, it took a lot of courage to share that with me. Thanks for trusting me enough. So you never talked to Terry about what really happened with the note?"

"No, neither one of us were mature enough to handle all of the rumors surrounding that night, so we just let things fall apart without a fight."

Just then Serena heard the timer go off on the oven, and she knew her cake was ready. "Hey," Tara said, trying to perk herself up, "that was a long time ago, and I'm over it now. I was just thrown off course by running into him today. Thanks for lending an ear." Serena said, "That's what friends are for." She patted Tara on the knee and headed for the kitchen.

Tara hurried to the bathroom after discovering it was almost five o'clock, and her mom would soon be home. She heard dominoes hitting the table in the distance and knew her father had found someone to play with.

As Tony recalled the conversation he'd had with Terry, he became angry all over again. He was surprised that he still carried the anger with him after all these years. When he and Terry met at the basketball court, Tony confronted him about the letter. Terry told Tony that he didn't write the letter and didn't know who did.

"How can you stand here and look me in the eye and tell me you didn't write it?" Tony asked Terry.

"Because you have to trust me. That is not my style, nor would I do that to Tara."

After becoming increasingly demanding of the whole truth, Terry revealed to Tony that Sheila had been writing him letters the entire time he and Tara were going out even after he told her to back off. The night that Tara lost her virginity, Sheila had been outside of Terry's window watching he and Tara making love. Terry explained that she seemed obsessed with him. He had been refusing her advances, and it seemed as if she became more and more determined to be intimate with him. Sheila was a beautiful girl with long thick hair that she often wore braided and had a reputation even today for getting what she wanted. Terry explained that after Tara left his house that night, he was getting out of the shower when the doorbell rang. His parents were gone for the weekend, and he figured it was Tara at the door. "Sheila was standing there in tears saying someone had tried to grab her while walking on the trail to her house. She saw my lights on and wanted to know if she could use the phone. Of course, I'm standing there in my towel, and she was becoming more and more hysterical. I reached out to her and held her, and soon the crying stopped. One thing led to another; and before I knew it, we were on the floor having sex. As soon as we finished, I was embarrassed by the whole situation and told Sheila she had to go and that it was a mistake. Now that I look back on that night, I know she was never planning to use the phone, and the whole story she told me she'd made up. I was trying to figure out a way to tell Tara what happened, but Sheila threatened me and became very violent if I were to ever tell her friend the truth. So I agreed to keep it a secret and went to school the next day like nothing happened. That's when the letter surfaced about what Tara and I had done and about her being with all those guys. I guess it was guilt that kept me quiet, and a part of me wanted to believe that Tara was cheating on me the whole time like the letter stated. Although the letter was supposedly written by Tara, I wondered about the validity of it. Tara stopped talking to me because she thought I had told someone about our night together. Of course, she knew the other part was made up, but she was more worried about what everyone else thought. I could tell she thought I was guilty and wanted nothing else to do with me. I wanted to tell her the truth so many times, but Sheila made it impossible because of what we'd done together. I messed up, and I was weak, but I still felt that I owed her the truth. Sheila threatened to make it seem like what happened was planned and I invited her over only moments after Tara had left. So you see, it was either leave well enough alone and let Tara stay mad at me or she'd find out that I slept with her best friend the same night she lost her virginity to me. Somehow I felt dealing with the rumor was better than Tara having to deal with double betrayal." Tony was in shock. Tara and Sheila had been friends since preschool, and Tara would give her last to Sheila or Carmen. Carmen and the girls became friends in grade school. They were inseparable; but after learning the truth about Sheila, he let her know he didn't care for her but never let on that he knew what she'd done. Now all these years later, he still felt that she was betraying his sister.

When Tara stepped out of the shower, she smelled the warm aroma of Serena's 7Up cake tickle her nose. The smell was so strong Tara's stomach growled as she tried to contain it. Looking over at the nightstand, Tara found a slice of cake and a glass of milk waiting for her. She smiled to herself and thanked God for a wonderful friend like Serena. As she finished the cake, she began to feel like herself again. She knew she only had minutes before her mom would pull up, so she slipped on her peach floral sundress with the back out and her peach sandals. The girls had planned to meet up with Carmen and Sheila to do some window-shopping and hang out at the mall before the party. Their time was cut short the day before when they went to the movies, and they wanted to maximize their time together.

Carmen had picked Sheila up to run a few errands before heading to the mall. On the radio, the girls heard Terry Jones was in town; and they both screamed with joy wondering if they'd get the chance to see him. "If we all hook up together, it'll be just like the old days before the split," Carmen said excitedly. They used to have so much fun together going to the movies on Saturday night and the skating rink on Sunday. "Those were the good ol' days," Carmen said. Sheila had been quiet and was staring out the window. She was deep in thought when Carmen interrupted. "Hey, Sheil, what's wrong?" she asked. Sheila offered a weak smile and said, "Oh, just thinking back to those days. We were such good friends, all of us. Life was so easy even though being a teenager we often looked at our parents like they were aliens or the enemy."

"Well, we're still all good friends regardless of what happened between Terry and Tara. Let's hope they've forgotten about the drama and moved on. We're all adults now," said Carmen.

"Yeah, you're right," Sheila said and returned her attention to the window. Carmen knew something was bothering Sheila, but Sheila was the type to keep things bottled up. She knew Sheila would talk about whatever it was that was eating at her in her own time. That was the way Sheila had always been, and Carmen respected that.

"Is that *the* Terry Jones you played ball with in school? He is a real legend." Melissa asked as she sat down by Tony.

"Yeah, we used to be pretty close during high school."

"Do you guys keep in touch now that he's all famous?"

"No, we don't go out of our way, but I'm sure we would hang out if we bumped into each other." Melissa had been asking Tony to take her to Putt Putt Golf since visiting it on their first trip to Fairburn. It was three thirty when they arrived, and there was nothing like the treacherous humidity the heat in the South can bring to any afternoon. They played a few rounds and decided to ride the bumper cars afterward. They were both worn out after being at the course for two hours. They welcomed the air-conditioned eatery next door as they grabbed a bite to eat. Tony realized he'd been so occupied with the thoughts from the past and his outing at Putt Putt that he'd not had much time to focus on Serena. He definitely wanted to see her at the party. He turned to Melissa and said, "I'm going to the party with my sister and friends tonight at the VIP."

"Oh, that sounds like fun. What time does it start?" she asked Tony as if she were interested in going. He looked a little surprised. Melissa never wanted to go out with him and his friends, let alone go to a party. That wasn't her thing, but Tony had a feeling he knew why she was interested all of a sudden. He tried not to show his disappointment and told her the party would start at ten o'clock. He left her in the living room watching the news while he headed for the shower and thoughts of Serena.

Tara found Serena and her dad setting the table and lighting the candles for her parents' dinner. Tara looked pleased that Serena was able to coax her dad away from his domino game long enough to help out with the surprise. "The chicken casserole looks delicious, Tara," her dad raved.

"Yeah, I think we did pretty good," said Tara.

"Did Serena let you sample her 7Up pound cake?"

"No, she wouldn't let me, said it would spoil my dinner. Do you think you could convince her otherwise?" They all laughed and heard the car door shut.

"That would be Mom," Tara stated. As she went out to usher her mom inside, Serena set the table; and Mr. Danston headed for the stereo. When Tara led her mother into the house, she was so excited and pleased that the girls had gone through all the trouble to fix her a full-course meal.

"You girls are amazing; this means the world to me." The music started as if on cue, and Mrs. Danston grew teary eyed. "Excuse me, I'll be right back," she said as she headed for the bathroom. Tara figured her mom was overwhelmed by the surprise and asked no questions. Mr. Danston assisted his wife to the table and pulled out her chair for her as if they were in a four-star restaurant. Serena was touched by this act of chivalry and immediately let out an ooh and aah. The girls laughed as they prepared the plates for Mr. and Mrs. Danston. The girls took their plates in the family room and watched BET while they enjoyed their home-cooked meal, and it was delicious.

On their drive to the mall, Serena had the chance to think about Tony and couldn't believe almost an entire day had passed, and she'd been so preoccupied with all the day's events that she hardly had time to think about him. Out of the blue, Tara said, "I think I'll invite Terry to the mall if he's not doing anything," as she picked up her phone and searched for his number. Serena guessed Tara had already saved Terry's contact info in her phone or she had committed it to memory. Serena smiled to herself wondering if those old feelings had resurfaced since their chance meeting earlier. They talked for a while and laughed as if all was forgiven, and she could see the tensed look leave Tara's brow, and it was soon replaced by a bright smile. After getting off the phone, Tara turned to Serena. "He's going to meet us at the arcade."

When Things Aren't As They Seem

The girls pulled up at the mall and looked around for Carmen's car. As they walked inside to the arcade, Tara's phone rang.

"Hello," she said, wondering if it was Terry standing her up.

"Hey, Tara." It was Tony. "Where are you? I called the house for you but got no answer."

"Yeah, Serena and I made dinner for the old people and decided to let them have the house to themselves tonight. We're at the mall right now meeting the girls to hang out. Why, what's going on?" Tara asked hesitantly.

"Are you coming to the party tonight?" Tony asked.

"Yeah, I plan to; what time are you showing up?" Tara asked her brother.

"I don't know yet; I'm trying to play it by ear." Tara knew Tony wanted to attend the dance unaccompanied.

"I should be there around ten o'clock, so look for me."

"Okay, I will." Tony was quiet, and Tara knew he wanted to talk to Serena, so she said, "Hold on, I'll get Serena for you."

He smiled and knew the girl on the other end of the phone truly had to be his sister. She was reading his mind now.

"Hey, Tony," Serena said cheerfully.

"Hey, lady, what have you been up to all day?"

"Just taking it easy. Tara told you about the dinner we cooked for her parents?"

"Yeah."

"It was great, and so we decided to hang out here at the mall until we head over to the party. Did Tara tell you she ran into an old friend today?" Serena was so excited.

"No, she didn't; anyone I know," Tony asked cautiously as he sat up.

"Terry Jones," Serena almost blurted out. "He looks even bigger in person," she went on. "I heard you guys used to play ball together."

Tony, not sure how much Serena knew, said, "Yeah, we used to be close." Tony started to drift in thought when Serena said, "Oh my god, he's here."

"Tara, look over at the stop sign, is that him?" Serena asked. There was a silver Lexus with twenty-inch rims turning and heading their way. A big smile spread across Tara's face, seeming to welcome the sight of Terry.

"Are you telling me he's meeting you guys at the mall?"

"Yeah, he's pulling in right now." Serena, noticing the change in Tony's demeanor, asked, "What's wrong, Tony?"

"Nothing yet," he responded as she tried to figure out what was going on.

"Okay, is there something I need to know? What's going on?" she pushed.

Man, she is very perceptive, he thought to himself as he heard himself say, "No, it'll be okay. Who else are you meeting at the mall?"

"Carmen and Sheila should be here any minute." That's exactly what he was hoping Serena would not say; but there it was within the next few minutes, all three of them would come face-to-face for the first time since their freshman year.

Tony knew he had to be there for whatever was to come. Melissa was still in the shower and would just have to understand. "I'll be there in ten minutes," Tony said; and before Serena could ask any questions, he'd disconnected. He told his grandmother that he had to leave and would be back as soon as possible and asked her to pass that message along to Melissa.

Serena stood there watching the second reunion for this couple today. Tara looked so happy to be in Terry's big strong arms. Serena didn't know what was going on with Tony, but she did know he would be there soon. As she walked over to meet Tara and Terry, she smiled as Terry picked Tara up off the ground and spun her around. They were close enough to kiss, but neither one made a move. Just as they welcomed her into their private meeting, Tara said, "You're already off the phone with Tony?" After hearing Tony's name, Terry asked, "So where is Tony these days?" Serena almost responded saying he would actually be there soon, but she refrained and let Tara explain that Tony was in town for the weekend from Columbus. Just then the girls turned to hear Carmen screaming as she ran toward Terry. As if the crowd already forming around the entrance to the mall wasn't enough attention already for Terry, Carmen's reaction to seeing him only exacerbated things. Now paying attention to the car parked beside Terry's Lexus, two big men in dark-colored suits stepped out of the Escalade adjusting their jackets as if they were strapped. They made it to the group's location within seconds as Carmen hung around Terry's neck as they embraced. Terry introduced his bodyguards to the group and let them know that these were his old friends from school. They held off the sightseers and fans while they finished talking. As Sheila approached Terry, Serena noticed how Sheila's body language had changed from being the usual flirtatious Sheila to possessing the demeanor of a choirgirl. Terry and Sheila embraced too; and while even that sent red flags up for Serena, no one else seemed to notice. Tara and Terry walked ahead while following the bodyguards into the mall. Serena was beginning to wonder if Tony was actually coming. Tara turned and looked back at Serena. "Aren't you coming?" she asked.

"Yeah, I'm ah . . ." She hesitated, not sure why. "I'm waiting on a phone call," she said, holding up Tara's phone. Tara immediately knew only one person would be calling Serena on her phone. She said okay and turned to go inside the mall with her friends. As soon as they were inside the mall, Serena began to look around the parking lot. She wondered whether or not Tony would bring Melissa. She mentally prepared herself to meet up with Melissa again. She wasn't too happy about it, but what could she possibly do? She was in Melissa's territory and knew she didn't have any rights to demand anything of anyone, especially Tony. As she watched for Tony's truck, she looked down to check the time when Tony came up from the other direction. She almost ignored him as he started in her direction. She was about to turn to go into the mall when Tony called out to her. Serena turned to look at the man walking toward her and was completely shocked to see Tony coming her way. She waved to him, and she waited eagerly for him to reach her. She was even more excited because he was alone. He looked really fresh with his faded blue jeans with a blue and white striped button-down. As he got closer, she could tell he had gotten his hair cut since she had seen him earlier. He looked really nice. As he approached, he flashed that million-dollar smile; and she melted. "What's going on?" Serena asked.

"Where's Tara?" Tony asked without answering her question.

"She's already inside the mall with everyone."

"Did Sheila show up?"

"Yeah, she was acting a little weird if you ask me."

"What do you mean weird, weird how?"

"She just seemed out of character when she came up to see Terry earlier. Maybe I'm just reading too much into it."

Tony seemed to be in deep thought once again and immediately said, "We've got to find them. I'll call Tara on her cell phone," he said.

Serena held up Tara's cell phone and said, "It won't do any good." He grabbed his forehead and looked worried. "Well, they're headed to the arcade. That shouldn't be too hard to find, right?"

"Okay, let's go," Tony said, grabbing Serena's hand and headed toward the mall.

Inside the food court, Carmen and Terry decided to stop for ice cream before going to the arcade. Tara was too stuffed from the big dinner and 7Up cake she'd eaten earlier. Sheila found herself very uncomfortable and nervous since arriving at the mall. *Why after all these years did this have to happen?* Sheila thought to herself. She could tell Terry was itching to come clean about the whole incident. Why did she agree to come inside the mall? She should have conjured up an emergency to get out of this. As she tried to figure a way out, the others talked about old times. It was only a matter of time before Terry would tell Tara everything, and she would lose her friend forever. As Tony led the way to the arcade, he noticed that Serena matched her stride to his, and they were tearing through the mall on a mission.

"Tony, will you please tell me what's got you so upset?" she asked. At first, he said nothing. "Here's the arcade," he said as he walked in ahead of Serena. Serena allowed him to search the arcade while she waited by the entrance as if they had planned their strategy prior to arriving at the arcade. As Serena tried to figure out what was going on, she felt Sheila had something to do with it; and Tony was determined to protect his sister. For this, Serena admired him even more for fulfilling his role as a "big brother." Tony exited the arcade looking left and right as he approached Serena. After a few minutes of silence, he said, "Did Tara ever tell you she dated Terry during her freshman year?"

"Yes, she did after we ran into him today."

"Did she also tell you that her freshman year was ruined by a couple of rumors that drove her and Terry apart?"

"Yes, she told me about that just today." Tony looked surprised and knew it must've still been painful for his sister to share such a traumatic time in her life with anyone. He was glad Serena was there for Tara.

"Well, Tara never knew how the rumors came about; but after some investigating, I discovered that her so-called friend had planted the letter."

"What? Let me guess—Sheila?" Tony nodded. "Why would she do something so awful to Tara if they were such good friends?"

"Sheila was jealous of Tara and Terry's relationship, so she slept with Terry that same night Tara had been over. When Terry told her it was a mistake and he had to tell Tara, she came up with this elaborate scheme to turn them against each other; and she was successful."

"That's why she's been acting so weird today. I'm so surprised Tara has not noticed."

"Yeah, it's going to break her heart to find out."

"Wait, why do you think she's going to find out? Is Sheila planning to tell her?"

"No, but I think Terry is. That's why I'm here. Terry actually told me about everything that had happened not long after the letter circulated. At that time, he felt Tara was better off thinking he'd boasted about their night together than to learn that not only did he sleep with her best friend the same night but she also started the rumors. I'm sure over the years he's felt like confessing to Tara, but the opportunity never presented itself, so what would possibly stop him from doing it today?"

"Does Sheila know you know what she did?"

"No, she and my sister were so close that Tara would've wanted to know why we couldn't get along and why I had done a 180 when it came to Sheila."

"Wow, that's gotta be a tough position to be in," Serena said.

"Yeah, well, I'll figure something out. I just felt that Tara would handle it better if I was nearby when and if it happened."

Serena thought about what Tony said; it made sense, and she was glad he was there with her.

"Okay, let's hit the arcade!" Carmen yelled as she stood up.

"All right, but, Tara, I need to talk to you alone," Terry said gently.

"Can it wait till after the arcade?" Carmen asked.

"Well, that's up to Tara." Terry and Tara were standing too when they noticed Sheila still sitting.

"C'mon, Sheil," Tara said, "what's up with you?"

Carmen saw the same odd expression on Sheila's face again for the second time today as she was waiting for her to respond to Tara's question. Sheila looked over at Terry and Tara. "I feel ill all of a sudden," she said, holding her stomach. Terry realized that Sheila knew he was going to tell Tara after all these years. He didn't feel sorry for her because she's had seven years to tell Tara but chose not to. Sheila looked as if she were going to throw up and ran for the bathroom. Carmen grabbed her purse and followed in pursuit of Sheila. Terry and Tara sat down again as Tara asked, "What do you want to talk to me about?" Tara had a good idea what Terry wanted to talk about; but after all these years, it was still somewhat painful to think about. Terry reached over and held her hands and had a very serious look on his face. He wasn't worried about anyone else overhearing the conversation, thanks to the secluded area they were in. He looked at his bodyguards, and they walked out of earshot of the conversation. Tara braced herself for what was about to happen.

Sheila was throwing up profusely over the toilet when Carmen stormed in. "Sheila, are you okay?" She went into the stall to hold Sheila and to pull her hair back so as not to get any vomit in her hair. Sheila couldn't respond. All she could think about was the hurt and disappointed look on Tara's face once Terry told her the truth. She could not believe this day had finally come, and yet she was still no more prepared today than she would have been seven years ago. Facing her friend and divulging her role of deception had been too painful to bear.

"I need to lie down," she told Carmen.

"Okay. Let's get you to the car. Can you walk?"

"Yeah," she answered, "but I feel really weak." The girls exited the bathroom and were about to head back thru to the food court, but Sheila couldn't face Terry or Tara, not knowing how much he'd already told her. "I need some fresh air," Sheila said as she turned and charged toward the exit door leading to the outside. There Carmen found a bench where she propped Sheila up as she reassured her that she'd be back in a flash with the car. Carmen pulled out her cell phone and dialed Tara's number but got no answer. She wondered if Tara had her phone on silent as she walked to her car.

Outside the arcade, Serena and Tony grew tired of waiting and decided to head to the food court for drinks when Tara's phone started ringing. Serena started digging in her purse for Tara's phone but didn't reach it in time. She pulled out the phone and looked at the screen to see "1 missed call." She figured it was for Tara and placed the phone back in her bag. As they walked by Finish Line, Tony stopped and said, "Let me go in to see if Tara's been in here." He walked up to the register and appeared to make small talk with the guys behind the counter. Serena began to worry about her friend and wondered how she would get through this.

Carmen reached her car and decided to try Tara again before she left the mall. She hated not being able to spend time with the group, but she had to get Sheila home. She dialed Tara again. This time Serena answered Tara's phone. Just then Carmen remembered Serena telling Tara that she was waiting for a phone call. "Hey, Serena," Carmen said, "where've you been?"

"I've been at the arcade waiting for you guys to show. Where are you?"

"Well, I'm actually in my car. Sheila fell ill, and she's on the bench waiting outside the food court's back entrance for me to take her home."

"What, is she going to be okay?" Serena asked, concerned.

"Yeah, I think so, but she said she needed to lie down. I was calling to let Tara know what was going on so they wouldn't be looking for us to return, but I totally forgot she didn't have her phone."

"Well, where is Tara now?"

"I'm not sure, but I left them in the food court. Terry had to talk to her about something, but Sheila got sick before we were clued in on the topic."

"Oh really, Tony's here with me. We'll head over that way now to see if we can track them down." The girls said good-bye as Serena tried to imagine what was going to happen next. She knew she had to get Tony right away. Carmen began digging in her wallet for the card Terry had given her earlier. She would try him on his cell phone.

Terry began with an apology to Tara. "I know I should've talked to you about this a long time ago, and I should have made you hear me out. I was a coward, and I'm ashamed of my actions." He was in midsentence when his cell phone rang. He looked at the caller ID, (205) 634-9999. He didn't recognize the number as he repeated it. Tara was surprised at hearing Carmen's number. "That's Carmen. Answer it," she urged.

"Hey, Terry, sorry to call on your cell, but I was trying to reach Tara, but of course she doesn't have her phone."

"Sure, hold on," he said as he passed the phone to Tara.

"Hey, Carmen, where'd you guys disappear to? Oh," Tara said. "Well, tell Sheila I hope she feels better, and I'll check on her tonight if it's not too late after the party." She hung up and handed Terry his phone back.

"Something wrong?" Terry asked.

"No, I think she'll be okay, but Carmen is taking Sheila home. She threw up all over the bathroom and felt like she needed to lie down." Terry kept his comments to himself and wondered if Sheila had finally developed a conscience after all this time.

Tony was still talking to the guys at the counter when Serena approached him. Whatever the conversation was about, it soon ended when Shawn and Corey laid eyes on her. Tony wasn't sure what the guys were focusing on, but they had obviously seen something of interest and began to come from behind the counter. "May we help you find something, anything, ma'am," Corey said as he walked up to Serena. Serena felt a little embarrassed to be getting so much attention from a man other than Tony in his presence. Tony turned to find Serena standing there. He had been so preoccupied with what was going on with Tara that he'd not really noticed how stunning Serena looked in her low-rise khaki capris and sky blue silk cami, which accentuated her beautifully sculpted upper body, but he did now. She had also changed her hair. *I guess she pulled her hair back for the dance, which actually made her look even younger.* Tony snapped out of his thoughts when he saw Serena's lips moving in his direction as if she were talking to him. Tony had been listening to his friends fall over themselves trying to assist Serena. Tony spoke up, "Hey, Serena, is something wrong?" The guys looked at him as if to ask, "You know her?" Tony picked up on their reaction and decided to introduce Serena to them. They shook hands, and Serena politely excused them by pulling Tony by the arm and leading him out of the store. She filled him in on the phone conversation she'd had with Carmen. Alarmed, Tony said, "We've got to get to her now!" This time they actually ran toward the food court. Upon arriving, Serena spotted the body guards and headed for them.

As Terry started with that night, he begged, "Please hear me out. You may never want to speak to me again, but I need to come clean with you about that night. Tara, I just want to let you know that I never meant to hurt you. After we made love and you went home, I had a visitor. I had just gotten out of the shower when I heard a knock at the door. Thinking it was you, I answered it. Well, one thing led to another, and I was unfaithful to you." Terry knew this was painful enough for Tara to hear, so he spared her the intimate details. "Well, right after that I knew I had made a terrible, terrible mistake, and I was trying to think of a way to tell you what had happened. I immediately told 'this person' that it was a mistake and that I had to tell you what I'd done." Tara begin to think back to that day as Terry explained what happened and tried to figure out who "she" could've been. She thought she and Terry would be together forever after that night, but the next day everything had changed. Now she knew why. "When 'this person' found out how I felt, she concocted this elaborate story and wrote the letter. Now that I think back, I know she had to have watched us from the window somehow in order to write such an accurate account of what happened between us." Tara's head was spinning now as she tried to put the pieces together. *Who could be so cruel,* she thought, *at the age of fifteen?* Tara felt hurt and relieved at the same time. Hurt because Terry had allowed himself to be intimate with someone else just moments after they'd shared so many intimate things. Relieved because she now knew that Terry shared what happened between the two of them with no one. "Did you believe that I'd been intimate with other guys during the same time I was dating you?" she asked as she braced herself for more pain. Terry was quiet for a while but eventually answered. "No, I didn't believe that, but I was feeling so guilty that I felt like I needed to believe you'd done something wrong for me to betray you the way I did. Tara, I hope you can find it in your heart to forgive me for standing by and allowing someone to come between us and hurt you so badly." Tara turned to Terry with tears in her eyes and said, "Why didn't you just tell me? We were such good friends. You should have trusted me more."

"I know. I just felt that with everything that had happened and everything that was in the letter, you'd suffered enough. I couldn't dare reveal such shocking details to you in the midst of your dealing with all that." Terry began to choke up. "What I couldn't tell you then would have changed your life forever; what I couldn't tell you then would have made you hate me even more; what I couldn't tell you then was that I slept with your best friend." There it was. It was finally out, and Terry was relieved. He watched Tara's face turn from an expression of pain to instant anger. "What do you mean you slept with my best friend?" She almost yelled. "What are you talking about? Is this person still my friend?" Terry put his head in his hands as he answered. "This can't be happening," she said as she began to replay everything that had happened over in her mind. At that time, she was only close with Carmen and Sheila; and they were there for her when she was going through all of the drama with Terry. Tara had lots of friends, but there were only two she kept in touch with even while living in Texas. She would make sure they talked once a month, sometimes more, and to think one of them had betrayed her friendship. Tara knew instantly which one of her friends had been there that night with Terry. She knew why her friend experienced a sudden bout of illness. She knew why Tony had all of a sudden started avoiding being around her. "Oh my god, this means Tony knows," she said aloud as she turned to find Serena and Tony standing a few feet away. Tara was so stunned by the news she didn't hear them walk up. One look at Serena and Tara knew that Tony had told her too. Tara grabbed her things and stormed out of the mall through the same exit Carmen and Sheila had taken. Serena knew Tara wanted to be alone, and she took a seat across from where Terry was sitting as he and Tony greeted each other. This was a lot for anyone to absorb. She had to put herself in Tara's shoes. She knew Tara was hurt, and she knew the next phase was anger. She needed some time alone to cool off before she went off. Serena was trying to calculate Tara's next move when she thought back to the conversation she'd had with

Carmen outside of Finish Line. "Oh my god, Tony, Sheila is waiting for Carmen at the back entrance of the food court. Tara's headed straight for her." Serena took off in a sprint. Tony processed what she was saying as he and Terry stood to race after her. "No, you stay here," Tony said to Terry. "She doesn't need to see you right now. I'll call you later." Terry said he understood. Tony was trying to catch up with Serena, but all he saw was her ponytail rounding the corner.

Tara reminded herself that what happened was in the past and they were all too young to make smart choices 100 percent of the time. She wasn't angry at Terry for playing a role in this whole thing. She was more disappointed in him because they were such good friends. Tara understood Terry's reasoning for not wanting the whole story to come out. At that time that could have destroyed Tara knowing she and Sheila had shared everything from shoes to clothes to makeup since they were four years old. That was what Tara could not excuse or forgive. It would be hard to hold sleeping with Terry against Sheila after all these years, but the constant lying and deceit could not be so easily forgiven or forgotten. She needed to gather herself. As she stepped outside, the gentle breeze felt good on her face. She headed for the parking lot and spotted Sheila curled up on the bench. She instantly forgot all of the sane thinking she'd just experienced. Yeah, she was mad at Sheila for lying, but she was mad as hell that Sheila invited herself over to Terry's house and practically begged him to sleep with her. The closer she got, the madder she became. Sheila had committed the ultimate betrayal. She'd had the audacity to spy on them from outside Terry's house and decided to ruin her *best friend's* reputation by spreading vicious lies. All of this and in seven years had not even attempted to tell Tara what she'd done. Tara realized the last seven years and maybe the years before also were a lie when it came to their relationship. Tara stood over Sheila, and Sheila looked alarmed. She could tell Tara had been crying and was upset. *Dear God, she knows,* Sheila thought as she attempted to stand up.

Carmen was pulling the car up when she saw Tara standing over Sheila in a confrontational stance. She jumped out of the car about the same time Serena busted through the back door yelling something at Tara. Before she could reach the bench, Tony was coming through the door in a full sprint behind her. "What is going on?" Carmen asked, "and where's Terry?" No one answered. They all watched in horror as Tara slapped Sheila and knocked her back down on the bench. Carmen ran to Sheila's side, and Serena pulled Tara away in Tony's direction. "I demand to know what the hell is going on?" Carmen screamed at everyone. It was clear to them all that Carmen had no idea what Sheila had done and was capable of. "Why don't you take *your friend* home," Tony suggested to Carmen. She noticed he'd referred to Sheila as her friend as if the group had turned on her. "Not until someone tells me something." She turned to Tara. "What gives you the right—" Before she could finish her question, Serena stepped in, "How dare she"—looking at Sheila—"stoop so low as to sleep with her best friend's boyfriend when they were dating? How dare she do all the dirt she's done to Tara and still have the audacity to look her in the eye without guilt or shame?" Serena knew it wasn't her place to speak in this manner, but she knew Tara was pissed, and losing one friend today was enough. Carmen had no knowledge of any of it, and she didn't want Tara striking out at her. Serena had nothing to lose, so she said what was on her mind. Carmen taking all of this in was literally taken aback. Her knees buckled as she learned of the news. She then thought back to earlier that day when she'd detected the odd expression on Sheila's face. *That's what the look was for. That's why she's ill, and it serves her right,* Carmen thought to herself. She couldn't remember all of the details of that day at school. What she remembered most was Tara's pain and embarrassment and how the three of them had a pity party that weekend and watched movies and ate junk food all weekend as Tara swore off men and vowed to be celibate until she was married. Carmen snapped out of her thoughts as Sheila rose from the bench and looked at her with the most pitiful, abandoned look she ever could have imagined. Although it seemed as if Sheila showed no remorse during the last several years for the role she played in the entire saga, Carmen believed she was genuinely sorry now. Carmen knew no one else was willing to assist Sheila in any way, so she turned to Tara and said, "I am so sorry. I had no idea." She trotted to catch up with Sheila and helped her into the car. She made a U-turn and drove away from the mall.

As Tara took a seat on the bench, she thought back to how perfect her morning had started and wondered how things got so screwed up. Although the whole ordeal had been shocking and somewhat painful, she was relieved to have everything out in the open. Now she finally had closure. Serena and Tony looked at each other and decided to give her some time alone; hopefully this time without interruptions.

Tara stopped them before they headed toward the parking lot and said, "Thanks for being here for me. Tony, I know this could not have been easy for you, but thanks for trying to protect me." Tony and Serena breathed a sigh of relief as they walked toward Tony's truck.

"That could have been malicious," Serena said, looking at Tony.

"I'd say Sheila got off real easy. It looks like the military has calmed Tara some, because had it been the old Tara confronting Sheila, it would have taken more than you and me to break up the fight they would have been involved in," Tony said as he shook his head. "That girl really got off lucky," he said with a chuckle as Serena shared a laugh for the first time in what seemed like days. Serena and Tony felt like a load had been lifted off their shoulders. Serena couldn't imagine Tony keeping quiet for all these years. She knew it had to really eat at him. They were both glad it was over. *Tara's strong and very resilient; she'll be fine,* Tony thought.

As he neared his truck, he pulled Serena into his arms and said, "Did I tell you how beautiful you look?" He felt like being open with Serena, and she was receptive. "No, you didn't, but I forgive you. You look quite debonair yourself," she said as she looked up into his eyes. She leaned in to feel the welcoming hardness of his toned and muscular body. He felt good. He encircled her waist and realized how nicely built she was. She had the perfect hourglass figure complete with the tiny waist, he thought as he stared down into her beautiful brown eyes. They held the gaze for a moment until Tony remembered he needed to call Terry and let him know everything was okay. Tony was going to get the number from Tara, but she was on the other side of the mall, and he wanted to update Terry. Pulling out Tara's phone, Serena said, "I think Tara saved his number in her phone. If not, we can check the last outgoing call and try to contact him that way." She handed the phone to Tony. He walked to the back of the truck and began talking to Terry, letting him know that Tara was okay but asked to be left alone for a while. He said he was as hungry as a horse and was going to visit the Piccadilly café before leaving the mall. He asked Tony to call him if Tara wanted to see him before she headed to the dance. As Tony hung up, he was headed back to Serena when Melissa showed up out of the blue watching him give Serena her phone. Serena was startled but didn't let on. She wondered how long Melissa had been standing there. *Did she witness the hug and near kiss?*

"Tony, I need to speak with you now," she said, not acknowledging Serena at all. Tony and Serena both knew this looked bad, but neither seemed too concerned. As Tony was about to walk away, he stopped in front of Serena and gave her a reassuring smile and unlocked the door so she could sit inside while he talked to Melissa. His action alone was consoling as she hopped into his truck with his keys.

"I want to know what was so important that you left me at your grandmother's over an hour ago without an explanation."

"Did Big Mama tell you I had to come to the mall?"

"Yes, she did, but my question is why didn't *you* tell me, and what was so important that you had to rush down?" she said, looking in Serena's direction. "What's going on with you two? Is she the reason for your being here?" This is why Tony hated discussions with Melissa. She asked fifty questions one right after the other without breaking enough for him to answer one. When he was able to get an answer off, she didn't believe whatever it was that he'd told her.

"Look," he said finally, "Tara needed me, and that's all I care to say right now. No need to worry; it's over now, and everyone's okay."

Melissa looked confused. "Well, if you're here for Tara, then where is she, and more importantly why are you here with Serena?"

This angered Tony. He offered her the truth, and now she was questioning him as if they were married and she'd caught him cheating. "Melissa, I've had a pretty eventful hour here at the mall, and I would rather not do this right now."

"Okay, since you don't want to tell me, I'll just go ask your *friend*," she said sarcastically. He grabbed her by the arm.

"Melissa, what did you hope to find coming here? Why didn't you call me? My cell phone is right here." It felt good to turn the questioning around on her. "You are not going over to Serena with your mess. You need to cool off! How'd you get here anyway?" he finally thought to ask.

"My friend from Peachtree City was in town and came by to get me." Tony didn't bother to ask who the friend was. "So are you ready to go?" he asked, a little annoyed. He would have to find Tara before he left. "It would be dark soon, and the mall would be closing in thirty minutes."

"What do you mean ready to go?" she snapped. "No, I'm going to leave the same way I came since you didn't bother to bring me with you."

"Like I said, my sister needed me; and if you can't understand that, it's too bad."

Tara walked up to the two of them right on cue and asked, "Is everything okay, Tony?" as she looked at Melissa.

"Yeah, nothing I can't handle; how are you holding up?" he asked with concern.

"Actually, Tony, I'm doing a whole lot better now. I just had to clear my head; it's all good. I'm ready to celebrate now and dance the night away," she said, breaking out in one of her dance moves. Tony laughed, forgetting Melissa was there, and knew Tara would be okay.

When Serena looked up to find Tara talking with Tony, she got out of the truck and headed over. "Hey, girl, you okay?" she asked as she approached.

"Yeah, I'm fine now." She reached out and gave Serena a warm hug. She then hugged Tony again and said, "Thanks again; I don't know how this all would've played out had you two not been here to have my back." They shared a relieved laugh. Serena was impressed with Tara's resiliency. She credited that to her flexibility and discipline instilled in her through the military. *That's my girl,* she thought. "Oh, let me give you your phone back."

After hearing and witnessing all of the exchanges, Melissa knew Tony had been telling the truth, and she felt bad. On the way over, she'd already promised Elva that she'd go to the dance with her since Tony wasn't communicating with her. Now she felt bad, but Elva would be back in a few minutes to pick her up on the other side of JCPenney. Tara turned to Serena. "You ready to head over to the dance?"

"Ready if you are," she said, smiling at her friend. As Tara looked out into the parking lot, she noticed that Terry's car was still there.

"Terry's still here?" she asked, looking at Tony.

"Yeah, he wanted to hang out in the hopes that you'd want to see him after you cooled off. I mentioned the dance to him, so he knows you're going to be there."

She laughed. "Thanks, Tony, I'll give him a call." Just as she flipped her phone open, Terry's bodyguards came out of the mall with Terry following closely behind, towering over them. The parking lot was about to get crowded because of the mall's closing, so Terry had to be extra careful. He'd already signed several autographs in the restaurant as he tried to pass the time waiting to hear from Tony. Tara started walking toward him as Melissa let out a little yelp. "It's really him," she said as she smiled from ear to ear. *This is unbelievable,* she thought as she got even more excited realizing she was going to meet a real-life NBA star. When Tara reached Terry, he reached down and studied her face to see if he would be able to converse with her without her going off. She received him with a gentle smile as he took a chance and leaned down bringing his mouth to hers and introduced a sweet toe-curling kiss right there on the sidewalk. "Do you forgive me?" he asked. Tara contemplated the question and said, "All is forgiven. It was all about closure, and tonight I got closure. Thanks for now trusting me enough to talk to me honestly." He knew that was a borderline low blow, but he deserved it, and besides, it was the truth. When they reached the group, Terry asked if they were ready to head to the dance. Realizing there was someone new in the group as he looked at Melissa, he then looked at Tony and Serena for an explanation. "This is my friend, Melissa," Tony offered as he introduced the two. Terry looked somewhat confused as he stared at Serena then Tony and realized they were not a couple. He could tell from their closeness that there was definitely some chemistry there. He reached out and shook Melissa's hand as he said hello.

"Well, Tara, would you like to ride with me, or do you want to meet there?" he asked.

"Ahh." Tara looked around at Tony and Serena. Sure she would like to ride with Terry, but she couldn't leave Serena hanging.

Terry, noticing the hesitation, said, "Either way is cool."

Tony spoke up, "Tara, you can ride with Terry; I'll make sure Serena gets to the dance in one piece." They all seemed stunned by this audacious offer.

Melissa fixed her mouth to contest the offer but realized what she'd told Tony before she found out what was going on. After all, she had boasted that she was getting to the dance the same way she got to the mall. She sure said it, and now she couldn't take it back, and Tony remembered it and held her to it. After Melissa realized everyone was staring at her, she said, "Yeah, I'd better go. I'm sure my ride is waiting on me." This let everyone know that everything was okay; but before she walked away, she approached Tony and reached up to kiss him before disappearing completely. She knew Tony would not pull away with such an audience as much as he may have wanted to. She turned now satisfied, smiled, and rounded the corner toward JCPenney. Tara simply shook her head and laughed at Melissa's attempt to take control over a situation she'd obviously lost control of. Serena smiled after Melissa walked away because she knew the kiss was for show and meant to send a message to her. Tony said nothing but turned to Serena and asked if she was ready. The two headed for the truck as Serena walked a few steps ahead of Tony. Since she still had the keys to the truck, she opened the door and took her seat. As Tony walked to the truck, he wondered what Melissa was up to. She was really showing him a side of herself that he didn't like. He wondered what Serena thought about the kiss. He followed her to the truck studying her walk and became excited because they were actually going to spend some time alone together on the ride to the VIP. She was getting into the truck while her mind was elsewhere. Tony closed the distance between them in a matter of seconds and studied her facial expression as he showed up out of the blue to assist her with closing her door. Serena was stunned to see Tony there standing in the open door as she took her seat. Was she that deep in thought, or had he been closer to her than she recalled? They made eye contact but said nothing. Both were quiet on the way to the VIP as Tara and Terry followed them with the bodyguards following Terry's car. The whole time Tony wondered what it would be like to kiss Serena. He even had a strong urge to as he closed her door to let her know that the kiss he received earlier was for show only and meant nothing. He didn't know her well enough to read her body language yet and wasn't sure what she thought about the kiss. He didn't want to insult her by trying to kiss her if she wasn't feeling it, so he refrained. It was the golden oldies hour, and a song by Guy was playing, and this broke the ice as the two of them sang along.

"What's your favorite song?" Tony decided to ask.

"Well, I have so many favorites because I really like old school; but if you asked me what my favorite song by Guy was, I could tell you without hesitation."

"Okay, instead of telling me, why don't you sing it; and if I know it, I'll join in. Tara told me you had a nice voice."

"Oh, did she? What else did Tara tell you?"

"Only good things," he said with a smile.

"All right, are you ready?"

Tony answered by turning down the radio. Serena cleared her voice and said, "I hope I can remember all the words." She started singing, "From the first time I saw your face, boy I knew I had to have you. Wanted to wrap you in my warm embrace—visions of your lovely face . . ." Tony joined in, and they harmonized while laughing and enjoying the fact that "Let's Chill" was both their favorite. Next they sang "Tenderoni" by Bobby Brown, and they knew all the words, and they began to realize they had quite a few things in common. Before they could work on another song, Tony slowed down and pulled into a large parking lot that was half full. "I guess we're early," he said, trying to read Serena's mind. She smiled and wondered when Melissa was going to pop back up. He turned the engine off and waited for Terry and his bodyguards to get their vehicles situated. He felt he had to do something subtle to let Serena know that the kiss meant nothing, so he reached over and took her hand in his. That was the sign Serena was waiting for, and everything was all right again.

As Tony scanned the parking lot, he saw Melissa headed his way. He took a deep breath and wondered what game she was going to play tonight. Serena was watching Melissa too. She pulled her hand away and smiled without saying a word. There was movement over in Terry's camp. He and his bodyguards were headed toward the building while Tara walked in the direction of Tony's truck. "Save a dance for me," he said, still smiling at Serena. She smiled back at the handsome man that seemed to occupy her thoughts more than he should as she opened the door and went to meet up with Tara. Tony sat in the truck until Melissa approached him. "Are you ready to go in?" she asked.

"Yeah, give me a few minutes." He didn't know how this night was going to turn out, but he wished he had more time with Serena. She'd be leaving tomorrow, and he didn't know if he'd ever see her again.

Tara and Serena were going to search for Derek and Vincent. The guys had agreed to pay their way in and for their first drink. Neither of the girls drank, so that was $3 the guys could save. As they entered the building, they decided to grab a table out in the lobby while they waited for the guys. "So how are you really?" Serena asked as the girls chatted.

"I'm much better now, thanks for asking. I'm more interested in what's going on with you. What's up with you and Tony? I can't believe you guys rode over here together without Melissa."

"Yeah, well, from what I understand, she invited one of her friends here; and I guess she felt obligated to ride with her. It gave me and Tony a chance to talk."

"Yeah, I know my brother—he's trying to lose Melissa so he can spend time with you. But ol' girl is suspicious. She should know Tony by now. That boy is going to do what he wants; and right now, that is to be with you. Did you see that kiss she laid on him before we left the mall? If that wasn't for show, I don't know what it was."

"Yeah, she's trying to send a message," Serena said. "I am definitely feeling your brother, but I don't want to cause any problems in paradise. If he and I were meant to be, it will be. He asked me to save a dance for him," Serena said, blushing.

"Believe me, he means it," Tara said.

"Well, I'm not expecting anything. I just want to get my groove on and enjoy our last night here."

"I agree," Tara said. "Let's check the parking lot for the guys before they think we stood them up." Terry met Tara before she reached the door. "Hey, what's up," Tara said as she studied Terry's face.

"Aw, something came up, and I've got to go. It shouldn't take me long. I'll call you when I'm headed back."

"Sure," Tara said. He reached down and kissed her cheek and left.

Melissa was still waiting on Tony to get out of the truck. She'd been standing outside his window since she got there and was beginning to feel ill. They didn't talk, but she could tell Tony was in deep thought. "Look, I'll be over at Elva's car. Come get me when you're ready to go in." When Melissa got to Elva's car, she was really beginning to get one of those nasty migraines, but she was determined to attend the party. "I just need to sit down and rest for a minute," she told herself after taking a seat in the back of the car.

"Are you feeling okay?" Elva asked.

"I'll be okay; give me a minute," Melissa mumbled.

When the girls walked outside, they saw Derek and Vincent sitting on the tailgate of Vincent's Tahoe talking to Terry as he headed to his car. Derek and Vincent had been to Florida to see Terry play a few times, but they were still excited to have him back in their hometown. The music was soothing to Serena's ears as she walked up and said, "Nice truck," fascinated with the twenty-inch rims, detailed paint job, and the thumping sound system. He also had the leather and wood grain package with a DVD player with the monitors in the headrests and land navigation. "Thanks," Vincent said, surprised as Serena took a walk around his truck touching the detailed paint job. Vincent smiled at Derek and Serena. "This girl acts like she knows something about rides." He laughed, watching Serena admire his truck. Before she could explain her love of automotive, Tara had already begun telling the story. "Serena absolutely loves nice rides, and she really thinks that rims are what make any vehicle. That hooptie she's got at home, she's always working on it." This surprised the guys as they looked at Serena, not believing Tara, but were impressed.

"Do you really have it like that, my sistah?" Derek asked.

"Is Uncle Sam paying that well?" Vincent chimed in.

"Well, the pay is okay. It's not about how much you make but how you spend or invest it."

"Well, we're not hating, but that Monte Carlo could never be a hooptie; it's a classic forever," Vincent said. They all laughed, and Serena was relieved the conversation was kept light. They decided to go into the party before all the food was gone. The guys paid their way as promised. The girls grabbed a table while the guys went to get some food for them.

THE LAST DANCE

Tony figured he'd better get inside if he was going to enjoy this night, so he called Melissa on her cell phone and told her to meet him at the front. Elva and Melissa walked to the front of the VIP and looked for Tony. Melissa was feeling a little better but knew it would only be a matter of minutes before she had a full-blown migraine with nausea. Tony paid for the girls as they went inside and grabbed a seat by the dance floor. He asked the girls if they wanted anything to drink as they took their seats. He met up with Derek and Vincent and gave them the customary brotherly handshake and hug. "Where's Tara and Serena?" he asked, looking around. Derek nodded in their direction and said, "They're sitting in the back waiting on us to bring their food." Tony looked in the direction but didn't see their table.

Serena noticed Tony, Melissa, and her friend walking in. She refused to let the sight of Tony and Melissa consume her thoughts the entire night. As soon as the guys made it back to the table, Serena asked Vincent to dance. Vincent placed the food down and held her hand as they made their way to the dance floor.

"I guess we'll get to dance on the next song since we can't leave the food here unattended," Derek said as he dug into his fries.

"Fine with me," Tara said as she realized she was hungry. As the two of them ate, they watched Serena and Vincent burn up the dance floor—both were very good dancers.

After Tony had made it back to their table, he noticed that Melissa had left the table. He figured she was out on the dance floor. As he scanned the area where Derek said they were sitting, he saw Tara and Derek, but no Serena or Vincent. Elva began to eat her food when Melissa returned from the bathroom.

"Feeling better?" she asked.

"No, but I'll be okay," Melissa said as Tony looked at her with concern.

"What's wrong, Melissa?" he asked.

"I'm getting another migraine. It must be from being out in the sun all day." She tried eating the chips and dip and finger sandwiches Tony had brought back with their colas.

"Did you take anything for it?" he asked.

"No, I left everything at your grandmother's house. I'll be fine," she reassured them both.

As Serena and Vincent danced, she noticed that he was a really good dancer, and everything he did came naturally. They were having a great time and working on their third song.

Tony felt the urge to dance and excused himself from their table as he walked over to Tara. Passing by the dance floor, he saw Serena dancing with Vincent. He had to admit they looked really good together out there on the dance floor. She was moving her hips seductively to R. Kelly's "Ignition." As he reached the table, he reached out to Tara. "C'mon, sis, let's show them how it's done." She took his hand and was led to the dance floor. After the second song, she was really glad the day was ending nicely. She got to be with her friends and brother at one of the biggest dances of the year. She and Terry were catching up on old times, and she found out who her real friends were. She couldn't ask for a better ending. She looked over at Serena and Vincent as they headed back to their secluded table. They were laughing and very jovial as they walked toward Tara and Tony. As soon as they were about to pass, the song ended; and the "Electric Slide" came on. The crowd was getting stirred up, and Serena and Vincent started chanting with the crowd as they joined Tony and Tara to dance to the "Electric Slide". They danced and laughed during the entire song. Tony was a really smooth dancer, and he had a matching attitude while clowning out on the dance floor. He and Serena ended up dancing beside one another, and they both enjoyed the closeness. At one point, he was really close to her as they were turning; and he put his hands on her waist. Serena didn't mind but knew she couldn't stand too much closeness as things intensified on the dance floor. When the song ended, Tony walked back with them to their table. Serena and Vincent ate while the five of them enjoyed each other's company. Derek was itching to get on the dance floor, so he and Tara headed out while Tony decided to go back to their table and check on Melissa.

Elva was out on the dance floor when he returned to their table. There was no change in Melissa's condition.

"Would you like to dance?" she asked.

"Sure," he said as she grabbed his hand and led him to the dance floor. After two dances, Melissa had had enough. Her migraine was approaching phase two—nausea. She headed to the bathroom as they were coming off the dance floor. Noticing Melissa practically running to the bathroom, Elva went in after her. She emerged minutes later to update Tony. "Melissa is not doing well. She needs to go home."

"Okay," Tony said, "do you want to take her, or would you like for me to?"

"I can drop her off since it's on my way." Tony walked the girls to Elva's car and told Melissa he hoped she felt better and that he'd see her when he got home. He knew she had to have really been feeling bad because she didn't grill him about what time was he going to come home. He watched them drive away and turned to go back inside.

Keith Sweat was playing when Derek grabbed Serena and said, "Come on, let's do this thing." Tara and Vincent followed suit. As Serena and Derek danced, he asked, "So you got a thing for my boy?"

"Who, Vincent?" Serena asked innocently.

"No, Tony," Derek clarified.

"He seems to be good people. Why do you ask?" Serena said.

"Just curious, it appeared there was something going on between the two of you today at Big Mama's. The two of you couldn't take your eyes off of one another."

"Oh," Serena said, thinking, *Was it that noticeable?*

"Yeah, I'm sure his girl saw it too."

"Well," Serena cut him off. "It's not like I planned any of that; it just happened. There was obviously a natural and instant attraction between us. Just know that I'm not here to cause any trouble. I'm here with Tara, and I intend to have a good time."

"I heard that," Derek said as he continued dancing. When the song came to an end, Serena wanted to be alone; so she told Derek she needed to rest. He didn't have any trouble finding someone else to dance with. When Serena made it to the table, she was actually relieved it was vacant. Tara and Vincent were dancing again. She needed some time to herself as she let her thoughts meander again, and once again they ended up on Tony. She thought about the events of the day and was happy she was able to spend some time with Tony alone. He had been the perfect gentleman, and she knew he was what she wished she could find in Texas. He was perfect for her—he had a beautiful smile including a set of flawless pearly whites. She loved being near him, and holding his hand earlier made her heart skip a beat. She loved the spontaneity she felt he possessed. Serena was deep in thought when someone pulled a chair up beside her and said, "Mind if I sit here?" She looked up and into his face; and to her surprise, it was Tony standing there, smiling down at her as he awaited her answer.

"Sure, please sit down." She glanced over at the table he and Melissa had occupied earlier and asked, "Where's Melissa?"

"Oh, she wasn't feeling well, so her friend took her back to the house."

"That's too bad; I hope she feels better soon," she said. Tony was not sure how to take what Serena had said; but after looking at her, he knew she was being sincere and liked her even more for being so considerate.

As they continued the conversation they'd started on the way over, they realized they had quite a few things in common. They both loved basketball and working out. They both had purchased homes, and both were very independent. The most ironic similarity was that they both attended GSU in Grambling, Louisiana, the same year. Their paths never crossed, but they missed each other by days. Serena arrived in the spring, and Tony left within days prior to the spring semester. She left to go into the army, turning down a two-year basketball scholarship. He returned home to become a firefighter. Both regretted the decision to leave school but had since accomplished their educational goals. Serena received her degree from Baylor University shortly after arriving in San Antonio. She had also been able to play basketball competitively while in the army. Tony decided to go to school on his days off, lunch hour, and some nights as he was awarded his degree from the University of Georgia. Both commended each other for never giving up and for a job well done. They made a toast to their accomplishments.

Serena looked out on the dance floor to see Tara and the guys still dancing, and Tara waved at her. Serena smiled and waved back. "I know this is none of my business," Tony started, "but are you seeing anyone back in Texas?"

Serena was pleasantly surprised at Tony's interest in her. "No, not anymore. I broke up a few months ago with a man I'd dated for two years."

"Do you still have feelings for this man?" Tony asked.

Smiling at his directness, Serena said, "No, I've gotten him out of my system and am just enjoying life now—no pressures. What about you and Melissa?" Serena asked, feeling it was her turn to learn more about his relationship.

"Well, it's complicated," Tony said, "but we have an understanding. She knows I'm not ready to settle down. She wants to get married and start a family, but that's not something I'm willing to do now or ever with her."

"And she's okay with that?" Serena asked, trying not to pry.

Tony smiled. "Look, I know you don't know me yet, but I would like to get to know you a lot better. I have no reason to lie to you. I've told Melissa how I felt several times, but she won't accept it; she keeps trying. It's almost as if she thinks if she hangs around long enough, she'll be able to change my mind. It's gotten so tense lately when we try to discuss it that it leads to a big fight, so we don't talk about it anymore. But that doesn't mean I've changed my mind." They were both quiet for a moment, processing the conversation they'd just had. Tara's phone rang as Serena looked over at the chair Tara was sitting in. Tara must have forgotten to take it with her. Tony turned to Serena. "Do you want to dance?" he asked as he held out his hand to her. Serena had felt a closeness to Tony that she couldn't quite explain or begin to understand. At this particular moment and time, she felt like the luckiest girl in the world as she took his hand and stood up. As they were headed to the dance floor, Tara and Vincent were headed to the table. Serena told Tara that she'd missed a call as she passed by holding Tony's hand. Before they found a place to dance, Keith Sweat's "Nobody" started to play, and they were both thrilled. Tony took her in his arms, and immediately she knew that her dance partner was no novice to slow dancing either. She enjoyed the moment as she and Tony eased into a nice rhythm. She loved the way he held her and never wanted to let him go. His hands were masculine but soft to the touch. Holding hands had been one of Serena's favorite forms of foreplay. When he held her hand earlier in the truck, she knew it was a form of an apology. Serena listened to his heart beating and began to get aroused by their closeness. She felt her hands sweating or maybe his hands were sweating, but she enjoyed every moment of it. "Thank you for sharing a part of your life with me," she said as they continued to move around the dance floor. Tony was a little surprised to hear what Serena said. He knew what she was referring to; but for a moment, he felt she meant something different altogether, something more serious. He wondered if she'd noticed that he'd misunderstood her statement. He was enjoying the dance the two of them were sharing, and he wanted to hold her forever. He knew the song was coming to an end but continued to move Serena around the floor. As if on cue, the deejay played a song by Midnight Star—"Slow Jam." This too had been one of their favorites as Tony pulled Serena closer as he placed his face beside her neck. He felt his hands sweating and hope it didn't bother her. He was deep in thought as he listened to the lyrics of the song and felt himself harden as he leaned closer to Serena. He was not embarrassed by his reaction to her, but he didn't want to offend her either. Serena wanted to dance with Tony forever; the way he held her seemed as if they were sharing much more than a dance. She got a whiff of his cologne and wondered if he was wearing Burberry. She had smelled it earlier in the day but was so preoccupied with everything that was going on she pushed the thought to enjoy it away. There was something about the way Tony smelled as his perspiration and cologne mixed together. She was completely turned on and began to hold him tighter as they swayed from side to side. Tony looked down at her, noticing the change in her, and the heat began to rise from the excitement each of them was feeling. As they moved with each other, Serena noticed that Tony had become sexually aroused; and this excited her. She continued to hold on and tried to remember each moment as it passed. The song ended, and they decided to take a break. They knew another dance could possibly lead to something neither one of them were sure they were ready for. The attraction had gotten stronger, and neither of them seemed to mind. They were just thankful to be in each other's company. As they headed for the table, Tara was getting off the phone.

"What's up?" Serena asked.

"Terry's on his way back. I didn't realize it was already one o'clock. The party's over at two o'clock. Well, at least I'll get the chance to dance with him at least once before we leave." Derek and Vincent had found steady partners out on the dance floor as Tony and Serena sat at the table, trying to calm their emotions down. The three of them laughed and talked. The girls enjoyed Tony's sense of humor. Tara and Serena began to discuss their trip home tomorrow and decided they would be on the road by eleven o'clock. They would take turns driving since they were both going to be up late tonight.

"Tony, maybe the next time I come I'll be able to take a trip down to Columbus and see your new house," Tara said.

"Well, you are more than welcome to come by anytime. You and Serena can come tomorrow if you want to," Tony said with a look of mischief. Serena was startled by Tony's directness and invitation to Columbus. Although she would never respond to the invite without Tara taking the lead, she felt a surge of excitement at the possibility of seeing Tony after tonight. Tara would have loved to visit Columbus to spend time at her brother's house, but she promised Serena that they'd be back on Sunday so they'd be able to relax and get things in order before Serena had to go to work on Tuesday. Terry walked over and joined the group as the conversation about visiting Columbus ended. The deejay announced the time one forty-five, which meant there'd only be a few more songs before the party ended. Terry and Tara stood up as if they read each other's minds and went out on the dance floor. Terry was so much taller than Tara. Serena wasn't sure people stared because they drew attention because of the big difference in their height or if they recognized Terry as the NBA player for the Miami Heat.

After a couple of favorites played, the deejay ended the night with "Let's Chill" by Guy. Tony immediately took Serena's hand and said, "Shall we?" This time there was something different about the way he received her. They held their gaze and finally turned toward the dance floor. Serena thought the whole time how perfect it had been to share the last dance with Tony on one of their favorite songs. As he pressed his body up against hers and drew her close, he rested his hands on her waist and placed his face next to hers with the warmth from his breath finding a nice place on her neck. She felt the hairs stand up on her neck as she raised her gaze to meet Tony's eyes. The whole night dancing with Tony seemed like a fantasy—never had anything so perfect happened to her before. They were still holding each other when the song was over. Tony gave her a gentle hug as if saying, "Thanks for sharing this evening with me," and Serena returned the embrace. *You're welcome,* she thought.

They all met up outside. Derek and Vincent had picked up two girls from the party and were headed to Wendy's. They said their good-byes to Tara and Serena and wished them a safe trip back to Texas. Terry was taking Tara to get her car so she could prep it for tomorrow. When Tony and Serena reached the truck, Tony walked to the passenger's side and opened the door for her. She was stunned but rather pleased with his belief in chivalry. She remembered he'd open the door for her earlier that day at the mall, but she was so worried about Tara that she barely noticed. Thinking back, she remembered he rose from the table as she excused herself to go to the ladies' room. *Wow, if this guy doesn't do something stupid to mess up this image I have of him, I'm going to have to convince Tara to take him up on his offer.* She laughed to herself.

Tony had been quiet since they left the club. He thought Serena was the "perfect girl." She did everything just right. *She's polite, she has very good table etiquette, she's intelligent, she is a lady, and I could really get used to this.* On a scale of 1-10, already Tony rated Serena as being a definite 8. Tony thought of two things she could do to receive a perfect score: if she reciprocated an act of chivalry and if her lips tasted as good as they looked. He often stared at her lips while she was talking and fantasized about being close enough to kiss them. He was in deep thought as he rounded the back of the truck heading for his door. Before Tony could reach the handle, the door popped open; and he almost jumped back in amazement as Serena looked up and smiled at him. She released the handle and returned to her seat. Tony hesitated before getting in the truck, stunned because she opened the door for him. After looking into Tony's face, she knew right away that he was shocked but pleased by her act of kindness, her act of chivalry. All he could manage to say was an awkward thank you. He wondered if Serena could read minds.

As Tony closed the door and started the truck up, he had to think back. The entire year he'd been dating Melissa she had never opened his door for him or done anything close to it. He was always expected to do for Melissa, and he wondered why it never bothered him that she took him for granted. It was probably the way her overbearing mother had reared her. She was an only child and always had people falling over themselves to please her. Her parents spared no expense on their baby girl. She lived in their guesthouse, and when she received her nursing degree last year, they bought her a Porsche. She didn't have to work because her parents paid all of her bills to include her car insurance.

"Tony, are you okay?" Serena asked, snapping him out of his deep thought.

"Oh, I'm sorry I was someplace else," he said apologetically.

"Please don't apologize for that," she said.

Why am I thinking about Melissa when I could be focusing my attention on this lovely lady sitting here next to me? Tony thought.

"Are you having second thoughts about giving me a lift to Tara's?" she asked, sensing something was wrong.

Tony looked over at her, clearly saddened by her question. "I could not think of any other way to spend this night than with you." They shared a warm smile, and with this he drove off, and they talked nonstop until they reached Tara's. Tony pulled into the driveway and cut the lights as he parked.

Serena turned to Tony. "I have to thank you for an absolutely perfect evening. I never imagined meeting anyone as exciting as you and becoming so close to you in such a short time. This entire day has been magically breathtaking, and I have you to thank for that." Tony's look became serious as he heard the sincerity in Serena's voice. "I could not have described my time with you any better than that," he said as they laughed again. "I can certainly say it was my pleasure." Serena wished the night didn't have to end. She knew this was a once-in-a-lifetime occurrence for her, and she wanted to end the evening with a kiss that was sure to be more memorable than anything else that had taken place between the two of them thus far. As they turned to face each other, Tony moved closer to Serena. Serena watched his eyes and his expression closely, not wanting to miss anything. His look of desire for her was so obvious and she hoped she returned the same passionate look. Tony reached for her cheek and slowly pulled her into his arms, as if moving slowly would help him to prolong the moment while remembering the kiss of a lifetime. He began to taste her lips with his wet tongue. Serena relaxed and gave in to him and allowed him to suck her lips. She stroked the back of his neck as he played with her lips. The heat between the two of them was easily noticed as the windows begin to fog. Tony offered her his tongue as she let out the most sensual, pleasurable moan. This excited Tony as he deepened his kiss by giving Serena his entire tongue. Serena accepted it and pulled it a little harder, noticing Tony's response to the deepening of the kiss. Serena was really particular about the way she kissed. She didn't quite understand how this man she'd just met knew how to kiss her just the way she liked it as he took her tongue inside his warm and inviting mouth. She could not have instructed him to kiss her any more pleasing than he had. Serena's nipples hardened as she became excited by the fact that Tony was so turned on by their intimacy that he had once again become aroused. They separated, as if trying to keep things under control, and sat back in the truck speechless.

"That was unbelievably extraordinary," she claimed.

"You are amazing, and I must say that was a first for me," he said.

"I've never responded that way before to a kiss," Serena said, still feeling the magic.

"I can't say I have either," Tony agreed. He turned to look at Serena with his head still resting on the headrest. "I want to see you again," Tony said out of the blue. "I hope I get a chance to see you tomorrow before you leave," he continued.

"What time are you leaving for Columbus?" Serena asked Tony.

"I will be leaving at ten o'clock. It's only a two-hour trip."

"Well, good night," Serena said, and she got out of the truck and headed for Tara's house. Tony watched her pull a key from her purse and walk up to the door. She turned to wave good-bye, but Tony was no longer in the truck. He had followed her up to the porch. Serena froze as he got closer, wondering what to expect. She backed up to the door and leaned up against the house as Tony towered over her and pulled her in for another kiss. As he pulled away from her, he smiled down at her and said, "I will see you tomorrow."

"I certainly look forward to that," Serena said with an English accent that made Tony smile. He sat in the truck and waited until the door was closed behind Serena before he backed out of the driveway.

Terry and Tara sat in the mall parking lot reminiscing about the good ol' days. Tara realized that he was still the same guy she fell head over heels in love with. They agreed to see each other again. Terry would be flying back to Miami on Monday night, and Tara was scheduled to leave tomorrow around noon. They had been apart for so many years because of a terrible and cruel prank carried out by her best friend. Tara wanted to make up for some of that lost time by spending some quality time with Terry. She wished they could stay another day. They said their good-byes as Tara pulled out from the gas station where she'd just filled up and checked out her car for their trip to Texas.

As Tony was backing out of the driveway, his pager started going off. He looked at the clock and noticed it was three thirty. The party was over an hour and a half ago. He knew it must be Melissa checking up on him. He decided not to answer it since he would be home in fifteen minutes. Tony wanted to use that alone time to savor the memories he and Serena had created that night, and that's just what he did.

"That looks like Tara's car," Tony said, passing by the twenty-four-hour BP gas station. As he passed, he discovered it was Tara's car pulling out onto the highway. Tony did a U-turn and caught up with Tara. She was still sitting at the end of the store's parking lot, so he pulled in and parked. Tara smiled as she backed into the parking space beside him. As they met up, Tara said, "What's up, bro? Where's Serena? Did she make it home okay?"

"Yeah, I made sure she was able to get inside before I left."

"Boy, you know that's not what I'm talking about. I mean give me the scoop, what's up with you two? You guys have been inseparable all night." Tony smiled from ear to ear, and then his expression changed to a serious expression. "Well, Tara, I can't explain what's going on, but I thank you from the bottom of my heart for bringing Serena here to Georgia. She is truly an amazing and beautiful person. Any man would be lucky to have her in his life." Tara's smile faded as she realized that her brother had fallen for Serena. "Tony, are you okay? Is that how you really feel? Where's my brother?" She attempted a laugh. Tara pretended to be shocked, but she knew her brother well enough to know that he was serious. "I've never heard you speak of any woman this way before. I can tell she seems really captivated by you too," Tara offered. Before Tony could respond, his pager went off again; and this time, he dialed Melissa's number.

Serena took a long hot shower in an attempt to calm her nerves. She had had the perfect evening and wished she lived closer to Tony. She felt that if he were closer to Texas, they could possibly have a chance to start a relationship. Serena snapped out of her thoughts when she remembered Tony *already had* a girlfriend. "What was I thinking? I need to be realistic," she said, scolding herself. "Even if we were closer, I can't impede his life and assume he would want it that way." Serena tried to push the thought of Tony out of her mind as she finished her shower.

"Tony, where are you? Do you realize what time it is?" Melissa asked on the other end of the phone. Tony looked at Tara, wishing he hadn't called Melissa. "I am at the BP with Tara gassing up the car. Why, what's wrong?" he asked.

"Nothing's wrong; it's just late, and I thought you said the party was over at two o'clock." She reminded him that it was four o'clock. Melissa couldn't resist. "Where's Serena? Is she there with you guys?" she inquired. Tony frowned at her audacity. "No, she's actually at home already." Melissa immediately felt relieved. At least they were not together anymore, and now he'd be coming home to her soon. She knew Tony was attracted to Serena, and there was nothing she could do about it; it was all karma. Thinking back to when they first met, she realized he had never looked at her the way he'd been watching Serena all night. "Look, I'll be leaving here shortly."

"Okay," she said as they hung up. Tony shook his head as he tossed the phone in the truck's window onto the seat without regard to where it landed. "What's wrong? Melissa's playing twenty questions again?" Tara asked. He simply nodded as he walked over to his sister and gave her a hug. "I'm glad you came home too," he said. "It's been too long." As they were pulling out of the parking lot, Tony leaned out the window and said, "I hope you take me up on my offer," and smiled as he drove off. Tara smiled and thought maybe it wouldn't be a bad idea after all.

After Tony hung up, Melissa tried to figure out why Tony was so fascinated with Serena. She immediately tried to compare herself to Serena. She was a pretty girl with the envious hourglass shape, but Melissa knew she was a looker too. Melissa had been blessed with large boobs, which Tony loved, and a decent-sized butt. She was about five feet ten, which was a few inches taller than Serena. She thought Tony looked at Serena as a "video vixen"; she would fit perfectly into the latest videos on BET. This didn't bother her so much, but Tony's response to this confident and poised stranger did bother her. Or maybe he's captivated by the material things that Tara's been boasting about. Whatever it was, Melissa knew Tony was slipping away from her, and she had to take control of things. She would have to reexamine things once back in Columbus. She hoped they'd have some time alone before she had to go to work on Monday.

Serena lay in bed trying to relax and focus on her to-do list when she got back to Texas. She hadn't checked her voice mail since she'd made it to Georgia. She heard Tara's car pull up and looked at the clock. *Four eighteen. We've got to get some rest,* she thought to herself, *especially if we are going to be on the road for fifteen hours later on this morning.* When Tara entered the room, Serena pretended she was asleep, not wanting to talk about Tony.

"Hey, Serena," Tara said, bursting in the room, "Oh, I didn't know you were asleep already."

"No, I'm just lying here," Serena said, changing her mind. She needed to talk about Tony and get it all off her chest so she could move on.

"I'm glad you had a good time tonight," she said to Serena. "I think my brother had an equally exciting time. Good thing Melissa left with a headache or the two of you may have never gotten the chance to connect." Serena sat up as she listened to Tara. "You know I think Melissa's days are numbered. I don't know why Tony even puts up with her. She is so spoiled, and she's always under him. If it wasn't for her falling ill, she would've been at the party giving you two the evil eye all night long."

Serena finally spoke, "Yeah, we had a very memorable night, and I am thankful to you for allowing me to share your family, especially Tony; he's perfect."

"Well, he thinks the world of you too. I think you are exactly what my brother needs. You are perfect for one another, and you seem to bring out the best in him." Tara could tell Serena had a lot on her mind; so with that, she said, "I'm going to jump in the shower before five o'clock strikes," as she smiled at her friend. "Good night."

Melissa was startled by the front door opening. She was so deep in thought that she'd not heard Tony's truck pull up. She pretended to be asleep when Tony entered the room since the lights were off except for in the bathroom. The bathroom light dimly lit part of the bedroom, Tony thought she was asleep so he didn't bother her. He began to undress in front of the mirror, facing away from Melissa. She watched him take off his clothes and remembered one of the reasons why she was attracted to Tony. He had the perfect body and was completely proportioned from his head to his toes. She vowed then to let nothing come between them. The light from the bathroom revealed Tony's erection as he stretched and headed for the shower. He never looked in her direction as he walked into the bathroom and closed the door. A few minutes later, she heard the shower running and began to wonder what led to his current condition. Before she could finish her thought, she heard a low moan coming from the shower, which grew louder as she sat up in the bed. She crept to the door to listen closer and opened it slightly. She could see his silhouette through the transparent shower curtain and saw him pleasuring himself. As she watched the grand finale, she knew he was thinking of Serena; and she felt ill all over again. She closed the door still in shock and crept back to bed. She forced herself to go to sleep so she wouldn't have to look at Tony. This time when Tony came to bed, Melissa had indeed fallen asleep.

FALLING IN LOVE

I t was eight o'clock when the sun glistened through the open windows and woke Melissa up. She realized she had fallen asleep before Tony came out of the bathroom. Being a light sleeper, Melissa figured she'd at least feel Tony getting into the bed next to her. She turned to steal a glance when she discovered he wasn't in the bed with her. She sat up quickly and found him asleep on the couch. She couldn't wait to wake him out of his peaceful sleep, so she stood over him and nudged him. "Why didn't you wake me when you got in?" she asked. Tony was dreaming he and Serena were walking on the beach when he woke to find Melissa standing over him, asking him something he couldn't quite make out yet. Grunting, he turned over. "Huh?" She repeated the question. "I knew you were feeling bad and didn't want to wake you after you'd already fallen asleep. Are you feeling better?" he asked, looking up into her face. He could tell she was perturbed, but he was tired and not in the mood to be grilled. Melissa continued. "So what time did you get in?" she asked as she began pacing the floor.

"I don't remember. I wasn't looking at the clock."

"Well, did you thoroughly enjoy yourself?" she asked sarcastically. Tony smiled before he realized that Melissa was staring at him. "Yeah, it was fun," he responded, trying not to sound too enthusiastic. Melissa was trying to read into the smile and was about to ask more questions when Tony sat up quickly and said he was going to check on his grandmother. Sometimes it took her a while to get her legs to cooperate with the rest of her body in the morning. Tony went in to check on her and grabbed the Bengay from her nightstand when he found her awake but still lying in bed. "Good morning," he said as he began to rub her legs with the cream. She patted his hand

and said, "Thank you," as she rose to go to the bathroom. When he returned to the bedroom, Melissa was in the bathroom brushing her teeth. Tony slipped on his jeans and T-shirt and headed to the kitchen to put on a pot of coffee. He escaped to the back porch to enjoy the sun.

Serena finally opened her heavy eyelids when she suddenly realized not only was she exhausted but starving. She had the weirdest but most romantic dream about walking on the beach hand in hand with Tony. She smiled at the memory of her dream when she got a whiff of bacon and eggs coming from the kitchen. This motivated her to get out of bed and get her things together.

Tony had always enjoyed watching the sunrise, and he loved being outside. It always brought him peace, and for this he thanked God. He gathered his thoughts as he headed back inside to say good-bye to his grandmother. He could hear Melissa moving around as she got her things together. He retrieved his bags from outside the bedroom door and headed to the truck. He found his grandmother sitting out on the porch. When he went back inside, he poured her a cup of coffee and prepared two slices of toast for her while he waited for Melissa to emerge from the bedroom. She turned to him and reached up for a hug as only a grandmother could do. She stared at him without saying a word. Then finally she said, laughing, "Tony, you really look happy. I can't remember if I've ever seen you this happy before." Tony was shocked to hear this coming from his grandmother, but he was glad to hear it. He wondered if Melissa could see it too. He thought of Serena and knew that she made him happy. "So when are you coming back, Tony?"

"I'm not sure, but I'm thinking about coming back for the Fourth of July. Hopefully it will be before the end of the summer if I can't make it in July. I will let you know as soon as I'm sure."

Melissa came out of the house with her bags and placed them on the porch. Tony took the bags to the car. "Well, Big Mama, thank you for having me. Take care," she said as she kissed her cheek.

"You take care too, baby," she said as Melissa headed to the truck. Tony came back for his final hug and kiss, and soon they were on the road headed to the Danstons'.

Tara was in the kitchen watching her dad moving around like he was born in the kitchen. He could make a mean breakfast and always made Tara's favorites when she was home. She looked across the table at Tonya who was going on and on about how she couldn't wait for her dad to finish cooking. She then requested five pancakes as Tara stared in amazement. Her baby sister had a big appetite to be so thin. Tara knew that Tonya could put away the five pancakes with side orders included. Tonya was fourteen but still the baby of the family and always got her way. Mr. Danston picked her up from Bev's this morning while he was out picking up groceries from the Food Lion. Tonya was excited to see Tara this morning before they left for Texas. They talked about Tonya visiting San Antonio when school was out. Tara promised Tonya that she'd look into the local basketball camps to see if there were any available slots. Tara thought it'd be nice to have family up for the summer. There were so many things to do in San Antonio.

Serena was cleaning up the room when Tara stuck her head in the door. "Hey, sleepyhead, are you feeling okay?"

"Yeah, I didn't realize my body was so tired."

"Yeah, you didn't move a muscle when I was in shower. I even packed my bags while you were asleep," Tara said as she'd noticed Serena had her bags all packed. The phone rang, and Tonya called out to Tara. "Come on and eat; my dad went overboard with breakfast, and it could take us all morning to finish off all that food," Tara said, laughing.

"Okay, I'll be right there."

They were the perfect family, she thought as Tonya stuck her head in to say good morning. She told Serena that she would be coming to Texas in the summer. "Make sure you bring your running shoes and your ball shoes," Serena said.

"You got it," Tonya said as she walked toward the door. Breakfast will be served in five minutes. Tara had registered Tonya for a two-week David Robinson basketball camp in San Antonio but was waiting to surprise her with it later. Serena was amazed at the relationship Tara and her baby sister had. Tonya was a very talented athlete who would really shine at the camp.

Melissa was on the phone with her job as Tony's thoughts landed on Serena. He was saddened by the thought of her leaving today. He tried to come up with ways of seeing her again while he sat on the porch. Nothing made sense, and besides, he couldn't just pretend Melissa didn't live in Columbus too. Melissa's cursing snapped him out of his thoughts. He turned to look at her. "What's wrong with you?" he asked, sounding alarmed.

After a brief pause, followed by a loud sigh, she said, "I have to go in tonight. Miriam called in sick; now I have to pull the eleven-to-seven shift." Melissa knew she would need at least five hours of sleep to function during her shift, which meant she needed to be down by five o'clock. Tony wasn't sure what he should say. He was thinking of inviting a few friends over and cook out tonight. "I guess we won't be having much of a Memorial Day celebration," Melissa said, pouting.

"Well, you won't be missing much. I'll save plenty of food for you if I can get in touch with the guys and pull this thing off," he said with a smile. Melissa said nothing because now she was in a funky mood, and all she needed to make matters worse was to see Serena. "Do you have to stop by your dad's? I really need to get home so I can get some sleep," she said. Tony was stunned by yet another audacious question.

"Ah, I've already promised him, and I would like to tell Tara good-bye. We will be home in plenty of time for you to prepare for tonight. Besides, he's cooking breakfast." This made Melissa smile because she's heard Tony go on and on about how his father would cook him the biggest and best breakfast when he came to town. Breakfast was fine, but watching Serena and Tony fall for each other right before her eyes was something she could do without. In a few hours, they would be back in Columbus; and things would be back to normal. Tony would normally be hungry by now, but this morning he didn't have much of an appetite, but he wasn't going to tell Melissa that. He needed to see Serena again before she left. The more he thought about it, he discovered he had butterflies.

Being a nurse had its advantages, but this wasn't one of them. Melissa changed her schedule to work on standby a few months ago. Not sure what she was getting into when she was in nursing school, she often thought of making a career change. Melissa didn't particularly care about being around sick people all the time. If it wasn't for her needing the hours to keep her license, she would definitely not be going in tonight.

As Tony pulled into the driveway, he began to wonder where Serena was and how he would react to seeing her after last night; more importantly, how would she react to seeing him? His butterflies worsened. What if things had changed somehow? He tried not to look worried, and he got out of the truck to open Melissa's door. Just then he realized he'd not given Serena his contact information. He told Melissa he would be in shortly as he went into his bag and dug for one of his business cards. He knew Tara wouldn't mind giving Serena his information, but he felt better doing it himself.

Serena slipped on her favorite yellow and orange floral sundress as she stood in front of the mirror. Her stomach turned slightly from nervousness. "Where did that come from?" she said to herself as she dismissed it and continued staring in the mirror. "This outfit is the perfect attire for my upcoming road trip." She found her matching floral hair tie and wrapped it around her ponytail. She put on her favorite orange sandals and said, "Now I'm ready for the road." She grabbed her bags and headed for the front. "Good morning, good morning," Serena said to Mr. and Mrs. Danston as she asked Tara for her keys. The girls were preparing the plates so she knew to hurry. Mr. Danston was at the kitchen sink washing the dishes. She wanted to get the bags packed and ready to go before she sat down to enjoy the morning feast. On her way to the door, she heard the doorbell ring. As she walked to the door, she saw Melissa standing there. Serena turned back toward the kitchen and said, "Melissa's here," as she smiled cordially at Melissa. Of course, she didn't return the smile or bother to speak, which didn't surprise Serena. As she approached the car, she wondered where Tony was. She popped Tara's trunk, and Tony looked up from the back of his truck. Both were surprised to see the other. "Good morning, what are you doing back there?" Serena asked playfully.

Tony smiled. "I was actually getting something for you," he said.

"Oh, something for me," she said with a curious look on her face.

"Yeah, I just remembered I'd not given you my business card, you know, so you can keep in touch," Tony said sheepishly.

"Oh, how thoughtful; you're right, I'd completely forgotten myself," she said as she reached into her bag and pulled out her own card. He walked over to Tara's car and lifted the trunk so he could put Serena's bags in. Tara had already placed her luggage in the trunk. They exchanged cards; and as Tony tucked his away in his wallet, Serena put hers in one of the bags he'd just placed in the trunk. "Thanks," she said as she closed the trunk. "Are you hungry?"

"I wasn't before I got here, but suddenly I'm ravenous." He smiled at her as the two of them walked to the house.

Love Happens

"Well, good morning!" Mr. Danston yelled from the sink to Melissa. "Come on in and grab a seat." He motioned toward the table.

"We already have your plate ready," said Mrs. Danston. Melissa said thank you and complied. Mr. Danston watched his son's face light up from the window when he talked to Serena. He could tell the conversation was somewhat intimate between Tony and Serena and wondered what was going on. Not wanting to draw attention to himself, he sat at the table waiting for them to come inside. Melissa was very quiet and seemed to be listening for the front door. She wondered what was taking Tony so long.

"So I hear Terry's in town," Mr. Danston said to Tara. Before she could respond, Tonya blurted out, "Yeah, we ran into him yesterday at the Food Lion, and he was all over Tara." Tara raised her eyebrows and said, "Thank you, Tara." The whole family laughed as Tara actually repeated the same story Tonya had. "Yeah, he's here for a ribbon-cutting ceremony at the new boys and girls' club being dedicated in his honor."

"What an honor; his parents must really be proud of him," Mrs. Danston said.

"Yeah, I'm sure they are," Tara said as she thought about all of the revelations of yesterday. "He's here until Monday; maybe you'll get a chance to see him."

Just then the front door opened, and in came Serena with Tony following closely. Tony watched her walk in front of him; and as her hips switched from side to side, he began thinking of last night. Serena took a seat at the bar as Tony paused beside her, still being caught up in his memory of their kiss last night. Serena looked up at Tony from the bar with a smile that was only meant for him. She then wondered if he was going to attempt sitting beside her since that was the only seat left. "C'mon over here; I have your plate all ready for you," Mr. Danston said to his son whose mind was obviously somewhere else. Melissa had her back to the bar and wondered what was taking Tony so long. She turned, realizing he had not heard his father. "Tony, your father is offering you a seat at the table," she said, irritated. As if on cue, Tara picked her plate up from the table and headed for the bar. "Tony, you can have my seat," she said as she stretched her eyes toward Serena, letting her know that the entrance they'd just made said a lot. Tony slowly turned away from Serena and realized he'd been the center of attention unintentionally. He took a seat between Mrs. Danston and Melissa and greeted them all good morning. Mr. Danston waited 'til everyone was seated. "Oh, gracious Father, thank you for this wonderful and blessed day. Thank you for allowing us to get up with able bodies this morning, Heavenly Father. Thank you for blessing a sinner like me with such wonderful children. Thank you for bringing us all together this morning to partake in this meal. Thank you for blessing me with my strong and steadfast better half," he said, referring to Mrs. Danston. "Lord, bless our two new additions to the family this morning as they are both special and will always be welcomed in my home. Finally, Lord, bless my two children as they travel on the dangerous highways today, Heavenly Father. Please protect them all and keep them safe, in Jesus's name I pray." They all said amen and began enjoying the breakfast before them. Serena was used to saying her grace, but hearing a powerful prayer like that before breakfast was somewhat overwhelming. She missed her family and wished they were as close as Tara's family seemed to be. She offered a prayer for her family before she started eating.

Mrs. Danston actually had Memorial Day off and had planned to go over to Big Mama's to grill some leg quarters and turkey burgers. Mr. Danston wasn't sure he'd be able to join them because he had to pick up his next load. "So what are you kids doing for Memorial Day?" she asked, looking at Tony and Melissa.

"Well, I'm thinking about having a cookout and inviting some friends over tonight." Melissa could tell that Tony's small get-together sounded as if it had escalated into something larger, like a full-blown party. She wondered if he decided to do that because she couldn't be there, so she watched him as he continued talking.

"Well, when do you go back to work?" she asked Tony.

"Luckily, I don't have to go in until Tuesday night." He didn't mention Melissa's schedule. Tony had been a firefighter since moving to Columbus three years ago and loved his job. It kept him in good shape, and most of all, he loved his work schedule. Twenty-four on and forty-eight off, which was how he was able to go to school and earn his bachelor's degree. He went on to say, "That means I can down some Coronas tonight and still be able to sleep it off tomorrow. Mr. Danston started laughing. "Yeah, don't down too many or you'll sleep through Monday." Tony looked at the girls sitting at the bar but began speaking to his father. "I've been trying to get Tara down to Columbus to see the house. This would be the perfect weekend. I just had the landscapers to come out a couple of months ago to plant flowers and hedges in my front and backyard. It's really beginning to look like home," he said with a tempting smile directed at Serena. Melissa almost choked on her food and quickly drank some water. *Did he just invite them to Columbus to see his house?* She was shocked because it was the first she'd heard about the invitation. She excused herself from the table and began to put her dishes away. She knew this could be a dangerous conversation, so she was more than ready to get on the road. She went to the bathroom to wash her hands and splash water on her face as if trying to wake up from this nightmare. While in the bathroom, she heard Tara say that they would love to go to Columbus and would do so today if Serena didn't have to go to work on Tuesday. Melissa almost jumped for joy. "Yes! Serena has to be back for work on Tuesday," she said with a sigh of relief. "You know we have a fifteen-hour drive ahead of us. If we leave by twelve o'clock, that puts us back in Texas at three o'clock on Monday morning. That'll give us the rest of the day to regroup. I wish we had more time," she went on. Tony looked at Serena with a sympathizing look. "Yeah, if you had another day, you could spend it with Terry, huh, Tara," Tonya joked. Tara smiled as she shook her head at her sister while everyone watched with interest. That thought had not occurred to Tara, but she would make sure she thanked her baby sister properly when the time was right.

Serena's head was spinning. *Had Tony just invited us to Columbus for a second time?* She realized he was serious, and she regretted having to work on Tuesday. She was surprised Tara even contemplated the invite because she had not seemed interested earlier. Serena figured Tara didn't want her to feel badly about not being able to stay longer because of her work schedule. She instantly knew this was why Tara hadn't seemed to take the invite seriously. Serena then began to think about the possibility of having one more day with Tony. Not to mention seeing a different part of Georgia and having the opportunity to see Tony's new home. She was so excited about what could have been. Well, Serena firmly believed that if something was meant to be, it would be. When Serena realized how deep in thought she was, everyone was up and clearing the table; and Tony was standing right beside her, looking down into her face. "Hey, lady," he said with a smile. She was startled by the closeness of his voice, and there he goes again calling her lady. Serena absolutely loved to hear him say that with his southern accent. It was an instant turn-on. "Hey, you," she said, standing up from the bar stool then realizing Tony wasn't backing away. He reached down and hugged her and said, "Have a safe trip." He then whispered, "Call me if you get lonely." Serena returned the hug and scanned the room for Melissa who was MIA. She laughed and told Tony, "Count on it!"

Melissa was walking up the hallway and witnessed the two of them embracing and laughing as if they shared a secret. Tony turned to Tara and said, as he hugged his sister good-bye, "I really wish you guys could come to Columbus, but I understand. How about a rain check?"

"Now that I can do," Tara said, hugging her brother.

Melissa said, "You guys have a safe trip," as she entered the kitchen. She was too thrilled they were going in the opposite direction and beamed with relief. She put on her best show and extended her hand to Tara, then Serena, and said, "Nice meeting you." Tara noticed the change in Melissa's demeanor and instantly felt like retaliating somehow. She knew this girl was playing games with her brother, and because she felt threatened by Serena, Tara saw her desperation and didn't like what she saw.

Tony and Melissa said good-bye to Tony's family and left for the truck. Mr. and Mrs. Danston decided it was time for their midday nap and said good-bye to the girls before disappearing down the hallway. The girls walked outside to wave good-bye as Tony and Melissa drove away. As Serena watched him drive away, she realized that she was really going to miss him. It was as if they had known each other much longer than two days. It felt more like two months, and yet there was so much more to explore with him. Tara had retrieved the cordless phone and was on the porch dialing her grandmother and noticed Serena still watching Tony's truck as he pulled out onto the main road. As Tara said good-bye to her grandmother, Serena took a seat on the porch hoping Tony had forgotten something, anything to give him a reason to turn around. It was eleven fifteen, and Serena reminded herself to check her messages before they got on the road. The breakfast had delayed their start time, but they would still make good time traveling on Sunday. Tara was hanging up with her grandmother and noticed Serena's long face. "We'll come back," she said to her friend, "I promise."

Serena asked, "Is it that noticeable?"

"I've gotta give Tonya some money for school; I'll be back in a sec."

"Okay, I'll be in the car; tell Tonya to keep working on that crossover," Serena said with a smile.

As Tony headed for the interstate, his thoughts were filled with Serena. He was hoping she watched him pull away from his dad's house. He had envisioned her watching him until the truck disappeared down the street but knew he couldn't risk looking back. *I'll probably never see her again,* he thought, and he felt his heart drop. *We had unfinished business. I wonder if it's possible to take a rain check on that,* he thought as he smiled to himself.

Melissa knew Tony was thinking about Serena. It was eleven fifty; and in ten minutes, the girls would be on the road heading west, she thought. She had been quiet since they left his father's house. She wondered if he'd noticed. Melissa knew whatever she had on her mind to say wouldn't be very nice, and it was getting harder and harder to contain. So if she had to talk during the trip home, she would make small talk. To break the silence, Melissa turned on the radio. Tony realized they'd been on the road for thirty minutes, and he'd not said a word to Melissa.

DETOUR

Listening to the music made him think about Serena even more. It was exactly eleven fifty-eight when "Let's Chill" came on over the radio. Tony couldn't believe it; of all the songs he had to hear at this particular time, it had to be the one he and Serena danced to last night. As he reminisced, he hoped Melissa had drifted off to sleep. He smiled to himself and began to replay that night over in his head again.

It was eleven thirty-five, and Serena was getting anxious to get on the road when Tara finally showed up on the front porch with Tonya. As Tara ran down the steps headed toward the car, Tonya waved from the porch yelling, "I'll see you this summer too, Serena." Serena smiled and waved back. The girls headed down the driveway and onto the main road. Tara turned to her friend and asked, "Are you okay?" "Yeah, I will be," Serena said. "I just need to get this out of my system." By this, Tara knew Serena was talking about Tony. "Tara, I am really thankful to you for inviting me to your home and even more thankful that I met your wonderful brother. I was able to spend some quality time with him, and he seems to be a great guy. I could probably go on and on about him," she said, laughing at herself. Serena had just confirmed what Tara had witnessed earlier in the kitchen. Tony seemed to be just as infatuated with Serena as she was with him.

The girls were headed for the interstate when Tara remembered she needed to check her tire pressure. It was too dark last night at the gas station to get an accurate reading, and she wanted to check the tires before getting on the road. Tara reached down to turn the radio up as she pulled over at the Shell station. "So what did you think about Tony's offer?" This question stunned Serena; she thought they were done talking about Tony, but before she could respond, Tara was jumping out of the car. She pondered the question and knew that if they attempted the trip to Columbus, they would be pushing it to make it back on Monday. If they would leave Columbus no later than five o'clock the next morning, they would make it to Texas around ten o'clock Monday night. Serena felt it was too risky especially with Monday being the busiest travel day of the holiday period.

Tara knew Serena wanted to be back by Sunday night, but she also knew the two of them were in the middle of something. She too wanted to visit Columbus to see her brother's house and spend more time on vacation, but she would leave the decision up to Serena. So she gave her some time to mull it over. It was eleven forty-seven when Tara got back into the car. "We're right on schedule," she said. "We'll be on I-20 in ten minutes." Serena was still quiet as Tara finished talking and pulled out onto the highway. Serena was thinking hard about seeing Tony again when "Let's Chill" came on over the radio. She gasped in disbelief. "I can't believe this." She felt overwhelmed as she listened to the song as if it were a sign telling her to go with her heart, which was pushing her to go to Columbus. How could she not pursue this feeling to see where it would lead her? Tara knew Serena loved this song and Guy, so they sang together as they often did when they listened to the golden oldies. Tara picked up her phone to call Terry before they got on I-20. Serena listened to the light-spirited conversation they were having. She thought back to everything that had happened with the two of them and was glad for the happy reunion. She felt they'd be seeing a lot more of each other now that everything was out in the open. Watching Tara talk on her phone reminded Serena yet again that she'd not checked her voice mail. She reached into the backseat to retrieve her cell phone. She had missed two calls, but no message was left. She checked her call log and found out that both numbers were from Texas. She decided to call her voice mail at home. She had three messages. One message was from her mother wondering where she'd disappeared to. Serena would call her as soon as she got off the phone. She'd been having so much fun that she'd neglected to call her mom. The second message was from a guy she'd just met. His name was John, and he was stationed at Fort Sam too. She would wait 'til later to return that call if ever. The last message was from Specialist Haley from her office. She wondered why Haley would be calling during the weekend. They never made it a habit to intrude on each other's personal time, so this alarmed Serena. *Oh no, something must be wrong.* The call came in on Saturday around noon, and she wondered if Haley still needed a favor. She pulled out her alert roster and found Haley's home number but got no answer. Next she tried her cell number, and she picked up. "Haley?"

"Yeah, hello," she said.

"This is Serena. You called and left a message for me yesterday."

"Oh, Johnson, what's up? Are you out of town?"

"Yeah, I'm actually getting on the road to head back as we speak."

"Oh, really? Well, I needed a favor."

"Go ahead."

"I have to go out of town on Wednesday, and I've cleared it with the clinic to work and be on call on Tuesday if you could do the same for me on Wednesday." Serena thought about the offer, and it would be more beneficial to her if she allowed Haley to switch duties with her. Working on Tuesday meant being on call at 1800 or six o'clock on Monday until midnight on Tuesday only because of this particular Monday falling on a holiday. Serena's head started spinning as she thought of all the possibilities. Tara had gotten off the phone with Terry and was now focused on her friend's worried expression. Serena said, "Sure, we can switch; just e-mail me a copy of the changed duty roster for my records."

"All right, that I can do," Haley said. "Thanks again for helping me out," she said as they hung up.

"No, no, no, thank you," Serena said out loud after she'd disconnected.

"What's wrong," Tara said, alarmed.

"Nothing's wrong; everything is right," she said excitedly. "You know that question you asked me before we stopped at the Shell station?"

"Yeah, about going to Columbus?"

"Exactly. What would you say if I told you that I don't have to report to work until Wednesday?" Tara was feeling the excitement. "So are you saying what I think you're saying?" Tara screamed. Serena's face lit up as she smiled from ear to ear. "Does this mean we are Columbus bound?" the girls said in unison as they laughed and high-fived each other. Both girls were ecstatic about their trip to Columbus as they bypassed the ramp for I-20 west. The girls were now headed south to Columbus on I-85. It was twelve ten, and they should be arriving in Columbus by two o'clock. Tara had called Terry to give him the news, and he was ecstatic. He cleared his schedule through noon on Monday and told Tara to expect him in Columbus by six o'clock that evening.

As Melissa watched the clock, she wondered if and when Tony would hear from Tara again. She hoped the girls didn't take him seriously and just decide to pop in unannounced. Well, one thing for sure was that she would have him all to herself when they got back; and since the girls were already on their way to Texas, she had time to work on Tony before the next opportunity presented itself to them. After hearing Tony tell his grandmother that he might be coming back for the Fourth of July, Melissa wondered if they were planning to meet up again in Fairburn. *That would be a total disaster. I'll just have to stay on top of my game,* she thought as she looked over at Tony.

Tony had barely said two words to Melissa, and they'd been on the road over an hour. Whatever the reason, he was thankful for the peace and quiet. He couldn't stop thinking about Serena and what could have been. He felt liked a school-aged boy again with his first crush. He remembered it like it was yesterday. Tia was the prettiest girl he'd ever seen in his eleven years, and he fell head over heels in love with her, and they were best friends until her family got transferred, and they lost contact. The difference was he was now a grown man and knew the difference between love and infatuation. "Tony, did you hear anything I just said?" Melissa finally spoke. Tony jumped at the sound of her voice.

"What is it, and why are you screaming?" he asked through clenched teeth.

"Why am I screaming, why the hell are you smiling? Let me guess, you're thinking about someone special," Melissa said sarcastically.

"Yeah, to be honest I was thinking about my first love." Melissa was appalled. How dare he mention that bitch? Before Melissa could further embarrass herself, Tony said, "I was thinking about my first love when I was in the fifth grade. Her name was Tia Delaney, and I would have done anything for her. We were the best of friends," Tony said as he laughed at the memories. He looked over at Melissa and saw she wasn't laughing. "What is wrong with you?" he asked.

"You are what's wrong with me." Tony tried to gather himself as he straightened up and glanced at the clock. It was twelve thirty; how long had he been daydreaming, and just how long had Melissa been trying to talk to him? He thought about Tara and Serena and wondered how far they were down the road. "Okay, Tony, obviously this relationship is not important enough for you to want to discuss. You are not here with me. I mean you are physically here but your mind is clearly elsewhere. Hell, I'm not sure where you are, and I'm not sure if I want to," she said. "Can we talk?" she asked pleadingly.

"Yeah," Tony said as he cleared his mind. "What's to talk about?" he asked.

"I want to know what happened in ATL. I know you are a friendly person and you get along with everyone, but you were a little too friendly with Tara's friend," she said, not wanting to say Serena's name. Tony took a deep breath, "Look, do we have to go through this again? According to you, I'm too friendly with everyone of the opposite sex, which also according to you is every attractive woman that I come in contact with."

"Oh, so you admit to being attracted to her," she said, still not saying her name.

"What I am saying is that every time you see me paying attention to someone who looks decent, you go crazy. And Serena is not an ugly girl," he said as if stating a fact for the record. Melissa ignored his last statement. "Well, Tony, I feel that you abandoned me completely this weekend, and you acted as if you were an escort for her. I know she is your sister's friend, but I think you went overboard, and I'm not sure exactly what happened between the two of you, but I don't like it."

"I'm sorry you feel that way, but you're blowing this thing out of proportion. I was trying to make sure she had a good time; and besides, you were not feeling well. What did you want me to do, stay at home because you were ill?"

"Tony," Melissa said, beginning to lose her cool, "I just want to know one thing, did you fuck her?"

"What!" There was no limit to the questions Melissa thought she could ask without hesitation. "What? Are you serious? Look, we've had our share of problems, and we've got a lot of issues to work on, but you are the one who's gone overboard. I'm tired and I'm finished with this conversation." Melissa was still watching him and waiting for him to lose his temper just as he always did when they were having a heated discussion. She was surprised by his tone and his comments. She knew she'd gone too far.

As the girls made their way to Columbus, they talked nonstop about their visit to ATL. Serena didn't want to make Tony her whole conversation, so she tried not to think about him and how excited she would be to see him again in a different setting. She was thrilled that she and Tara could spend the evening with the men that held their interest. While her thoughts drifted back to Tony, she heard Tara's phone ring in the background but was too deep in thought to really notice what was being said. Serena then wondered how Tony would react to their surprise visit and if the magic they shared would continue or was it now past tense. As Tara hung up the phone, she looked over at Serena. "Earth to, Serena," she said and began to laugh. "Okay, where, or shall I say, who is on your mind?" As she looked at Tara, she knew there was no need to answer. Tara knew exactly how Serena felt and was happy for her and Tony. "Okay, well, we have about forty-five more minutes to go. I guess we should let him know we're coming," Tara said and smiled as she began to dial Tony's number. Serena's heart fluttered and palms began to sweat and her stomach felt queasy trying to anticipate Tony's response to the news. Suddenly she had cold feet, and the whole ordeal had become a bit overwhelming. "Tara, do you think Tony's going to be upset by our showing up unannounced?" Tara looked at Serena and laughed but saw that Serena wasn't laughing. "Hey, what's going on? Are you having second thoughts?"

"Yeah, I guess you can say that. I just don't want to show up when he has already decided that we aren't coming, and we totally ruin whatever he has planned."

"Look, I know my brother, and I know that he would love for you to come to Columbus, and whatever plans he has or had will either be changed or we'll be included. Don't worry so much." Serena felt a little better but wouldn't feel completely at ease until they actually okayed the trip with Tony.

When Tony made it to Columbus, he had already made a few phone calls to get the party started and had formulated a list of things he'd need in order to carry it out. He stopped at his local Kroger's to get the food items for his Memorial Day cookout. Melissa decided to stay in the truck to figure out her next move. Tony had only been gone a few minutes when his cell phone started ringing. Melissa knew how Tony felt about his privacy, and he hardly ever went anywhere without his cell phone. *He must really have a lot on his mind to leave his phone,* she thought. Melissa knew he would not appreciate her answering his phone, but he wouldn't have to find out. So she reached over and answered it. "Hello," she said into the phone.

"Hello, who is this?"

"This is Melissa. Can I help you?" As she responded, she knew right away that it was Tara on the other end of the phone.

Tony filled up the shopping cart with ribs, chicken, turkey burgers, hot dogs, charcoal, and suddenly wanted something sweet. Nothing would satisfy him more than Serena's homemade 7Up pound cake that he'd sneaked a piece of after breakfast that morning. He immediately began looking for cake flour, butter, vanilla flavor, and tried to think of anything else he might need to put it together. He was having a craving and wasn't sure about some of the ingredients. He smiled to himself because that would give him an excuse to call Serena. He knew the most important ingredient was a can of 7Up. He smiled at the thought of hearing her voice. He figured he'd make a mess out of the cake since he had never attempted to bake anything before, not even after moving into his new house. Somehow he'd hoped that baking Serena's 7Up pound cake would make him feel closer to her. When Tony heard about Serena baking her family's 7Up pound cake from scratch, he was really impressed. "Do you think maybe one day you'll bake one of your famous cakes just for me?" Tony replayed the conversation over in his head as they sat across from each other at the dance. "If the opportunity ever presents itself, I would be honored to treat you to my family's secret recipe." She described how she mixes her ingredients, not stir. She was very meticulous in describing her knack for mixing the ingredients. "Whatever you do, don't ever substitute bottled 7Up for canned 7Up. The only time my mother ruined a 7Up pound cake was when she used a bottled 7Up." He laughed at the seriousness in Serena's expression as she described the incident. Sometimes Tony felt closer to Serena than he ever had to Melissa. He loved listening to her talk with so much passion. Serena smiled as she thought about Tony moving around a kitchen with an apron, whipping up a cake. As he stood in line to check out, he was even more excited now about calling her. He reached for his cell phone and was alarmed to find it not in the case on his belt. He placed his items on the conveyor belt as he tried to remember the last time he'd seen his phone. He must've been in such a hurry that he'd left his phone in the console. This bothered him because it was out of character for him to be so careless.

"Melissa," she repeated as if in shock, "this is Tara; where's Tony?" Melissa knew there was no way to get out of this one, so she spoke as casually as she could muster. "Oh, he's in Kroger's picking up a few items for tonight. He should be out shortly. Is there a message?" Tara wondered how long Melissa had been answering Tony's phone and if he was even aware. Trying to keep the concern out of her voice, "No, no, there's no message; just tell him to call me as soon as possible," Tara said.

"Is there something wrong? Did you guys get off okay?" Melissa said, prying.

"No, nothing's wrong; and yes, we made it out of Atlanta without a hiccup," Tara said deceptively. "Just tell Tony I'll be expecting his phone call," she said, trying to end the conversation.

"Okay, sure," Melissa said as she thought, *Right after I've made wild passionate love to him and make him forget about Serena.* "I'll tell him right away," she said, hanging up. She wondered if it was necessary to erase his last incoming call. Probably not, but she needed to cover her tracks, and she deleted the call before putting the phone away.

Tony headed to the truck after spending over $200. He overspent because the whole time he was thinking about Serena and not monitoring how much he was putting in the shopping cart. Melissa was startled after seeing Tony head toward the truck. She decided to get out and help off load the groceries after seeing the number of bags he had. As Tony approached the truck, he saw Melissa hop out of the truck and waited at the back for him to get there with the groceries. *That's strange,* he thought as he got closer. *She never helps with the groceries.* She was always the first to jump in the car and turn the AC on while the bagger or Tony would load the bags. Tony again had a weird feeling since being away from the truck. *Maybe she was trying to apologize for the argument earlier.* As soon as the truck was loaded, he got into the driver's seat as Melissa eased into her seat. She leaned over and kissed him warmly and seductively and finished it with a nibble on the ear. Tony was shocked by her demeanor since they'd not said two words since their discussion earlier. Tony didn't return the kiss, but he didn't push her away either; he was still in shock. Once she sat back in her seat, he said, "Are you okay?" as the curiosity got the best of him. "Sure, I'm just ready to get home and get showered and take off these clothes," she said, licking her lips and rubbing her breasts. Now Tony knew why she was acting so weird. She was inviting him over to her place to make love. After all, they'd been away from home two days and had not been together intimately. Tony didn't believe in having sex in his Big Mama's house out of respect for her. So whenever they were faced with those circumstances, they would make love the moment they returned to Columbus to make up for lost time. Well, that was before this last discussion and before Serena. He went to start the truck but remembered he'd left his cell phone in the truck. He immediately looked in the console and looked to see if there were any missed calls rather than ask Melissa. The screen showed no missed calls, and he was disappointed. He thought the girls would have called by now. If they left on time, they would have been on the road two hours. He promised himself he would call the minute he dropped Melissa off. He then smiled to himself and wondered if his memory proved to be accurate while shopping for the cake ingredients. Melissa noticed the smile and hoped it was for her. Melissa held her breath while Tony checked his phone. She was relieved when he put the truck in gear. She couldn't tell him that Tara called because he would be totally pissed to know she was intruding on his personal right to some form of privacy. They would have plenty of time to chitchat with each other. After all, their drive was at least twelve hours. She tried to rationalize. It would without a doubt ruin their homecoming lovemaking session. *Maybe afterward I could tell him, but not a moment sooner,* she thought as they headed to her house.

"I cannot believe Melissa had the audacity to answer my brother's phone. For as long as I can remember, Tony never allowed any of his female or male friends for that matter to answer his phone." This bothered Serena, but she kept it to herself as Tara was already mad enough for both of them. It was two o'clock, and the girls were arriving in Columbus. They both freshened up and tried to look lively as they entered the great city of Columbus, which they'd heard so much about. It had been an hour and still no word from Tony. Serena began to wonder if his plans had changed. She had a bad feeling about things since Melissa answered Tony's phone.

Tara had never been to Tony's house; she had just gotten bits and pieces since talking to Tony this weekend. She knew it was on the west side of town near the fire station where he worked. Tara figured she'd call her parents and let them know about her change in plans and see if they could assist her with directions to Tony's house.

As Tara got off the phone, she assured her dad that she was going to keep calling Tony with the hope of contacting him before they popped up. Just then the girls came to a Target store, and she told her dad that they were stopping to buy a few items. "Serena and I are going to spend most of our time in Tony's swimming pool," Serena heard Tara say. She had forgotten about Tony's pool and the fact that she didn't have a bathing suit, but Tara had everything covered.

Tony was almost at Melissa's. He passed her parents' home and headed back to the guesthouse where she had been living since finishing high school. As he pulled into the driveway, his phone rang. Melissa immediately tensed up, hoping it wasn't Tara again. She had to keep him occupied so he wouldn't answer the phone before they made it inside. She let the bottle of water slip from her fingers and land on top of the console where she knew Tony had stored his phone. He stomped on the brakes, and the truck came to a screeching halt. By this time, they were only a few feet from the parking space. "Oh, I'm sorry," Melissa said, as she listened to the phone stop ringing, "let me run inside to grab a towel." She searched for her keys and hurried inside to retrieve a towel. By the time she got back to the truck, Tony was cleaning up the spill with some cleaning towels he kept in the back of his truck. She apologized again this time for being clumsy. He looked at Melissa strangely and wondered why she seemed so anxious. "Don't worry, it didn't do any damage," he said, reassuring her. Tony reached into his console without warning and opened his phone to see who called. He smiled as he looked at the number on the screen. "Hmm, Tara called; I wonder if everything's all right," Tony said out loud. "Oh," Melissa said as her heart began to beat so loudly that she couldn't hear what else Tony was saying. Tony was anxious to talk to them both. "C'mon, Tony, you can call from inside," Melissa said convincingly. She knew she had to get Tony inside because once she did, he would be all hers once again. Tony was about to clip the phone on his belt as he normally did when his phone announced that he had one new message. "You go on in; I'll be right there." He didn't want to check his message or talk in front of Melissa at this point especially with her acting weird. As he dialed his voice mail, Melissa hurried inside, wondering what the message from Tara would be. She had begun to work on her story as to why or how she had forgotten to give him the message. When he rushed in the house, Melissa wasn't sure what to expect, so she just stood there in shock. "Hey, I need to call Tara right away. I'm going to run home and put this meat up before it spoils, and I'll be back later."

"Tony, are you sure? You know you can use the phone here; and if you want to store the meat, you know you can put it in the freezer in the laundry room." The cake flour and flavor would be fine out in the truck while they revisited each other. Melissa wondered why seeing those items in the shopping cart alarmed her. Now she knew Tony had absolutely raved about the 7Up cake he had eaten earlier. He was so impressed that Serena had time to master the skill of baking and be a full-time soldier. She wondered when he was going to ask her to bake it. Melissa had forgotten Tony was standing there still trying to get to his place. "No, I'd better get home and check things out before tonight." Melissa immediately brushed up against Tony and moved in a way that no man would mistake for anything other than what it was. Melissa wanted intimacy, and she couldn't wait. Tony was flattered by her desire for him, but it was all about timing, and right now there was somewhere else he needed to be. As he rushed to his truck, he began to dial Tara's number, but there was no answer. She'd only called five minutes ago, and now she wasn't answering. Tony grew concerned.

As the girls chose their bikinis, they grabbed sunscreen and flip-flops that matched their swimsuits. Target was their favorite store, another thing the girls had in common. On their way to the car, the girls' level of excitement increased astronomically. "We'll be there in fifteen minutes," Tara said. Her dad had given her directions, and Serena wrote them down. *We would soon see Tony,* Serena thought as the butterflies returned. Just as they drove off and got onto the main road, Tara's phone was ringing, and she was overjoyed to see that it was Terry. She answered the phone cheerfully and talked for a few minutes as Serena made sure she made all the right turns. As soon as Tara hung up, Serena said excitedly, "Okay, Tara, we are getting really close now; and we need to try Tony again." Tara checked her phone and said, "Oh no, I missed his call. We must've been in Target."

"Did he leave a message?" Serena asked.

Tara checked; and sure enough, there was a message: "Hey, it's Tony; I'm just making it home. I had to drop Melissa off, but give me a call when you get this message." The message was playing on the speakerphone, and Serena could hear the concern in his voice. Just hearing his voice made her heart skip a beat. *Here it is; I'm within five minutes of seeing this man that I am falling so hard for, and he doesn't even know I'm coming. I would be so embarrassed if he would not welcome me with open arms.* "Oh my god, Tara, I am getting cold feet." Tara turned on Cherry Grove until they passed the fire station. "Tony's place should be a few blocks from here. Don't worry, Serena, everything's going to be just fine; trust me," Tara said as she tried to reassure her friend.

Tony wondered how far the girls had made it and how they were doing as he unloaded the last bag of groceries. He looked at the cake ingredients and started smiling at the memory of Serena. Well, it had been twenty minutes since he left the message. Maybe the girls stopped for a bite to eat. He prepared and seasoned the meat and let it sauté in his special homemade sauce. He jumped in the shower and fantasized about Serena and wondered if she would send him a picture when she got back to Texas. He felt so stupid when he remembered he always carried a disposable camera in his truck, and he could've looked at Serena twenty times a day if he wanted to. He washed his hair and shaved but was in no hurry to part from his thoughts of Serena, so he let the hot water pour over his head and run down his muscular chest until it reached the shower floor. He got excited just thinking about Serena and the dances they shared. His dream was abruptly interrupted by the phone ringing. As he stumbled out of the shower half drying himself off, he didn't bother to look at the caller ID before answering the phone. "Hello," he said. Just then the doorbell rang. *Who could be coming over this early,* he thought to himself as he said, "Hold on." He placed the phone on the bed and headed for the door. He slipped on some shorts and slippers but wasn't dry enough for a shirt and went to the front door expecting to see one of his neighbors.

As the girls rounded the corner to Azalea Drive, they spotted Tony's truck in the driveway. *Surely he was home alone or at least without Melissa for the moment,* Serena thought as they neared Tony's driveway. She not only had a serious case of butterflies, but the closer they got, the more her knees trembled, and her palms began to sweat. Tara pulled into the driveway and sent Serena to knock on the door. As

Serena got out of the car, she almost lost her nerve; but she knew she only had a little more than twelve hours left to spend with Tony. So she walked to the door and cleared her throat as she held her breath while trying to remain calm. She knocked on the door twice but got no answer. Tara decided to call his home phone again. *He had to be inside or nearby,* Tara thought as she dialed his number. After looking around at Tony's small but quaint porch, she discovered a doorbell and suddenly felt foolish for not noticing it sooner. She pressed the doorbell and turned to see if Tara had made contact. Just as Serena turned around, she heard the door open and felt a presence. As she whirled around, there he stood in a pair of white cotton shorts with blue slippers and a solidly built chest still dripping wet from what she hoped was the shower.

Melissa was getting antsy wondering when Tony would make it back. After all, he just needed to put the food away and take a look around. He'd been gone almost an hour, and she'd gotten herself so worked up that she was about to explode. She needed at least five hours of rest to make it through the night shift. "Maybe I should go over rather than wait here." She began to pack her overnight bag for what would be more like a few hours rather than overnight. "I'll surprise him," she said to herself as she began singing while she packed her belongings.

Tony must have been hallucinating because the visitor on his front porch looked like, smelled like, and sounded like Serena. As he stood there awestruck, his confused look must have sent a mixed message. Before he could say anything, Tara called out to Tony from the car as she held up her cell phone and disconnected. Tony smiled from ear to ear knowing now that what he saw standing before him was real and not a mirage. Seeing his award-winning smile, Serena lightened up as she returned the smile. Tony immediately reached for her hand, looking at her as if to see if it was okay. He hugged her so deeply and warmly, and she reciprocated. He repeatedly asked, "What are you guys doing here? I thought you'd be in Birmingham by now. Why didn't you leave a message to let me know you were coming?" He asked all of these questions while still holding on to Serena. Tara closed the car door and started walking to the house smiling at the reunion of her close friend and her dear brother. Tony could feel the pounding in Serena's chest as they separated. "Are you okay?" he asked, looking concerned. "I hope I didn't get you wet." She stepped back and said, "I'm fine now." He returned the smile. Tara stepped up and said, "You are the hardest person to track down." Tony was clearly stunned at what he was hearing. "I know we should've told you we'd changed our minds," Serena offered.

"No, it's fine; I'm glad you two are here. I was wondering what was going on, but we kept missing each other."

"Okay," Tara interjected, "are you two lovebirds going to stand there holding hands all day, or are you going to give us a grand tour?" Serena and Tony looked at each other, not realizing they were still holding hands. It felt so natural. "Yeah, come on in, and I'll show you around." Tony led them into the house and headed straight for his favorite room. His den/theater room was just off the kitchen. "Watch your step," Tony warned as they stepped down into the dark room. It was absolutely magnificent. There were posters of movies on the walls in nice black frames, and the room was windowless. "How perfect!" exclaimed Serena. There were three rows of black leather theater seats complete with oversized cupholders. The carpet was burgundy, and it was set up just like an actual theater, from the big screen to the aisles on either side of the seats lined with illuminating lights. Tony had added his own touch and covered the aisles with clear vinyl runners to protect the carpet. In one corner of the room, he had two vending machines: a soda machine and chip and candy machine. All of the items cost $0.25. "Oh my goodness," Serena exclaimed, "how perfect!"

"You have a popcorn maker? This is so cool," Tara said as she lounged in one of the theater seats. "This is the perfect getaway. I think every house needs one." Tara and Serena both agreed. Off the theater room, there was a short hallway with a bathroom on one side, and the other side led to the deck and pool. They walked out the back door and were amazed to see the beautiful bean-shaped pool filled with the clearest blue water. He even installed a showerhead out on the patio for use before and after the pool. The flowerbeds at the back of the yard were breathtaking. The backyard was huge and was enclosed by a privacy fence. After they finished the tour of the backyard, they headed inside where Tony showed off his kitchen. The floors were covered in alternating black and white tiles. His dining room table was black lacquer with pewter candleholders with black and white striped candles and matching accessories. The girls were astonished at the beauty of this bachelor's home. Serena was thoroughly impressed by the tasteful décor. The three bedrooms and living room all showed well, and all were large and spacious. After the tour, it was almost three o'clock; and while they were touring Tony's bedroom, he grabbed a T-shirt to put on. Tony heard Serena's stomach grumble and realized that none of them had eaten since breakfast. As they went back up to the kitchen, Tony decided he'd make lunch for them. As Tony prepared tacos, Mexican rice with fresh cilantro, the girls sat at the dining room table and relaxed. "So where's Melissa?" Tara asked while Serena looked on curiously, having forgotten all about Melissa. "Oh, I dropped her at home," Tony said. Serena knew Tara had heard the message Tony left saying he'd dropped Melissa at home. She figured it was a good way to bring her up to see how much he knew about her first phone call to him. "I was helping her get her bags inside when you called. Sorry I missed your call. Had I known you were coming, I could've already had lunch ready." Serena believed him too. He sure knew his way around the kitchen and looked good in his kiss-the-chef apron. *I wanted to do just that.*

"What do you mean?"

"I called more than once," Tara said as she stared at Tony.

"What do you mean? What time did you call?"

"I'm not sure of the exact time, but it was shortly after we made up our minds to come here."

"I'll prepare the table and get the drinks ready if you don't mind," Serena said, wanting to get away from the conversation they were about to have. Tara went on to explain that Serena had received a message about not having to work on Tuesday, and that's when they decided to come to Columbus and called him to let him know. As she looked through the cabinets trying to orient herself with where everything was, she completely tuned the conversation out, not wanting to be involved. Serena noticed cake flour and vanilla flavor and wondered what Tony had planned to do with it. She recalled him saying he never tried to bake anything since he was a teenager trying to prepare his mom a birthday cake when he inadvertently set the cake on fire. She made a mental note to ask him when he finished talking to Tara. As Tara went on and on, Tony was still puzzled about the missed phone call. The only time he'd been away from his phone was when he was in the grocery store. He remembered checking the missed calls, and there were no calls. Tara's phone rang, and it was

Terry, so she excused herself and took the call outside. As Serena took a seat at the table, Tony seemed lost in thought, so she gave him some time to think. "So, Tony, what were you going to do with cake flour and vanilla flavor?" Serena asked, smiling. Tony was embarrassed that she'd discovered them but answered with a smile. "I was actually going to try to bake one of your 7Up pound cakes. That would give me an excuse to call you," he said with a cunning smile.

"I would hope that by now you know you don't need an excuse," Serena said, returning the same seductive smile.

"Oh really, well that's great news," Tony said.

"If you want me to bake you a cake while I'm here, I'd be more than happy to."

"Will you really?" he asked.

"Of course, I'd do that for you."

Just then Tara reentered the room. "Tony, one of the reasons I was calling too was to see if it was all right with you for Terry to come here." Tony looked surprised. "Terry's coming here?" he repeated. "Yeah, that's cool I've already made a few phone calls, and I'm going to start grilling some ribs and chicken around five thirty. I'm keeping it small. I've invited about twenty people over, so I'm sure he will be welcomed, and I don't have a problem with it. Whatever makes you happy," he said with an approving smile.

Tony fixed the girls' plates and placed them on the table; he sat down, and they began enjoying the Mexican feast he'd prepared. Just as they started eating lunch, the phone rang. Tony ignored it and said he would check the caller ID later. "Tony, when did Melissa start answering your phone?" Tara asked out of the blue. Tony choked on his iced tea; and after clearing his throat, he asked, looking confused as if Tara were mistaken, "What do you mean answering my phone? Melissa doesn't answer my phone." The girls immediately looked at each other. "Well, she did today while you were in the grocery store," Tara continued. He knew right away what Tara was saying was true. *That explained her strange behavior at the store and why she seemed so nervous when I came back to the truck,* he thought to himself. His eyes widened and his brow frowned as he recalled taking the time to check for missed calls when he returned to the truck; there were none. He couldn't believe Melissa tried to cover up answering his phone by deleting the call. He stood up immediately and excused himself from the table. The girls looked at each other and decided to clear the table. Serena took out the butter to soften for the cake. Tara left to grab their bags from the car while Serena finished up in the kitchen.

Melissa had gotten her uniform ready and was preparing a snack before she left for Tony's. *I'd better call before I leave in case he's on his way over. I'd sure hate to prolong our meeting,* Melissa thought to herself, beginning to daydream about their upcoming lovemaking session. She decided to pack her car and stop by the washroom to throw a load in the washer. While she was out, Tony called but got no answer. It was getting late, so he figured she'd fallen asleep. When Melissa returned, she didn't bother to check her messages. She didn't notice the message-indicator light flashing as she called Tony from the wall phone in the kitchen. She called and let the phone ring several times, but no one answered, nor did the voice mail pick up. *That was strange. Why was Tony not answering his phone?* Melissa started panicking. *What would possibly keep him from answering his phone? Maybe he was on the other line; maybe he was talking to Tara. Maybe he knows.* She decided to try his cell phone, but he didn't answer, so she left a message.

When Tony returned, he seemed a little more relaxed. "You okay?" Serena asked, still sweeping the floor as she spoke to Tony. When he didn't say anything, she turned around to look at his face; and he was smiling. "Yeah, I'm fine. What are you doing? Girl, you don't have to clean for me."

"Well, it's not for you. It's out of habit; and besides, I don't like making a mess or leaving my mess for someone else to have to clean. That, my friend, is the discipline my mother instilled in me long before the military reintroduced it to me in basic training," she said with a smile, and they both laughed. He didn't seem concerned about the phone call earlier, and Serena was relieved. She didn't want him to be upset. This was the first time they'd been alone since the dance, and it felt good. Neither of them said anything for what seemed like an eternity. As Tony began pulling the meat out of the refrigerator, Serena was gathering the items for the cake. As they moved in sync and in silence, Tony said, "You look good in my kitchen." He leaned over and kissed Serena on her soft, succulent lips, and she welcomed the kiss she had longed for since the night of the dance. She smiled but said nothing as they continued working. They both seemed surprised by the passion they both experienced with the kiss. As they parted, Serena's nipples hardened; and suddenly, she had the desire to kiss Tony again. She wondered if he felt the same way too. Suddenly, his cell phone rang, and the spell was broken, or so she thought. "Would you like to come out back with me?" he asked. Serena smiled and was puzzled by his lack of interest in the phone call. "Yes, that sounds great. The butter is melting, and I just need to preheat the oven to 375 degrees."

"Consider it done." He walked over to turn the oven on. He turned to her and took her hand as he led her outside.

As Melissa jumped in her car, she tried calling Tony again on his cell before she arrived. She could not calm the nervousness she felt as she began to shake. She wondered why he never came back over or at least called to say he wasn't coming. As she locked up the house, she let her mind race with all sorts of wild thoughts and began to panic. She wondered if he knew, and if he did what story would she tell him if and when he asked her about the phone call. When Melissa turned down Azalea Drive, her heart sank as she glared at the car sitting in Tony's driveway. It was Tara's Honda Civic. Melissa was livid. *What were they doing here? They're supposed to be on their way to Texas.* Her mind began to race even faster. *I can't believe he didn't tell me.* "How dare they try to pull this one over on me," she screamed as she hit the steering wheel with her fist. She came to an abrupt halt and jumped out of the car, leaving her purse in the front seat with her windows down. She was so concerned about what was going on behind closed doors that she nearly ran to the house. She wished she'd thought to bring Tony's extra key that she'd been keeping in case of an emergency with her so she wouldn't have to announce herself by ringing the doorbell.

Tara decided to call Terry to find out how his trip was going. He told her he was about an hour away and that he couldn't wait to see her. While Tara was on the phone with Terry, she had another call. She was surprised to see the number on the screen, but she didn't answer the call. She told Terry to be careful and she'd see him shortly. She wondered why Carmen was calling.

As soon as Terry hung up with Tara, he dialed his mom in Florida. He knew his cousin Karen lived in Columbus now and had been since graduating high school. It would really be great to see her on this impromptu visit to Columbus. Had it not been for Tara, he didn't know if he'd ever venture to Columbus on a personal visit. He dialed his mom, but she wasn't home, so he left a message. He knew she always checked her messages when away from home. Karen worked in the medical field, but Terry wasn't sure what her occupation was.

Tony stood and held Serena's hand as she lowered herself onto the deck. As they sat on the deck's edge with their legs hanging over the side, she looked up into his face and for a brief moment, thinking how warm and kind he'd been since the moment she'd met him. This was like a dream come true, and she wanted to savor this moment forever. She'd wondered if this feeling was something that would last or would it fade away as their relationship progressed. She quickly pushed the thought away, reminding herself that she was headed back to Texas tomorrow. It was easy to not think about Melissa as long as she wasn't around, but she knew that absence wouldn't last forever. Serena knew she'd better conduct a reality check and soon. On their way out, Tony had turned on the stereo so that they could enjoy the music while out back. Will Downing was in the background crooning, and this seemed to set the mood. Tony and Serena were enjoying the music and each other's company. The tranquility of the beautifully landscaped yard while listening to the splashing water in the pool was like heaven. They talked about Tony's job as a firefighter and how he knew he was destined to do what he does. Serena talked about her enlistment into the army and how she enjoyed the challenges of being in the military.

"I called Melissa earlier after Tara told me what she'd done to question her about the call. When I looked at my phone, the call had been completely erased from the call log. There's no way it was an accident, and it really pissed me off." He sat quietly for a moment.

"Well, what did she say?" Serena asked.

"She didn't answer, and I'm not sure if she's already resting before she goes in tonight or if she's out and about. I don't know why I'm telling you this. I guess I just want us to always be up front with one another. This so-called relationship I'm in is based on lies and deceit, and it has been from day one now that I think back on it. I don't mean to put all of my business out there, but I do want you to know that Melissa can be crazy sometimes."

"Hey, there you are!" Tara exclaimed. "I didn't know where you'd disappeared to. I talked to Terry, and he'll be here shortly."

"Good, let me get the coals ready; and by the time he gets here, we should be able to start smoking the meat." Tony heard a car door close, and it seemed to be coming from his front yard. They all stopped and listened and heard the doorbell ringing.

Tony was already headed to the door when the doorbell rang again. He looked through the peephole and discovered it was Melissa, and she looked pissed. Tony was not ready to have this discussion now. He'd already told Serena how he felt about the whole deceptive ordeal. Today he wanted to focus on Serena and not be in a foul mood all day because of Melissa's trifling ways.

The girls wondered if it was Melissa at the door. Serena tried not to worry about what was going on at the front door. Tara asked Serena if she wanted to play cards later on. "Sure, does Terry know how to play?"

"Is he from the South?" Tara asked, laughing.

"Yeah, I guess I wasn't thinking."

"Okay, Serena, what's on your mind?" Tara asked, feeling something was bothering her. So Serena filled her in on some of the things they talked about, mainly about Melissa.

Melissa stepped forcefully into the foyer as Tony opened the door. "Aha, I knew she was here, and you're trying to play me!" she screamed at the top of her lungs. "You and that bitch had this planned all along, didn't you? Well, this is going to stop right now," she commanded. Tony grabbed Melissa by the arm and led her to his bedroom. "Girl, what is your problem?" he asked, trying not to raise his voice. "Do you know that girl well enough to be calling her a bitch? What if she heard you?"

Tony seemed really concerned that I had insulted Miss Serena. This worried Melissa. *Why is he taking up for her, and he's seeing me,* she thought to herself. His behavior further annoyed her. "I don't give a damn if she did hear me. She is in my territory now, and I'm not having it. There's no way I'm going to let some trifling hooker you just met interrupt what we have and disrespect me at the same time."

"Girl, what are you talking about? I did not know they were coming, but you knew that I had invited them." Tony felt weird having to defend Serena's honor in her absence when suddenly he remembered the incident with the phone call and became irate. As he tried to contain himself, he said, "Melissa, I'm not doing this with you today. My sister is here, and we are not going to have all this unnecessary drama in my house." Tony's phone rang; and as he answered it, he began laughing and talking as if nothing was wrong.

Melissa didn't know who was on the other end, but whoever it was, was coming over for the cookout. Tony walked into the bathroom and began washing his hands while he assured them that they'd be eating around seven o'clock. The phone call gave them a much-needed break. When Tony hung up, he turned around to find Melissa standing in front of him. She had gotten undressed and was standing before him in her birthday suit. Melissa knew it was Tony's weakness. She also knew Tony loved spontaneous sessions and knew her timing couldn't be more perfect. She walked over to him and gently pushed him onto the bed and straddled him.

Tony was not in the mood to forgive Melissa just yet. He wanted her to learn her lesson and stop being so suspicious and accusatory of his every move. As he lay underneath Melissa, he looked at the way her breasts hung so beautifully, not too big and not too small. She smelled of Victoria's Secret mixed with a musty feminine smell. Normally this would drive him crazy, but today it had no effect on him whatsoever. He was not amused nor aroused and wondered why he'd not been interested in taking advantage of this opportunity.

Terry called Tara while the girls were still sitting on the deck. "Hey, do you remember my cousin Karen?" Terry asked and continued. "She's here in Columbus. I'm going to drop by her place. It's not far from Tony's. I was going to stop by the store to pick up some Corona and Courvoisier afterward. What would you and Serena like to drink?" He told Tara he'd be there in about an hour after taking her order. Serena began to miss Tony and wondered what he was doing; he'd been gone at least ten minutes. She knew it was Melissa at the door. Serena began to feel sick inside as her heart began to pound faster and faster. The thought of Tony being intimate with Melissa or anyone for that matter really bothered her. As reality began to set in, she knew her place and would never forget it nor put herself in this situation again. She needed to do something to get him off her mind and quick. She didn't want him to think she was some kind of crazed fatal attraction. Tara got off the phone after she noticed the ill look on Serena's face. "Serena, are you okay?" Serena tried to perk up, but it was no sense in trying to hide her feelings from her friend of two years. She knew whatever she did, she couldn't let Tony see the disappointment that she felt inside. "Do you think Tony would mind if I started on the cake now?"

"No, I think he will be pleased. I'll come with you," she said as they got up from the deck. "We can go for a swim when we get the cake in the oven if you're ready."

"Sure, that's the second best idea I've heard all day." She managed a weak smile. Serena turned to go inside not knowing what to expect. She stopped by the stereo and found a local jazz station. Jazz was where she visited when she needed to forget about things that troubled her. It always seemed to relax her and put her in the zone she wanted and needed to be in. Jazz always did the trick; and for that, Serena was forever grateful. Tara had stepped out to get the bathing suits and the rest of their bags from the car when she noticed a car parked in the driveway that probably belonged to Melissa. Now she was getting concerned. *What was going on with Tony and Melissa?* she thought as she locked up the car and headed back inside. Serena let the sounds of Kenny G take her to a trouble-free land, and she even found an apron. She felt at home as she mixed up the ingredients and moved through the kitchen light on her feet to the music. "No worries," she said, convincing herself. She even had enough time to prepare a tossed salad complete with tomatoes, onions, green peppers, and cucumbers. She hoped Tony would not mind.

Was it because of Melissa's deceit or because he had work to do before sunset for the cookout? Maybe it was because he had a special houseguest that he so desperately wanted to get back to. He couldn't figure it out and felt that he was wasting time. He lifted Melissa up from the bed and told her to get dressed. Melissa was shocked and broken at the same time over Tony's refusal to make love to her. He'd never reacted that way before. She began to feel embarrassed but mustered up enough courage to ask him what was wrong. "Nothing's wrong. I just can't do *this* right now. You need to get dressed." Silence fell upon the room, and he noticed Will was no longer playing. Jazz was always a welcomed pastime for him. As Melissa got dressed, he went to the bathroom to wash up so that he wouldn't carry her sexual aroma back out to his guests, but especially to Serena. He decided to change shirts too just in case. As he turned the water off in the sink, he heard someone moving around in the kitchen. He wondered how long someone had been in the house. He left Melissa in the room to get herself together while he made his way to the kitchen. He heard the jazz radio station on, and this made him smile. As he entered the kitchen, he could not have imagined a more comforting sight than to see Serena moving around in the kitchen with his apron on, like she was supposed to be there. He smiled as he stopped to admire her. Tara was coming back into the house with her hands full when she stopped in her tracks and watched Tony watch Serena dancing around the kitchen with a look of adoration. Tara smiled as Tony stood there quietly. Serena spun around to dance over to the table and was startled when she discovered she had an audience. She wondered how long they'd been observing her. Her goal was to lose herself in the music, and she had accomplished that. She laughed the most sensual laugh and said, "Boy, am I glad I don't talk to myself." The three of them shared a laugh. She canted her head to the side and said, "Hi there," to Tony, as if all was forgiven. He responded, "Hey, lady, are you finding everything okay?"

"Yeah, I got it covered."

Tara put the bags down. "Tara, do you need some help with the bags?"

"They're just a few more."

"I'll come with you," he said as they left Serena in the kitchen putting the cake in the oven. Serena looked out the window and saw a cute red convertible in front of Tony's house. She figured that must've been Melissa's car.

Serena watched Tony and Tara laugh and talk when she noticed Tony had changed shirts. This puzzled her; *why would he have to change shirts unless he'd gotten it dirty somehow.*

She wondered where Melissa was and what she was doing. Before Serena could finish that thought, she heard Tony's bedroom door open.

As Melissa got dressed, she heard the three of them in the front laughing. She wondered how this was going to play out. She'd made a fool of herself, but only in Tony's presence. She heard the front door close and took a peek out the window and saw Tony and Tara at Tara's car. Serena must still be inside. Melissa immediately knew how to get back at Serena and let her know who was running the show. She took off her bra and walked into the front with her blouse buttoned up the wrong way, letting Serena take a look at her prized possession. The state of her shirt was to confirm to Serena that she and Tony had been intimate.

As Serena was loading the dishwasher, she could see Melissa walking up the hallway not taking her eyes off of Serena. Serena swallowed hard and kept waiting for Melissa to say something. Something about the whole incident made Serena think that Melissa and Tony had been intimate. Serena had to keep reminding herself that whatever the two of them had was there before she was. Serena knew she would be totally out of character to have an attitude with either one of them. She spoke to Melissa as she got closer to the kitchen. Melissa hesitated; and before she could speak, Tony and Tara were coming in with their bags. Melissa almost opened her mouth to ask if they were spending the night at Tony's, but she knew they were, and she didn't want to make herself look any worse than she did already.

"Are you ready for a dip in the pool?" Tara asked Serena.

"Yeah, I'm ready if you are," she said with a big smile on her face. Cooling off in the pool was what she really needed. Having the oven on and preparing the cake had Serena overheated. She and Tara started toward the back. Serena turned to Tony. "Do you mind if I take a shower?" Melissa held her breath as she waited to hear Tony's answer. "Sure, you can use my shower in my bedroom. You'll be waiting forever on slow poke," he said, teasing Tara. Tara threatened her brother and went into the guest bedroom with her bags while Serena headed down the hallway to Tony's room. This was not what Melissa expected, but it was Tony's house. Melissa felt she needed some fresh air and headed for the backyard. "Melissa," Tony called, "what's wrong with your clothes?"

"What are you talking about?" she asked as she looked down at her feet and said oops, as if she were surprised to find her clothes in disarray. Tony wondered if Serena had noticed that Melissa wasn't wearing a bra, not to mention she buttoned her shirt up wrong. He dismissed this. "You left your windows down and your purse in your car." Melissa seemed shocked at her carelessness. "We'll be having more company soon." Tony continued. "Do you plan to put your bra back on?" Melissa looked stunned that he would ask her to do that. He knew exactly what Melissa was up to.

Tony went to the storage shed to retrieve the lighter fluid. He decided to check the refrigerator for cold soda and water. He was running low on sodas and would have to restock it before the guests showed up. He used the phone in the storage shed to call Justin to pick up some things from Party City. There was a Party City on his way over, so Tony figured he wouldn't mind. Justin knew he was good for the bill. Tony started the fire on the grill and took a seat on the deck and waited for the coals to get ready. Melissa joined him and sat under the big umbrella in the huge chair. He heard a car pull up, and he went around to the side of the house and opened the fence that led to the front yard. There he saw Terry getting out of a Cadillac Escalade and went out to greet him with their usual brotherly handshake and hug. "Man, you are just in time," Tony said.

"Yeah, I figured you'd want some of my help with the grilling," Terry said, boasting. "I wish I could've gotten here sooner."

"No, you are just in time. Tara's inside changing into her bathing suit. Come on around back."

"Wait, I stopped by the package store and picked up some drinks." Tony grabbed the Coronas, and Terry carried the other bags. Terry followed Tony to the deck and commented on the beauty of Tony's house and was thoroughly impressed with the pool. "Man, this is really nice," Terry kept saying. He was surprised to see Melissa lounging on the deck. He spoke to her and placed the drinks on the deck as he wondered whether or not she lived there with Tony. He went to check on the coals while Tony went out to restock the refrigerator in the storage building. Tony wanted to keep the girls' drinks in the refrigerator in the house so only they would have access to them. His guests would know that whatever was in the storage was theirs for the taking, but what was kept inside was off limits.

As Tony was in the shed moving drinks from the shelf to the refrigerator, Serena and Tara came out onto the deck. Terry grabbed Tara and gave her a big hug. He spoke to Serena as she made her way off the deck on to the poolside. "When did you get here?" she asked.

"I just drove up about five minutes ago."

"Good," she said, "perfect timing." As she chatted with Terry, Melissa raised up from her comfortable position to get a good look at her new competition. Serena was definitely built perfectly for a two-piece, and she knew Tony would soon notice too. Serena felt like a million dollars after a nice long shower, and now she was ready to soak up some sun and enjoy the pool.

Melissa couldn't take her eyes off of Serena. *Her abs are nice and cut, and oh my goodness, not the video booty. Tony is really going to lose his mind when he sees her.* Good thing Melissa had her dark sunglasses on so Tony wouldn't know that she was staring at him while he watched Serena.

Tony watched the girls come out of the house. He saw Melissa staring at Serena with her mouth open. He laughed to himself and thought, *She'd better close her mouth before a fly flies in.* He knew why she was staring, and he couldn't blame her. God had truly blessed this lady with all the right curves in all the right places, and she certainly was different from anyone else he'd met before. Whatever it was, it peaked his curiosity. Serena had the body of a goddess, and her pretty brown skin looked good in the bright yellow two-piece she wore so well. Melissa was staring so hard that she didn't notice Tony staring at her. Melissa was startled to see Tony coming up the steps to the deck and wondered how she missed his initial reaction to seeing Serena. She knew he was attracted to Serena, and there was nothing she could do about it. Tony had brought beach towels out of the storage building and handed one to Tara. "Are you joining us?" she asked her brother.

"Not now, maybe after I get the meat on." He then took the second towel over to Serena. *Oh, how gentleman-like,* Melissa thought as she stared watching and waiting for anything out of the ordinary to happen between the two of them.

Serena looked up to see Tony coming out of the storage building with towels and thought he has everything covered. That was one thing they hadn't thought to pick up at Target. As he went over to Tara, she could see Melissa eyeballing him. She looked pissed. *Well, looks like she found her bra,* Serena thought. She began to think about the offer Tony made to her. He had offered his shower in his room. Serena thought that was a very nice gesture. When she took a look around the room, it appeared neat and tidy just as it had before Melissa came over. She was beginning to question whether or not the two of them had been intimate. *Why would Tony offer his room if he'd just made love to another woman in his bed prior to my going in? Why would Melissa make the grand entrance she had without her bra?*

"Hey, lady, are you okay?" Tony interrupted. He was standing right beside her, leaning down to talk to her.

"Hey, where'd you come from?" she said, smiling up into Tony's eyes. She could still see the look of concern on his face. "I'm fine," she reassured him. He handed her the towel, and she thanked him.

"I'll be back; I gotta get the meat on the grill," he said as he turned to go in the house. Serena eased into the water, and Tara soon joined her. Tony came out to the deck with one pan of meat; and before he turned to go back inside, Serena yelled from the water, smiling, "Tony, will you please check the timer on the oven, pleaseeee? I don't want to ruin your cake." Melissa listened to the exchange; "your cake," the words echoed again and again in her head. *Why in the hell is she baking a cake for my boyfriend?* Melissa thought to herself and became furious. *When did they decide to do all of this? It's almost as if they had planned this whole day.* Melissa stopped in the middle of her thoughts—*Tony bought the ingredients when we stopped at the grocery store earlier.* She began to wonder how much of this was a coincidence.

Tony smiled at the sound of Serena's enthusiastic voice as she asked him to check on the cake. She didn't want to ruin it, which I doubt was possible. He didn't bother to look at Melissa as he headed inside. He knew she'd want to discuss what that meant too, and he didn't have the time or the energy to have another discussion. Before he headed out back with the tray, Justin pulled up with a carload. He was followed by Darrin and Kenny. There were only three vehicles, but somehow twenty people climbed out and were headed toward the house. He grabbed the remote to the big screen in the theater room and put on *Scarface*, which was one of his favorite movies. He then went over to start the popcorn machine up just in case any of them needed something to snack on while waiting for the food. He kept the popcorn machine preset; and in fifteen minutes, they would have enough popcorn for everyone. Tony loved to entertain. He looked in on the cake, and it was shaping up quite nicely; it had forty more minutes. He set his watch as he walked to the front door. Tony smiled and welcomed his guests as he led them thru to the theater room and out back. He allowed the guests to use the bathroom off the theater room, which was also close to the back door. He loved entertaining but always set the ground rules for his friends, and their friends so that there were no misunderstandings. They respected Tony and knew that if they caused problems while at his place, it would be their last visit. His close friends knew that to be true, so they only invited the well respected when they came over.

Melissa looked up a little when the others joined her on the deck. She was beginning to hate her job more and more. She would soon need to get a nap if she planned to stay up during her shift. As Tony stepped out on the deck, he introduced Terry, Tara, and Serena to his friends. All were big hits. Of course, they were all going crazy over seeing Terry Jones up close and personal. They couldn't believe he was actually doing the grilling. Justin and Darrin had heard Tony talk about playing ball with Terry in high school; now they were meeting him in person. They were also excited to finally meet Tony's baby sister who they'd heard was in the military. "And this is Serena, Tara's friend. She and Tara are both stationed in Texas." The guys were falling over themselves to get a closer look as Serena and Tara were hanging on to the side of the pool. Tony realized he'd forgotten to take the girls' drinks inside. "Justin, can you take these drinks and put them in the refrigerator and also bring the meat out of the refrigerator to Terry?"

"Sure," Justin said, "I'll get it." Justin was one of Tony's closest friends, and Tony trusted him. He would normally help Tony grill the meat when they had cookouts. He soon returned with another huge pan of meat and stopped to assist Terry at the grill. Tony was standing beside Terry checking the first batch they'd put on. The meat sizzled as they placed it on the grill. Serena was getting hungry just from the sweet aroma of smoked meat. That was something she was used to doing at home with her family when she was fortunate enough to get there for a holiday or two.

As Tony walked away from the grill, he saw they had everything under control. He went inside to get his swimming trunks on. He was stopped by Melissa on his way to the pool. "Baby, aren't you going to spend some time with me before I have to leave?" she asked, trying to sound persuasive. He sat down in the chair next to Melissa, and this seemed to make her happy. He heard Justin tell Terry that he could go to the pool if he wanted to and that he'd watch the grill. Terry was more than happy to be getting some time with Tara, so he headed to the pool. Melissa began to think back to how she found Tony's room. She wondered if he and Serena had been intimate. He seemed really distant even as he sat two feet from her. Serena saw Tony sitting by Melissa, and she wondered if he was being forced to sit there. She tried not to stare at the strained look on his face.

"What time are you going to lie down?" he asked Melissa, trying not to seem too pushy.

"I need to be resting no later than seven o'clock. I really need to go now." It was almost six o'clock.

"Well, if you need to lie down, you can go climb in the bed," he offered.

"I might just do that," Melissa said as she placed her head on the back of the chair and closed her eyes. "I'm going to take a few laps to cool off." She agreed and seemed a little calmer now. Tony took off his shirt and walked toward the pool.

Serena watched Tony remove his shirt and was sure her mouth dropped open. His chest was built so beautifully, and he had very broad shoulders. His abs were ripped beyond a six-pack, and she liked what she saw. Not only was his chest finely built, but his legs were fine and muscular too. She had obviously not taken in the whole package when he gave them the tour earlier, but now was her chance to get an eyeful. "Serena," he called out, bringing her out of her thoughts, "the cake has twenty minutes." She reached down to set her watch and waved as if to say thank you. As he turned to check on the grill, Serena got a glimpse of his supermuscular calves and almost winced. She had gotten worked up just by watching this man walk half naked toward the pool. She needed to cool off and fast, so she swam to the far end of the pool and just admired the beauty of Tony's magnificent backyard. Serena held her breath as Tony headed her way. She was wondering how to react to this total package that was headed straight for her. She almost turned to go in a different direction to put some distance between the two of them. Serena felt her nipples harden, and she began to feel her insides tighten. She started fantasizing about the gentle kiss they shared earlier in the kitchen. *Where is he going, and what the hell am I doing licking my lips at the sight of him? How could I forget that this is someone else's man? And that someone else is probably looking right at us. I am losing myself over this man in front of all these people as if nothing else mattered. Oh god, he's coming right for me.* She tried to look away. *This boy is sexy as hell, and he ain't even mine,* she thought to herself as Tony finally reached her. She turned to put some distance between them. She couldn't take it anymore. Serena went underwater and swam as far away and as fast as she could. When she surfaced, she thought of the cake and turned to ask Tony how the cake looked when he checked on it earlier, but she couldn't find him. Tony had eased into the pool and saw Serena with her back to him, so he went underwater, and just as she turned back around, he surfaced. Serena was stunned to see Tony right in front of her and almost screamed. "Where'd you come from?" she asked, already knowing the answer, but she didn't want the moment to be more awkward than it already was. There was no escaping this man or his obvious desire to be near her. Tony had either been blessed with this body or he had a very strict workout regime and diet because he was unbelievably breathtaking.

The feeling was mutual. As Tony approached her, he was trying to read the expression on her face. She looked stunning in yellow. The bathing suit fit her perfectly, and the tie behind her neck was perfect for showing off her muscular arms and shoulders. Tony was immediately attracted to Serena when he met her for the first time in Atlanta, and she was fully clothed. Now that she was scantily dressed and exposed her beautiful brown skin, he was instantly drawn to her. He loved the way the ties met at the nape of her neck and the way the top gently squeezed her breast to show just enough cleavage. Her arms were cut and toned, her abs were flat and tight, and her legs were beautifully shaped. It was obvious she frequented the gym on a regular, and this turned Tony on so much that he couldn't turn back now even if he wanted to. *Wait!* he said to himself, *where is she going?* He wondered if she could read his thoughts somehow. He wanted to get to her fast.

"Hey, lady," he said as he found himself face-to-face with her.

There's that word again, Serena thought as she smiled at him.

"Where are you running off to?" he asked, surprised by the fact that he'd said that out loud. It was not like they were the only two people in the pool. In addition to the eight people in the water, Terry and Tara were huddled together in the five-foot water. They seemed to be really enjoying each other's company. They both knew this was a rhetorical question. He knew what she was doing. She was trying to keep things under control, but he couldn't stop doing what he was doing. He was drawn to her, and she knew it. *This could be dangerous,* thought Serena. Just then she noticed the change in music. Melissa had gotten up and was returning to her lounge chair. She had just taken her seat and obviously felt the need to change the soothing jazz music to a hip-hop radio station. Tony and Serena both smiled at the gesture. *Melissa knew we were getting a little too comfortable and wanted to change the mood,* Serena thought as she smiled to herself. She realized Tony was smiling back at her, and it didn't have innocence written all over it. Serena's watch started beeping as if on cue. "It's time for me to check on the cake," Serena told Tony, who was completely lost in his thoughts of Serena. "I'll be back," she said, getting out of the pool and reaching for her towel. Tony dunked his head. When he surfaced, he watched Serena dry herself off as his mouth watered once he saw what she was working with. Serena had the roundest, most attractive apple bottom he'd ever seen, and he was completely thrown by this and instantly felt himself aroused. What had gotten into him? Tony watched Serena wrap the towel around her body and head for the house. He knew Melissa was watching him, and it seemed as if every guy in the backyard and some of the girls admired Serena's killer body.

Before Serena made it to the door, Melissa made sure she made eye contact with her and gave her the most contemptuous look she could delve up. This was to let her know that she didn't approve of what was happening between Tony and her, nor did she appreciate it. This time, Serena didn't avoid contact because it was clear that Tony was the aggressor, and she didn't feel guilty at all, so she gave a cordial smile as she entered the back door.

The cake was beautiful. She'd found an electric Sunbeam mixer in Tony's pantry and used it to mix the ingredients. Normally she would stir the ingredients by hand, but she didn't want to completely exhaust all of her energy preparing the cake. Using the mixer allows enough batter left over to make a sample cake. So she took both out of the oven and allowed the smaller cake to cool before putting in on a platter and taking it out to the poolside. She didn't know the people in the theater room but offered them some cake anyway. As she exited the house, she spotted Tony on the edge of the pool still in the water. Terry and Tara were digging around in the storage building. Darrin and Justin were bringing tables out. She walked up to Tony and said, "Would you like to sample the 7Up cake?" He smiled and said, "Yeah, but I'm not in a position to get out of the water yet." Serena wasn't sure what that meant, so she walked over to Tony with the platter. Her back was to Melissa as Tony opened his mouth and took the piece of cake Serena was offering. After he'd taken all the cake he wanted, he kissed the palm of Serena's hand seductively. Serena was so shocked she laughed out loud and found herself putting distance between them once again, and she was not looking back this time.

As she glanced in Melissa's direction, she noticed the chair was empty. Tara watched Tony and Serena teasing each other and read Serena's mind as she scanned the area for Melissa too. "She left," Tara said, answering Serena's unspoken question. Serena was relieved Melissa had not witnessed what had just taken place.

She grabbed a lounge chair and applied sunscreen while she enjoyed the sun. She watched Terry and Tara play around, and she smiled at how the two of them interacted with ease and comfort. Melissa appeared from the side of the house, and Serena was relieved to be out of the pool near Tony. She marched right over to Tony, and before long Tony was following her back into the house. She wondered what was going on, but she soon had company coming her way. After all, she was the only person in that direction, and she just happened to be sitting by two empty chairs. After chatting for a few minutes with Kevin and Louis, she learned that they were close friends with Tony and had been since he moved to Columbus. They asked all the general icebreaker questions, and Serena asked a few questions of her own. Tony reappeared on the deck less than ten minutes and once again headed her way. She didn't see Melissa trailing behind him and instantly relaxed. Her company noticed Tony coming too and made room for him to join the conversation. Tony made small talk with them, but all he really wanted to do was spend some time alone with Serena. *What was I thinking inviting all these people over,* Tony scolded himself. "So where's Melissa?" she asked while Kevin and Louis excused themselves.

"She had to go get some sleep for her shift tonight."

"Oh, I thought she was off until Tuesday."

"No, she got a phone call before we left Atlanta saying she had to go in." Serena couldn't think of anything else to say. She didn't know if she should jump for joy or plant a warm wet kiss on Tony's sweet lips. Tony couldn't read Serena's expression, but he'd hoped she was as excited by the news.

MAGIC

The food was about to be served as Serena appeared from the back room where she had taken a shower earlier. Tony was out by the pool. Tony was forever amazed at Serena's beauty and couldn't keep his eyes off of her. She had on a sleeveless peach floral linen dress that tied at the nape of her neck showing off her chiseled back. She replaced her gold earrings with her one-karat diamond earrings complete with silver and diamond-studded accessories. She'd repinned her hair in an updo, which complemented her face and also accentuated her back. Tony had showered first and changed into his khaki shorts and green polo shirt with brown sandals. As Serena approached him, she noticed how the backyard had taken on the form of an outside dining area complete with tables covered with white tablecloths. Justin and Kenny were setting up the last table when Serena stopped and stared in amazement at the beauty of the setting. There were two white candles perfectly positioned on every table. *How romantic,* she thought as Tony approached her. "Where did all this come from, and what's the special occasion?" she asked in a surprising gasp. Tony gave her a peck on the cheek and said, "Thanks, for fixing the salad and the cake," as he led her to the last table that was strategically placed for privacy. He did all he could to keep from brushing up against her or taking her in his arms and tasting her full, sensual, and inviting lips. He was glad that she was pleased. He didn't know if he could tell her it was all for her. He wasn't sure how she'd take it. So he said nothing as he pulled her chair out to seat her.

Serena was taking it all in. She was focused on the flickering of the candles. Serena had a thing for candles, and she noticed the change in the music. This time Luther Vandross could be heard in the background, crooning as he always did. She really loved Luther and had all of his CDs. Tony watched the smile spread across Serena's face when she heard Luther Vandross come on. *It wouldn't hurt to throw on some Levert or Teddy Pendergrass either,* Serena thought. They were among her favorites too. She was thoroughly impressed with the entire scene. Who would've guessed the candles would've been scented too? There were two more chairs at their table, and Serena wondered who'd be joining them. Tara and Terry had disappeared, and the others were beginning to take their seats at the table too. As they began their meal, there was yet another change in the music, and this time it was Guy. *Oh my, what is this man trying to do to me?* she thought as she enjoyed her meal. *The chicken and brisket were perfect. The salad was quite tasty too, if I must say so myself,* Serena thought. Someone had prepared a potato salad, and it was simply delicious. Tony and Serena were enjoying the music and meal when Terry and Tara joined them halfway through the meal. "Mind if we join you," Tara asked.

"Not at all; we've been waiting for you two to show up." Neither one said anything, but Serena knew that Tara was glowing, and it wasn't from taking a swim. She knew they'd been intimate, and her face was absolutely radiant, and Serena was happy for her friend. "Tony, you remember my cousin Karen Scott, right?"

"Yeah, I remember Karen a.k.a. the Brain." The three of them laughed, remembering exactly why Karen was dubbed as such. She was a straight-A student whose favorite subject was science. "Well, I saw her today. She lives not far from here."

Tony looked confused. "What? She lives in Columbus?"

"Yeah, she actually works at Quest Lab and Research over on Ratcliff." "Yeah, I know that place. How long has she been in the area?"

"Since high school," Terry said proudly. "She works as a lab tech, and you know that's right down her alley."

Tony said, "Yeah, well, tell her I said hello and if she ever needs anything to call me. I'm in the book."

"Okay, I'll do that. I'm going to try to get Tara over to see her tomorrow before she leaves; maybe have breakfast or something." As the three of them engaged in a conversation about the good old days, Serena drifted off into her own little world. *If Tony's orchestrating this entire night, I could only imagine what would happen next.* Not wanting to rush anything and spoil the moment, Serena relaxed and savored each moment with Tony.

They were finishing up when Tony's cell phone rang. He excused himself and took the call. It was Melissa wanting to know if the party was over. She still wanted to be intimate and wanted to know if she could get a quickie in before driving to work. Tony was indeed horny and fully prepared to be involved intimately, but the someone he was thinking of was not Melissa. She accepted defeat and told Tony good night.

Tony was back in a few minutes with a more relaxed look on his face, and Tara noticed it too. They looked at each other but said nothing. Tony seemed to answer the unasked question by saying, "Melissa's on her way to work, and she told me to tell you all good night." Tara and Serena shared another look; this time they both smiled and again said nothing.

All of them should have been exhausted from partying last night, but all were wide awake. There was an air of liveliness, and Tony and Serena seemed rejuvenated by the possibility of making a love connection. Resting would have to wait because the next musical group to come on was the Gap Band, and Tony extended his hand to Serena, and it was a repeat of last night. The others had eaten, and the tables had been put away. The oversized patio had become a dance floor that several other couples decided to take advantage of too. Next Midnight Star and everyone's favorite played, "Slow Jam," and the dance floor was packed. Even Terry and Tara came up for air to reminisce on this chart topper from the good old days. Serena melted in Tony's arms for the rest of the night. Tony was enjoying the closeness of their bodies and felt the softness of her breasts against his chest. Her whole body tingled, and she felt the heat rise from Tony's body as they danced. She wasn't sure if it was the Courvoisier she'd been sipping on or because Tony was holding her so perfectly. Neither Serena nor Tara were drinkers, but tonight was special. Tara and Terry had decided to catch a late show at the theater just down the street. "Okay, be safe," Serena told her friend as she finished her dance with Tony. She was glad Tara and Terry had reconnected. She was even more excited about being in Tony's arms.

After the last guests left, Tony and Serena began to clean the inside. Everyone pitched in to clean the outside near the pool and the grounds before leaving. The leftovers had already either been given away or put away in the extra refrigerator in the storage shed. Since everyone had departed, the two had the entire house to themselves. They turned off all the lights and decided to have cake and coffee in the theater room. They both agreed on watching one of their favorites. Serena had seen *The Five Heartbeats* over ten times but enjoyed it more each time she saw it. As the movie started, Tony reached over and took Serena's hand. He held it for a while, just long enough for his heart to skip a beat. Their hands were on fire and began to perspire, and neither one of them pulled away. Tony felt himself getting worked up as he wondered if Serena was as turned on as he was. He felt the entire weekend since meeting Serena had been one awesome dose of foreplay, and boy, was it powerful. He caressed Serena's hand and gently placed it near his mouth where he kissed the palm of her hand like he was out in the wild and was starving to taste her as the passion ignited between them. Serena responded with a moan, and Tony was pleased, so he kissed her wrist and smelled her perfume and wondered what kind she was wearing. Whatever it was, it was driving him mad. Serena reached over and kissed Tony's ear and played with his lobe for a while, and he was very responsive, and he shivered as she began to lick and nibble on his neck. This was driving him absolutely crazy. He had not had this type of response to any of the foreplay he'd ever experienced with anyone, and he knew he had to have Serena.

It had been six months since she'd broken up with her last boyfriend and almost two months since she'd been intimate with anyone. It was only nine fifteen, and they hadn't seen one minute of the movie. Serena didn't want to rush this moment and wanted to slow things down a bit. She excused herself and stood up slowly. Tony took her hand and pulled her to him with his face resting on her chest, and he felt her nipples harden through her dress. Tony was even more turned on by this appreciating the softness of her body. She felt her knees buckle, and Tony caught her before she lost her balance. They both looked at each other and parted just enough to see the other's burning desire and the longing for more. "I'll be right back," she gasped, as the air seemed to leave her body. She turned and practically ran to the bathroom to put some distance between them once again. She washed her face and brushed her teeth as she tried to get a grip. She wondered what would happen next. Her head was spinning with anticipation, and she hoped she could contain her eagerness. Her emotions were working overtime as she exited the bathroom. When she rounded the kitchen corner, she noticed that Tony had disappeared. He was now positioned near the couch in the living room, which was completely darkened except for the two candles Tony had lit. Jodeci was playing low in the background, and Serena appreciated his knack for romance. As he lit the third candle, he turned to see Serena standing there watching him. He was so caught up in the moment. He smiled at her, and she noticed right away there was something more serious about his demeanor. Serena took a seat on the couch praying they'd strike up a conversation. She felt they could talk about anything; and at this point, she needed a distraction. He was a very knowledgeable man who wasn't overly opinionated. Tony took a seat as they began chatting and laughing, sometimes nonstop. Occasionally they'd just listen to the music. The mood seemed lighter, and Tony looked like himself again.

Tony was setting the mood in the living room when it suddenly hit him that Serena would be leaving tomorrow, and this saddened him. She was not going four or six hours away. She would be fourteen hours away, and he didn't know when or if he'd ever see her again. He didn't want to bring it up, so he stayed away from the subject as he lay in Serena's lap on the couch. "So, Mr. Walker, when do you think I'll see you again?" Serena asked as if she were reading his mind or his earlier mood. He sighed and looked into her eyes. "That's completely up to you," he stated, waiting for a reaction. Serena, surprised by the answer, thought immediately, *Sounds like he wants to see me again,* as her heart raced. Feeling like a school-aged girl, she asked, "What if I want to see you on my next four-day weekend?"

"That would be Fourth of July," she said, smiling down at him.

"Do you think you'd be able to make it back to Atlanta?" he asked. "We're having our family reunion at the community center near Tara's." Serena considered and decided it was possible. "Yeah, I would have to come back to the East Coast to see you. I just don't want to be in the way of what you and Melissa have. How about this," she said. "Once I leave, you'll have time to determine whether or not this is something you really want to do." She was trying to give him a way out because the last thing she wanted to do was put herself in a bad situation. After all, she'd been there and done that. "Okay, we'll both give it some thought and see what happens," he said. Both were pleased with the conversation, and both seemed to be deep in thought. Serena took Tony's hand and caressed it over and over again. She began touching his face as he turned his face into her hand and kissed the palm of her hand with more passion than before. He closed his eyes and accepted whatever she did to him because it brought him internal joy. Serena began caressing his face and chest as she studied his expression; taking her finger, she began to play with his lips tracing them with her fingertips. Tony shivered as this thoroughly aroused him. Neither one of them knew how much more either of them could take. Serena bent down so that her face was millimeters from Tony's. She held his face, and she began to trace his lips with her tongue. He allowed her to tease his lips until he felt the urge to take her tongue into his mouth and kiss her deeply. This excited Serena, and it must've excited Tony too. Serena gently unbuttoned his shirt and was enjoying the close-up view of his beautifully built chest. She knew he wanted more, so she watched his face as she kissed him and slowly unzipped his pants. They walked slowly to his bedroom as he stopped by the stereo inside the bedroom, and there it was playing to her surprise. Teddy Pendergrass was singing "Turn Off the Lights." He had thought of everything. They walked over to his oversized bed with a bookcase headboard that featured lights in the top and a huge mirror in the headboard. As Tony stood there at full attention, he turned Serena's back to him as he gently kissed her neck and untied her dress, allowing it to fall to the floor. He stood there admiring her beautiful body, her curves coupled with her sexy intimate apparel. He felt compelled to kiss her sculpted back and shoulders, and finally he kissed her apple bottom, and this time she moaned. He sat her on the bed and fell to his knees. Serena was completely exposed to this man she'd just met, and yet she felt like she'd known him forever. She reached down and finished taking his shirt off and was finally able to touch his bare, muscular chest that had teased her all day by the poolside; and it felt great. Tony was very blessed, and his body was an absolutely beautiful sight. Once she couldn't resist waiting anymore, she pulled him down on top of her; and with one quick move, they were both sent into oblivion. Neither one of them wanted it to be over, so they tried slowing things down and took their time. This was a fantasy come true, and neither one of them could have asked for a more compatible and pleasing partner.

They held each other for what seemed like an eternity, but in reality, it was five minutes before they drifted off with Jodeci still playing in the background. She remembered glancing at the clock when it was one thirty. She hadn't heard Terry and Tara come in, and she hoped they hadn't heard everything that had just happened. She was too tired to worry about it tonight as she closed her eyes.

It was seven o'clock when her alarm clock went off. Serena immediately felt a sense of sadness knowing today, in just a matter of hours, she'd be packed up and headed to Texas. She couldn't prolong the inevitable. She gathered herself and looked around the room trying to get her bearings. She smiled as she remembered the intimate moments she'd shared with the amazing man lying in bed beside her. As she thought of the day ahead, she turned over to sneak a peek at Tony, wanting to freeze the moment in time. As she quietly rolled over, she let out a surprised giggle, as she looked right into Tony's eyes. He was already awake, but Serena could not recall hearing him wake up or move around. "Good morning," she said as she continued to laugh at herself.

"Good morning yourself," Tony said as he leaned over and kissed her lips gently, not taking his eyes off of her for one second. She saw a familiar expression as she studied his face and knew instantly that he was thinking about what was to come too. "You hungry?" Tony asked.

"No, but I'll take coffee and cake to tide me over for a few hours."

"Okay, I think I can manage that." He smiled but didn't move. He reached over and took Serena's hand while replaying last night's magic over again in his head. Serena could only imagine what Tony was thinking about. She knew this would be a night she'd never forget. She drew his hand to her lips and kissed him lovingly.

As Tony started toward the bathroom, Serena went next door to get her travel outfit and overnight bag. As she reentered the modest-sized bathroom, she hung her sundress in Tony's walk-in closet just inside the bathroom door. She placed her bag on the floor and her necklace on the hook behind her dress. When she exited the walk-in closet, she turned just in time to see Tony's beautiful naked body entering the shower. She was relieved when Tony closed the door, hoping she could mask her desirous expression she was sure had been plastered across her face. She stopped at the sink and allowed her skin to exfoliate while she brushed her teeth. She had hoped he would be exiting the shower soon so she wouldn't have to wonder if he wanted to be intimate with her. After last night, she'd wanted more this morning but didn't want to push too much. He may even be having second thoughts about her and last night. Reality may be setting in.

Inside the shower, Tony wondered if Serena still found him desirable the morning after. He was aching at the chance to be close to her again. She'd caught him watching her this morning, and he didn't mind. Serena was an incredibly passionate and beautiful person, and he longed to be near her. "Are you okay, Serena?" he asked. "Are you coming in?"

"I'll be right there," she said as she rinsed her face and patted her skin dry. She opened the shower door and was impressed with the size of the shower. It was big and spacious with a built-in bench, which was where she found Tony sitting. He was looking every bit of the seductive man he'd been the night before. Serena pinned her hair up so it wouldn't be a total mess after the hot shower. As she began to wash her body, she relaxed and closed her eyes and allowed herself to be lost under the steady stream of hot water.

Tony had given her all the time he possibly could without going crazy. As she turned in his direction, she kept her eyes closed, wondering what he was doing. Tony knelt in the shower and pulled her close to him. He felt Serena tremble under his kisses as he continued to explore her. She couldn't remember experiencing anything so erotic before. She began to relax, and this time her knees gave out, and Tony had to catch her.

Tony was glad Serena didn't object to the way he was kissing her. He was not able to continue and stood up quickly, bringing Serena up with him. He kissed her deeply, and she returned the same passion she'd possessed the night before. Tony was surprised by her actions. He reached over and turned the shower off, not wanting her to get drenched. They were so turned on by the beauty of their intimacy, they'd began making music of their own as they collapsed in each other's arms. Tony reached over and started the shower again while he watched Serena cleanse her perfect body.

BACK TO REALITY

B y the time Tony stepped out of the shower, Serena was fully
clothed. He smiled as he continued to dry himself off. His
alarm clock sounded, startling him and bringing him out of his
fantasy. Serena noticed the change in his demeanor but didn't
question him. Tony knew it was seven forty-five, and Melissa normally
showed up at the same time every morning after she'd pulled the
eleven-to-seven shift. After dressing and listening closely to the sounds
of the house, he realized someone was knocking on the door.

Serena was gathering her things when she thought she heard a
knock at the door. Surely it was her imagination. *Who'd be coming
over this early?* she thought to herself. Realizing it was not quite eight
o'clock, she could think of only one person showing up at this time.
It was Melissa. That must've been the look she'd seen on Tony's face
after his alarm had gone off earlier. Before they had a chance to
say anything, they heard a sound outside Tony's bedroom window.
"Tony, come open the door," he heard Melissa say as she began to
tap on the window. The tapping changed to frantic knocking on the
outside of the bedroom. As Serena got her things together to go
to the guest bedroom, she could hear Melissa's voice change from
coaxing to hysterical demands. "Tony, are you in there," she said as
she banged louder. This girl was going to wake up the neighborhood
if he didn't let her in soon.

Serena listened to Melissa's ranting as she packed her belongings.
She wondered how long she'd been knocking because she seemed more
than a little upset. As Serena packed her things up, she said nothing to
Tony for fear of being heard. She didn't want to add to his problems
either, so she headed for the bed to collect her intimate apparel. Now
Melissa was screaming, and Tony was dressing hurriedly. Melissa ripped

the screen off the side window as if she were going to climb in if she found the window unlocked. Serena and Tony listened to her huff and puff as if she had been crying. She began pushing up on the window. Tony was dressed now; and after they both made up the bed, Serena exited the room. He held his breath, hoping he'd remembered to lock the window after he entered the house through that same window last week because he'd locked his keys inside. The window wouldn't open. Serena had made it safely into the guest bedroom, and Tony was straightening up the room and spraying air freshener before hurrying up the hallway to the front door. As he walked up the hallway, he looked at Serena and wondered what she was thinking and immediately felt sorry for putting her in this predicament. He was glad she wasn't interested in a confrontation, and he felt relieved.

As Serena reached the guest bedroom, she watched Tony as he started for the front door. The last thing Serena wanted was to make a mess of Tony's life and leave him there alone to face whatever was to come. He turned and reached for her, and the two shared a warm and gentle embrace as if they understood each other.

Tony opened the front door and looked out in search of Melissa. As he walked around the house, he saw Melissa standing on a chair, still trying to pry the window open. "Melissa," he yelled, not as loud as he wanted to. "What are you doing?" he said in a loud whisper. "Girl, come inside and stop making a spectacle of yourself." Melissa immediately jumped down off the chair and almost ran toward him.

"So you just had to fuck her, huh?" she screamed at the top of her lungs.

"What?" Tony asked roughly as he grabbed her arm and headed for the porch.

"Get your hands off of me; I want to see Serena."

"Wait, I'm warning you right now; you need to calm down and get yourself together," he admonished her. "If you have anything to say to anyone, it'd better be to me." Melissa turned and stormed off into the house.

Tony was a very private person and didn't appreciate that kind of attention. He would have to put a stop to this rampage because the last thing he wanted was for Serena to be involved in any mess, or was it called a love triangle? All he could think about was protecting Serena.

After Serena closed the door, she quickly put her things away and put her bags by the door ready for the trip home. It was eight o'clock, and she'd never thought to check on Tara, so she crept out into the hallway and heard sounds outside like someone was dragging something. She heard the front door close and figured Tony was headed out to find Melissa. As she dismissed what was taking place outside the house, she opened the door to the other bedroom and found Tara's bags packed and by the door; but Tara was nowhere to be found. There was a note written on the pillow: "Got up early and went to get breakfast at IHOP with Terry and Karen. We'll be back by 9:00." Serena smiled knowing her friend was okay. That gave her an hour to spend with Tony if she was lucky. The initial plan was to be on the road by ten o'clock so they'd be arriving in San Antonio by midnight or shortly after. Serena wasn't sure if the plan had changed, but if the military taught her anything, it was to always be prepared for everything, and that she was. Now she needed to move fast as she turned up the hallway glancing at the windows as she passed by. She'd made it to the kitchen and put on a pot of coffee. After setting the table, she headed for the deck. As Serena slipped out the back door to feel the sun's warmth and the morning air on her face, she heard Melissa's loud voice coming in the front door, with what sounded like footsteps closely behind her. Serena wanted to give them some privacy to discuss whatever it was on Melissa's mind. Serena prepared herself and was once again ready for anything. As she sat on the deck, she felt the gentle southern breeze on her skin. She stared into the blue of the pool and reminisced about the candlelight dinner she and Tony had shared just a few short hours ago. She had such a wonderful and complete evening, and now it was time to face reality. She reached into her bag and found her cell phone, which was also her PDA. She checked her schedule for upcoming appointments and responded to a few emails she'd missed over the weekend. Luckily, there were no other messages. She was ready to return to Texas, but she wasn't so sure she was ready to leave Tony. Inside, she could hear Melissa's voice as she was opening and closing doors. It seemed as if she were conducting a room-to-room search. *I wonder if she's looking for me,* Serena thought. "Okay, it's time," she said to herself and stood up to go back into the house. Obviously, she'd completed the search, or Tony put a stop to it.

Serena washed fresh fruit and arranged the fruit in a serving bowl and placed it on the table. She decided to cut a slice of cake for Tony and herself as she placed the cake next to the cup of coffee she'd prepared for him. They were so loud they didn't hear Serena moving around in the house. Serena didn't want to start eating without Tony. So she walked over to the stereo and found the jazz station and turned the volume down low. She found the morning paper just inside the kitchen and figured Tara had gotten it from the driveway. She decided to read the paper until Tony and Melissa came up for air. She was surprised by her own calmness and would do what was necessary to protect Tony. Suddenly, the house grew quiet as if they were being tamed by the magical sounds of the smooth jazz playing over the radio.

"I want to know how you thought you'd get away with this and keep it from me!" Melissa yelled as she headed for the hallway. Tony followed quietly, not knowing what to expect. He was so pissed by Melissa's antics he didn't notice the aroma of coffee drifting from the kitchen as he entered the house. Melissa headed for the guest bedrooms first and saw Tara's bag by the door but no Tara. She went so far as to look in the closet as well. She then headed for Tony's bedroom, and Tony followed her in and shut the door. "Melissa, just what are you expecting to find?" he asked, but she didn't respond. She saw no signs of Serena, so she kept looking and went into the bathroom until she found proof of Serena being in Tony's bed. Melissa kept searching as Tony watched in amazement. She was acting like a deranged psychopath, and he'd wondered how and when she felt she'd found proof of Serena being there. She stormed out of the room and was headed to the room where Serena was. Tony was running out of patience and felt his temper on the verge of flaring. Tony closed the distance between him and Melissa quickly and grabbed her by the wrists. "Look, you've gone too far, and I want you out of here now. You've overstepped your boundaries by showing up here acting like a mad woman and causing my neighbors to peek out of their windows wondering when they should call the cops. You need to go home and get some rest."

Now Melissa was sure he'd been with Serena last night. Tony was being too protective of her. She just needed proof of her presence in his room. She had had enough of Tony's deceit and wanted to confront them both about the time they shared last night at the cookout. No one had said a word to her about the two of them, and they didn't need to. Melissa's mind was racing as she jerked her arms from Tony and headed to the door again. This time she was able to get back into the room where she locked herself inside. She tore through the trashcan looking for condom wrappers. She checked the toilet for used condoms not yet disposed of, and she found nothing. She tore open the closet door, and there it was as clear as day—an unfamiliar piece of jewelry hanging on a hook just inside the door of Tony's walk-in closet. Tony was listening from outside the door as he asked Melissa to come out. "Aha!" she screamed. "I knew it. I knew this bitch had been up in here, and I'm so sick of your denials." Tony was listening to her accusations and wondered what she could have possibly found. He then began to question whether or not he'd collected all of her personal items after their shower that morning. Melissa yanked open the door and stormed out of the room. Tony reached for her to restrain her but knew it wouldn't take much for things to get physical. He began to think Serena was nowhere to be found as Melissa conducted her search of the premises. He wondered where she'd disappeared to. The last thing he wanted was for the two of them to be at each other. He was deep in thought and became concerned that maybe she'd left the house without his knowledge. He headed for the kitchen after Melissa and wondered what proof she had.

Serena had begun to think Tony and Melissa had made up. It had been quiet for at least five minutes, and her coffee was getting cold. Her mind began to wonder as she scanned the newspaper and reached for her necklace. She made it a habit to twirl it and run her fingers over it whenever she had it on. "Oh my goodness, what did I do with my necklace?" She didn't even remember taking it off. Did she lose it or had it fallen off somewhere? The last time she remembered having it on was . . . Serena knew immediately and was alarmed as she replayed the last time she'd had it on over in her mind. It was in Tony's bed. Serena hoped it was tucked away safely under the covers out of Melissa's reach. She remembered picking it up from the bed before heading to the shower. She remembered! She had placed it on a hook in the walk-in closet before heading to the shower.

She turned and saw Tony following Melissa up the hallway. He looked troubled, and she dismissed the look, assuming Melissa had pushed him too far. "Good morning," she said, greeting Melissa and Tony. But before she could offer her coffee and cake, Melissa quickened her strides and was in the kitchen standing over her. Tony quickly inserted himself between the two of them as he told Melissa she needed to go home. "No, it's time for you to 'fess up!" Melissa screamed. Serena looked back and forth and wondered if Melissa had seen the two of them in the room. *Could Tony have told her about last night?* "I told you all I needed was proof that you two were fucking, and now I have it." Serena looked taken aback and immediately replayed her actions this morning. She had retrieved her clothes, shoes, and, more importantly, her things from last night. *What could Melissa have found? Was it a condom or the wrapper? The only other thing it could have been was if this bitch had a hidden camera in the room.*

Tony pushed Melissa away and said, "Melissa, you need to leave."

"So what are you going to do to me, Tony, if I don't?" she asked nastily. "You're going to put me out for this bitch." She spit her words at Tony. Until now Serena had been willing to take some bashing because inside she knew she was wrong, but being called a bitch was crossing the line, and she quickly snapped out of her serene environment. "What did you just say," Serena said raising her voice. Tony knew the side of Serena he was now seeing was one he had not yet encountered, and Melissa was still sticking with her accusations. "How dare you attempt to insult me and approach me with your immature insecurities." Melissa wondered if Tony was going to step in, but she remembered she still had the proof. "Insecurities, huh, what about this!" she said, holding the necklace up. Tony looked at the necklace Melissa dangled in the air wondering what she'd found. Serena's necklace. Serena recognized the doubt and hesitation in Tony's eyes and stepped up to claim what was hers. "Oh, my necklace," Serena said calmly. "Thank you for returning it to me. I've been looking all over for it. Tony, where'd you find it?" she asked as if to let him know that if this was all the proof she had, then she's got nothing.

"He didn't find it, Ser-e-na! I did, and guess where I found it? Oh, let me help you," Melissa said sarcastically. "In the bed! The bed that you shared with my man last night!"

Before she could respond, Tony stepped in. "Melissa, I find that hard to believe," he said calmly as if he had caught on.

"I don't have any idea why this would be in Tony's bed," Serena added. "I do remember leaving it on the hook last night in his closet."

Melissa cut in. "What the hell were you doing in my man's room last night!" she screamed as she directed the question to Tony, but Serena wasn't finished. "Melissa, I really think you need to take Tony's advice and go home and get some rest because it is obvious you're suffering from sleep deprivation."

"Okay, that's it," Tony said as he grabbed Melissa's arm. He'd had enough. "You need to leave now. You've been acting deranged since showing up here this morning. Either you can walk out that door yourself or . . ." It was Serena's turn to interrupt. She didn't want Tony to say anything out of anger that he may regret later. "Now even if I felt like your questions warranted an answer, I wouldn't play your game because there is a way to do everything. What we're doing now isn't very ladylike, and I don't appreciate your accusations." Melissa instantly felt as if she were losing control and being lectured by Tony's houseguest. "Since I am a houseguest of Tony's and if *he* were to wonder how that necklace turned up in *his* room, I'd explain to him that I took it off last night when I used his bathroom to shower. "This," she said as she took the necklace from Melissa and held it up, "is not something I normally get into a chlorine-filled pool with." Melissa's mouth dropped open, and she couldn't believe her proof had been dismissed so quickly. She was thoroughly embarrassed and had completely forgotten about the shower last night. She wanted nothing more than to be on her way. As Serena finished her closing argument, she turned to Tony as if Melissa were invisible and asked how he liked his coffee, gesturing to the table where the coffee, cake, and fresh fruit waited. Serena moved over to the table as Melissa stood in front of Tony completely humiliated. "Melissa, would you like coffee and cake?" Serena asked in her most cordial voice. Melissa didn't bother to look at Serena, but she gave Tony a look that could kill as she turned on her heels and stormed out as Tony watched her head for the door and closed it behind her. He waited to hear her car start up and watched her pull away before he turned to face Serena. She was still waiting for Tony to tell her how he liked his coffee. He was so still and quiet Serena wondered if he was upset with her, Melissa, or the entire world. He quietly took a seat at the table and turned to face Serena as the plate she placed in front of him startled him. *When did she have time to do all this?* Tony thought. "I take two creams and two sugars," he said while smiling in disbelief. Tony had already dismissed the morning's excitement and wondered how she would have reacted if she were in Melissa's shoes. As she poured Tony another cup of coffee and placed it on the table, Tony grabbed her hand and looked at her apologetically. "I am so sorry you had to go through that. It was so unnecessary," he said with a little smile.

"No need to apologize," she said, returning his smile. "Let's enjoy breakfast."

Terry and Tara met Karen for breakfast. *Karen hadn't changed much,* Tara thought as she approached their table. She was still thin and looked like a teenager. The only thing missing was her braces and glasses. Tara later found out that Karen was now wearing contact lenses. "Hi," she said as she took her seat. "It's good to see you after all these years," she said, smiling.

"Yes, it's been a while, and you have not changed a bit," Tara said, complimenting her. The three embarked upon their high school days for the next hour over pecan waffles. Karen had a three-year-old son and was engaged to be married in September. Her flower girl was the daughter of one of the bridesmaids. She was trying to keep the wedding party small, but it seemed that after every meeting with the coordinator, they found the need for one more person. "Well, one thing that's not changed is the date," Karen said jokingly. "She seems really happy," Tara said to Terry as they were waving good-bye and watching her drive off.

"Yeah, Karen is doing really well for herself," Terry said as he looked down at her business card. Karen promised to send an invitation to the wedding that was going to be held in Atlanta.

As he took in the beautiful table setting, he still wondered how Serena found the time to prepare this meal. As if reading his mind, Serena smiled and said, "While you were in the back." Tony nodded and said, "I see," and that was the last time either of them mentioned the incident.

After breakfast, the two sat on the deck and laughed and talked, not wanting to think about the inevitable. In a few short hours, they would be separating; and neither of them were ready for that. They were laughing so hard when Tara showed up in the doorway. "Well, good morning, you two." They both turned around and found Terry standing behind Tara, and both were glowing. Serena said good morning and glanced down at her watch. It was eight fifty-eight, just like clockwork. Tony got up to hug his sister and shake Terry's hand. "So how was your breakfast with Karen?" Serena asked.

"Oh, it was great. She's getting married this year," Tara said excitedly.

"Oh, really." Terry said, "Yeah, she's getting married in Atlanta in September."

The girls packed the car up and were saying their good-byes to Tony and Terry. They were going to play dominoes after the girls left. Serena shook Terry's hand and was surprised she got a hug in return. As Terry and Tara said their good-byes, Serena turned to look at Tony and wondered if the sadness she felt inside mirrored the sadness she saw in Tony's eyes. She slowly walked up to him. "Well, Tony, it's been great. I really mean that. Thanks for inviting me." They had already said their good-byes earlier. He reached out and held her hand and said, "You are welcome to come back anytime." He released her hand as he gave her a gentle squeeze, and that was enough for Serena.

The girls pulled away at exactly ten o'clock and were listening to Mary J. Blige's *No More Drama* CD as they headed down the highway. The girls talked nonstop for the next seven hours about everything. Tony had called twice, and Terry was now on his third phone call with Tara. Serena had filled Tara in on the drama with Melissa. She was so proud of the way Serena handled herself and said she wished she could've been a fly on the wall to witness the showdown. Serena smiled to herself as she drifted off to sleep. When she woke up, they were in Dallas. She knew Tara was tired, so she took over the driving duties while Tara dozed off. Tara thought about the conversation she and Tony had. He wanted to confirm Serena's story about not being attached. *I know my brother, and I knew enough to know that he was crazy about Serena. He is afraid of stepping out on a limb and being so open and apt to getting his heart broken. I reassured him that Serena is a very honest and giving person. He is trying to be careful not to make a fool of himself.* While chatting with Tony, he admitted to her that he was missing Serena already.

It was the second week in June, and Serena and Tony talked to each other at least twice a week and on Saturday and Sunday. She called Tony mostly at work. There were a few times there had been an actual fire, and Tony had to leave in a hurry. She knew he loved his job and wondered if he'd consider a location change if things ever got that serious between the two of them. For now, she was only thinking and planning to herself. She wanted Tony to bring up the subject so she didn't seem too desperate. Melissa's name never came up. Serena knew that Melissa was there before her, and Tony had never mentioned that he was going to break things off with her. So Serena wanted to play everything by ear but also stay mentally and emotionally prepared for anything. She knew that she could easily be in love with Tony but also knew that you can't be in love all by yourself. She was a very patient person and willing to wait for Tony.

Melissa and Tony's relationship had been strained since the incident with Serena. Melissa knew she'd messed up and blown things out of proportion. It had been six weeks, and they'd seen each other only on days he was off. Melissa knew the relationship would never be the same again, but she still wanted to try. She stopped over four days after Serena left just to talk to Tony, and he was very unresponsive. They had been intimate a few times, but it wasn't the same. She knew he'd lost interest in her, but she wasn't ready for the relationship to end, so she kept making herself available. Melissa felt if she continued to be there for him, he would eventually come around. The Fourth of July was only a few weeks away, and they had not made any plans. Melissa decided she would surprise Tony with plans of her own.

LUST OR LOVE

Tara and Serena sat at the Day Spa getting their pedicures and manicures and talked about the upcoming weekend. The Fourth of July was here already, and Serena couldn't wait to see Tony. They'd been talking constantly since she'd left Georgia in May, and not a day passed without her thinking about him. Serena was driving to Georgia this time, and Tara was of course going to accompany her to see Terry. He had agreed to fly up from Florida. As the time neared, Serena got more anxious. She was so excited about finally seeing Tony again after six weeks. They didn't have any concrete plans yet, so the girls were playing everything by ear.

Lying in bed with Melissa complicated his thoughts more each time they were intimate. He had not officially broken it off with Melissa, but he felt that things would never be the same between the two of them again. He wondered if she sensed the change in their lovemaking since he'd slept with Serena. Serena was constantly on his mind, and there was nothing he could do to remove her from his thoughts. Even when he was working, he thought of Serena and longed to be with her. He and Melissa never talked about that day again, but he knew they both still relived that day in their minds. He had made plans to see Serena for the Fourth but had not discussed the Fourth with Melissa at all. He knew she'd wonder why she wasn't going to Atlanta, and he needed to come up with an answer and soon. As he walked out onto the deck, he reminisced about Serena's last visit and couldn't wait to see her again. His feelings had grown since the last time they spent time together, and he could get used to seeing her on a more regular basis. He wondered if she'd thought about being stationed at Fort Benning? Melissa opened the door and joined Tony on the deck, bringing him out of his deep thoughts.

Tara and Terry were keeping things hot and heavy. Tara was happier than Serena ever remembered, and this pleased Serena. They were making plans to take a cruise together the next summer. Serena had never been on a cruise but had always dreamed of going. She had applied for her passport and decided she would vacation in Jamaica for her very first cruise. Now the only question was when and with whom. The closer the weekend got, the more uncertain she was about seeing Tony. They had been in contact with each other, but she felt something had changed. It wasn't anything Tony said or did. She just had an odd feeling about their trip to Georgia, and it was one that she couldn't shake.

The girls signed out on leave Wednesday at midnight. As the girls got closer to Atlanta, they were ecstatic about their trip. They were looking forward to being back in Atlanta and should be pulling in around early afternoon. Traffic was very light since they chose to drive through the night before traffic got too bad. "Do you have any idea what the guys are planning for this weekend?" Serena asked Tara.

"No, I'm still waiting on Terry to divulge that information to me. He and Tony are trying to surprise us, so I don't want to spoil it for them." The girls chatted and worked a crossword puzzle together when they weren't on the phone with one of their guys. They had five days off and were looking forward to spending the Fourth with the guys. Serena wanted to ask Tara about Melissa but didn't want to put her in the middle of anything. She would have felt intrusive if she were to ask Tony, so she didn't. She regretted this more the closer they got to Atlanta. The girls pulled into the local Food Lion around three o'clock. They picked up wine, cheese, crackers, and other necessities for an impromptu picnic they'd planned for the group. There was a Big Lots next door where they found a picnic basket, plastic ware, and wineglasses. Terry would soon be arriving from Miami. His flight was supposed to land at three o'clock. He'd planned to meet Tara at her grandmother's shortly after that. Tara and Serena decided to take the guys out to an Earth, Wind & Fire concert Friday night. Neither of them had a clue that the girls were planning any of this. The concert started at nine o'clock, but they wanted to be seated by eight fifteen.

Tony was on his way and would probably beat them to his grandmother's house. Serena had spoken with Tony several times, and he seemed just as excited as she was about their reunion.

Serena still had not mentioned Melissa; and she felt that if there was something that needed to be said, Tony would do the honors.

As they pulled into the driveway at Tara's, Tonya was waiting outside for them. The girls got out of the car and were hugging each other as if they'd not seen each other in months. Tara mentioned their plans for the evening to Tonya, and of course, she wanted to do something to help. Tara asked to borrow her CD player and picked up some D batteries at Food Lion. As Tonya walked from the back of the house, Serena said, "What's that delicious smell?" Tonya handed Tara the CD player and several CDs. She turned to Serena and said, "I've just baked a large pan of fudge brownies for you guys to take on your picnic." Serena's face lit up. "Oh, what a wonderful surprise. That was so sweet of you. Thank you!" she said as she hugged Tonya again while Tara looked on. "Way to go, sis. I'm going to enjoy having you in Texas with me. I hope you got your bags packed." Tonya smiled and stood by her sister. "I've been ready since the last day of school. My bags are packed and ready to go," Tonya said, laughing.

Tony had talked to Serena at least five times today, and he was really looking forward to seeing her. He'd been missing her since she'd left Columbus, and he longed to be near her again. He was unsure about what to expect. He and Melissa had pretty much ended their relationship since Serena and he spent time together. Things were never the same between them, and he knew why—he'd fallen in love with Serena and could only hope she loved him too. It had been two weeks since he'd talked to Melissa. After she'd found out he was going to Atlanta without her, they'd had a big fight that ended in a shoving match and Tony putting her out of his house. The neighbors got a show that night, and Tony was relieved no one called the cops. He wondered if Serena still looked the same. She never got around to sending him any pictures after she left. This time Tony was going to make sure he would have pictures of her and them together because he brought his camera with him and three rolls of film. He was prepared for this visit as he smiled to himself, pulling into his grandmother's driveway.

FOURTH OF JULY FIREWORKS

I t was three forty-five, and the girls packed up Serena's car with the picnic basket and other necessities. Serena was familiar with Tara's neck of the woods and took the wheel as they left for Big Mama's. Since they'd been driving all night, Tony suggested they park Serena's car and use his truck. The girls turned into the driveway and saw Tony getting out of the truck.

Serena's heart skipped a beat as she held her breath and watched Tony sitting with one leg out of the truck as if he'd just arrived. When he heard the car in the driveway, he got out of the truck and squinted against the sun, wondering who was pulling in. *This man even looks good squinting,* Serena thought to herself as she watched Tony. He wondered who would be driving up in a black car. He saw the Texas plates and smiled from ear to ear, realizing that the black Maxima belonged to Serena. He walked to the car as they parked and headed straight for Serena's door. She turned the car off nervously and watched Tony approach. She didn't know whether to get out and scream as she ran into his arms or if she should wait for him. Before she could ask Tara what she thought, Tara had jumped out of the car to greet her brother, leaving Serena alone in the car. She was waiting for a cue from Tony. He was happy to see his sister and hugged her as he watched Serena behind the wheel of the car. He wasn't sure what to make of the expression on her face. He walked over to the driver's door while Serena gathered herself, removed her seat belt, and reached for the door handle when she realized Tony was reaching for the handle on the outside at the same time. They both stopped and stared at each other for what seemed like minutes. Tony broke the ice by breaking out into this huge smile. Serena saw the familiar million-dollar smile complete with the most perfect set of straight white teeth and began to melt right before his eyes. As Tony opened the door, Serena beamed back with the same warm and beautiful smile he fell in love with. Both were unsure of what to do next. Serena stepped out of the car as Tony shut the door. She felt like the same school-aged girl again on her first date. "Hey, lady," Tony said, still smiling. Serena's heart softened, and that was all the welcome she needed as she stepped into his warm embrace. "Hey there yourself," she said into Tony's neck. The hug was all they needed to know to confirm nothing had changed between them.

Inside they chatted with Big Mama, and she was excited to see them all again. They were sitting around in the living room when Terry knocked at the door. They had been laughing so much they didn't hear him pull up. Tara went to the door and without hesitation kissed Terry as they greeted each other. Tara had considered dating Terry seriously again. They'd not only rekindled the love they once shared but had become close friends again and talked almost every night since her trip home in May. Serena knew Tara was already serious about Terry because she had stopped seeing Kevin who was stationed at Fort Sam Houston with them. They had met at the movies a few months back and started seeing each other. Tara knew he was seeing someone else also and figured it would always be that way with him, which made it easier to cut the ties.

As the two of them walked into in the living room, Terry approached Big Mama and gave her a big hug. She knew right away who he was and claimed he hadn't changed a bit. But everyone who went to school with Terry or knew of him during his teenage years knew he'd grown almost two feet and was no longer the skinny kid who used to sporadically slam-dunk on his opponents and throw their balls out of the gym. She asked how his parents were since they relocated to Florida. "Everyone is fine, and I couldn't be happier being surrounded by family." Terry's parents moved to Florida when he started playing for the Miami Heat. They kept their home in Atlanta but built another home outside Miami to be closer to Terry. With their professions, it wasn't hard for them to relocate. Terry's mom was a schoolteacher, and his dad was a coach. They'd found jobs in Dade County within their first week there. They made it to all of Terry's home games and would often catch some of his away games when they fell on the weekend.

Tara had to convince Tony to let her drive his truck. They'd loaded the truck with the picnic basket and blankets while Tony and Terry caught up. The guys sat in the back while Tara and Serena sat in the front. The wine was on ice now and should be completely chilled by the time they were ready for it. When Tara pulled into the parking lot and killed the engine, Tony asked what was going on. Serena looked back and smiled and said, "You'll soon see." As the girls grabbed the things from the back, they led them to a picnic area by the water; they began to see the picture. They spread the blanket out on the ground and took a seat. It was a very calm evening for this time of day. Most people were just getting off work, and the teenagers were gathered around the basketball court. They took the route less traveled so Terry wouldn't get hassled by the kids, who were sure to recognize him.

They enjoyed the sandwiches, chicken fingers, and potato salad they'd picked up on their way. The wine, along with the crackers and cheese, tasted great and was a perfect lead into the brownies Tonya had baked. Tonya had outdone herself and even added pecans. Serena loved pecans, and they finished off the entire tray of brownies.

They were all relaxed and stuffed at the same time after finishing off the wine. Terry and Tara headed for the water where they found a nice rock to sit on. Serena and Tony took a walk around the park, enjoying their time alone and the gentle breeze as the children laughed in the background. Tony reached for Serena's hand as they enjoyed one another's company. "I really missed you," he said to Serena.

"Well, that's music to my ears because I missed you too." They both smiled but once again wanted to take things slowly. Serena and Tara had taken leave and wouldn't have to leave until Sunday or Monday. That gave Tony and her four full days together. They made their way back to the playground and sat in the swings as they chatted. Tony was enjoying life in Columbus and his job even more. Serena was happy to hear it, but she also felt somewhat saddened by his comments. She felt she could really love Tony, but a long-distance relationship was not her thing.

Tony was elated to be lying on the blanket next to Serena, enjoying the sunset. The girls brought an extra blanket, and it came in handy. Terry and Tara shared the other blanket and had drifted off to sleep. Serena was thinking of the concert they would attend on Friday night. They hadn't told the guys of the news yet but hoped they could attend. "So what are your plans for tomorrow?" she asked Tony, surprising him. After considering the question, "I don't have any plans for tomorrow, lady; why, do you have something in mind?" he said with that mischievous look that always led to something else. Focusing on the business at hand, she was pleased to hear his answer. "Well, Tara and I got you and Terry tickets to the Earth, Wind & Fire concert."

"What?" Tony asked as he sat up. "Earth, Wind & Fire are in town tomorrow, and you got tickets?" he repeated as if he thought he heard wrong.

"Yeah, Tara did the research at work one day, and we've already purchased the tickets. I hope you are available." Tony smiled. "Of course I am available for you," Tony said. She was happy he accepted the invitation, but she wondered if he was still seeing Melissa. If so, where was she this weekend? "I am yours this entire weekend," he continued. Serena thought that statement confirmed what she'd believed. He was still seeing Melissa, and he was free for this weekend. She smiled and tried not to show her disappointment. As the stars came out and the streetlights came on, the bugs and frogs were creating music of their own. Serena missed Oklahoma and spending nights outside on her front porch. Tony reached over and was staring down at her. "Are you okay, Serena?" he asked, his voice full of apprehension. She smiled up at him. "I'm fine; I'm just glad to be here with you. I wouldn't trade this for anything in the world." This made Tony happy, and he considered asking her about transferring to Fort Benning. He was afraid of the answer, so he decided to kiss her instead. He bent down and pressed his lips to her warm soft lips. Serena looked up at him and returned the kiss.

Tara and Terry awoke around nine thirty and found Serena asleep in Tony's arms as he watched her sleeping. The park closed at ten o'clock, so Tara and Terry started packing up while Tony stirred Serena out of her sleep. Waking up to see Tony hovering over her was like a dream come true. *Lord, where did this fine man come from?* she thought to herself as she had an urge to pinch herself.

"Hey, sleeping beauty, it's time to go."

"Did I fall asleep? Oh my, what time is it?" After Tony told her it was nine thirty, she knew she'd been asleep for over an hour. She had to have really felt comfortable to be sleeping outside in a public park. Tony helped her up, and they joined Terry and Tara in the truck. "So we're going to see Earth Wind & Fire tomorrow, huh, Tony?" Terry asked after getting the okay from the girls.

"Yeah, this is one concert I am really looking forward to," Tony said.

"I've never seen them before, but I hear they put on a great performance," Terry said. They continued talking about the concert as Tony drove away from the park. Serena and Tara sat in the back, discussing what they were going to wear.

Melissa knew Tony was going to meet Serena, and there was nothing she could do to stop him. They'd grown apart since she showed up on Memorial Day acting like a madwoman. Although they'd been intimate since then, it was as if Tony was just going through the motions. She knew it was over, but she wasn't ready to let him go. Now he was gone, and she had to work Friday. She knew he'd be at his grandmother's on Saturday because it was the Fourth of July. She would have to come up with a plan to get Tony away from Serena.

Tony and Serena said good night as she and Tara left for Tara's parents' home. Terry had left for his parents' home and had a list of things to do around the house on Friday before the concert. Tony had a similar list for his grandmother. He had to prepare the yard and the grill for the cookout on Saturday and remove some trash from around the house. His grandmother had at least five bags of clothes that needed to be delivered to Goodwill. Tony didn't mind doing anything for his grandmother.

Tara and Serena awoke to Mr. and Mrs. Danston's voices at six thirty. They were getting ready for work and were talking over coffee and the newspaper at the kitchen table. Tara got up to say good morning. "Well, it's about time we lay eyes on you," Serena heard Tara's father say. "Hey, Daddy, hey, Mama," Tara said as she hugged them. Serena soon drifted off to sleep again. It was ten thirty when she awoke again. This time she heard the basketball bouncing on the court, and she knew it had to be Tonya out getting her exercise in. She lay there and began to think about Tony and the evening they had planned together. Terry and Tony were going to pick them up at five o'clock for dinner at Jacques. It was one of Atlanta's finest restaurants and required a coat and tie. Serena knew Tony was going to look nice in whatever he decided to throw on; after all, this man had been truly blessed in more than one area. The phone brought her back to the present as Tara opened the door. "Good morning, it's for you," she said, handing the phone to a confused Serena. "Hello," she said into the receiver. "Good morning," Tony's voice returned the greeting, sounding as sexy as ever. She was glad to hear Tony's voice so early in the morning and wished he were lying next to her. "You know, I've reached for the phone three times already to call you but decided not to because it was so early." He knew she was tuckered from her trip to Georgia and didn't want to disturb her beauty rest. He'd just finished cleaning the yard and was heading to Goodwill. "What color are you wearing tonight?" he asked Serena.

"I am wearing a semiformal blue and black dress."

"That's perfect," he said. "I'm going to rent a tux today and wanted to be sure of your colors." Serena smiled as she considered his thoughtfulness. "Okay, well, I'm going to finish up here and come back to relax before tonight. I'll pick you up at five o'clock on the dot," he said.

"I look forward to seeing you," she said, smiling as he hung up. "What's up with Tony," Tara said walking through the door.

"Nothing, he was just confirming my colors for tonight."

"Oh, how sweet," Tara said as she watched Serena's face beam with happiness. "How about the three of us go into town for something to eat," Tara suggested.

"Sounds good, let me jump in the shower."

Melissa had it figured out. She would have to do something drastic, and she knew just what story to tell. She thought long and hard about it. Even if she and Tony never got back together again, she would make sure Serena wanted nothing to do with him ever again. It was four thirty, and she wouldn't get off until seven o'clock Saturday morning. She had her car packed and would be leaving for Atlanta the minute she got off.

Terry and Tony arrived promptly at five o'clock in the backseat of a white limo. The girls were so excited they beamed with joy. They were thoroughly surprised by the thought of being chauffered around town and to the concert in a limousine. Their reservation at Jacques was for six o'clock. Tara was dressed in a wine-colored gown that accentuated her physique. It was low cut with a swag neckline and showed just enough cleavage. Terry was tall, dark, and handsome in his silver tux with a wine-colored cummerbund. His Stacey Adams' shoes were burgundy and silver, and they both looked like they belonged on the cover of a magazine. Serena was not disappointed watching Tony pose for pictures in his black tux looking like he was on top of the world. Tonya agreed to be our photographer for the evening. The black and royal blue were perfect colors for them. Their eyes locked from the moment he stepped out of the limo. He was stunned by her beauty and had almost forgotten where they were going. They all were dressed so nicely they could have very well been attending a wedding. Tony noticed how the dress hugged Serena in all the right places. She wore a pair of black stilettos that had to be at least four inches high, and he was immediately turned on. Her skin was radiant, and her legs were beautifully shaped as she stepped toward him. The dress had fitted long sleeves that featured an oval opening showing her sculpted chest. The back of the dress was enough to drive any man insane. There were two straps crisscrossing a few inches below her nape. There was an even larger oval outlet that continued down just millimeters from her butt, exposing her strong and toned back. All the feelings he'd had after first meeting her came flowing back to him all at once, and he felt goose bumps all over his body. It was sexy, and Tony was aroused. He was shocked by his response, but he was no fool. Serena was a beautiful and seductive woman who could have any man she wanted. He gave her a quick kiss on the cheek. "You look stunning," he said as he walked her to the limo.

"Thank you," she said. "You are really wearing that tux, and I am honored to be on your arm." She smiled up at Tony as he led her to the limo while Terry and Tara watched from their seats in the limo. They were seated across from Tara and Terry when Tony presented Serena with the most beautiful red rose. Serena looked at Tara, and she was holding her red rose too. The chauffer closed the door, and Serena reached up to Tony and gave him a warm kiss to say thank you.

When they arrived at Jacques, they were given a tour and took tons of pictures. This time the tour guide acted as their photographer. It was almost six o'clock as they headed for the dining room entrance. After they were seated, they enjoyed the live band while waiting for their food. Serena had never been to Jacques before, but it was absolutely beautiful inside and out. There was a mixed crowd, and everyone was dressed to kill. Serena noticed she'd gotten a few looks from men and women and hoped her dress wasn't too much for the restaurant. As Tony led her to the dance floor, he must've sensed what she'd been thinking. "Serena, did I tell you how beautiful you look and how perfect you are for me?" he said, staring down into her beautiful brown eyes. She looked radiant, and he wanted her to know that and be completely at ease. Not knowing how to respond, Serena smiled. "Yes, you have, and thank you for making me feel comfortable."

He went on. "You are the envy of every woman in here tonight regardless of race, wealth, or class; and I am honored to be here with you." She needed to hear that and was grateful for the compliment. She held him closer while his hand rested on her exposed skin in the oval opening. His hands were warm and inviting as they sent chills through her body. At this moment, she wanted to kiss him but decided against it, not wanting to cause a disruption in this upscale restaurant. As they danced, they noticed a group of fans who'd been sitting a few tables away from Terry and Tara had finally made their way over to their table. When Serena looked again, Terry was signing autographs in the middle of people dining at Jacques.

"Why don't we give Terry and Tara an outlet?"

"My thoughts exactly," he said as they headed for their table. Terry soon led Tara to the dance floor, which was where they remained until their food was ready.

After dinner, Tony and Serena spoke quietly at their table since they had some time alone. "Serena, have you ever thought about transferring to the East Coast?" he asked with an all-too-familiar look on his face. Serena knew Tony was serious, and she was hopeful that maybe he felt the same way she did. She wanted to take their relationship to the next level, but it would be hard if they remained states apart and he kept Melissa around. She was speechless, not sure where he was going with this line of questioning. So she played it safe with a straight face. "Yes, I've thought about it before, but I kinda like being close to home." She decided to take their conversation a step farther. She looked at him and smiled. "Have you ever considered possibly relocating," she paused, "maybe down South?" She knew by his reaction that they were trying to get a feel for what the other wanted out of the relationship. Serena knew she only had a few days with Tony and didn't want to waste time beating around the bush. She knew she and Tony had found something special in each other, and she wanted to further explore whatever it was. "You know, Tony, I am up for reenlistment next summer, and I'm almost certain Fort Benning has a position for me. I would love to do some checking around, but I'm sure it is possible." His face lit up after hearing the news. Not only was it possible, she seemed as if she would actually consider relocating to be near him. "Would you consider coming to Texas?" she asked again, this time more directly, which surprised Tony yet again. He never knew what she would say next, but she never disappointed him. All the feelings and thoughts he'd experienced were mutual. He wondered if she already loved him too. He smiled this time, almost laughing. "Serena, I would follow you anywhere if you would have me." The smile disappeared from his face and was replaced once again by the most sincere and gentle expression. He reached out and took her hand in his and kissed it gently. He wanted to share a real kiss with her but didn't want to make a spectacle of himself just yet. Hearing Tony say he was willing to leave Columbus to be with her could have been a confirmation of Melissa no longer being in his life, but she needed definite answers from him, so why stop now? "Tony, I don't like to pry, but I need to know if you and Melissa are still in a relationship." This time Serena was serious. Tony knew this would come up, and he was prepared to answer her questions honestly. He squeezed her hand and said, "No, Melissa and I are no longer seeing each other. I am not seeing anyone, and I would like to start working on our future together." Serena thought she was going to faint. *Did he just say* our *future together?* She blinked hard, trying to replay his exact words over in her head. This was the best news she could have hoped for. *This man wants to be with me,* she thought as she laughed loudly, not caring who heard or saw her. They met in the middle of the table and shared a warm, sensual kiss they'd been trying to avoid. This time they couldn't restrain themselves anymore. They were about to embark upon a newly united journey in life, and they couldn't be happier. "I would like for you to meet my mom tomorrow in Savannah," Tony said slowly as Serena stared at him. She wasn't sure if she was having problems with her hearing, so she looked around the room at the nearby tables. The band was still playing music, but she couldn't make out what tune they were playing. Everything was in slow motion. She thought *this can't be real* and turned back to Tony with a confused look on her face. When she finally focused on Tony, he was no longer in his chair but in front of her on one knee, presenting a ring to her. "Serena Johnson, will you spend the rest of your life with me?" Serena's heart stopped, and her hearing came back all at once in a rush, and she realized what was happening. Serena looked around the room, quickly searching the dance floor for Tara and Terry. The buzz in the restaurant was a jumbled noise that seemed light-years away. The food and wine must've gone to her head because now the room was spinning, and everything around her was in slow motion. Finally as the room spun in Tony's direction, she found Tara and Terry standing behind him. *Why is everyone staring at me?* she thought when she suddenly remembered why she was holding her breath. She let it out all at once and found Tony still on one knee looking as handsome and patient as ever. He had proposed to her, and he was still waiting for an answer. He held her hand as she noticed how beautiful the ring was. It was a two-carat princess-cut diamond with a wide platinum silver band. The diamond was sparkling brilliantly in the light. The whole room was quiet now with all eyes on her. An answer, that's what Tony was waiting for. He was still smiling as he held the ring out to her. "Yes, Tony, I'll marry you," she said in barely a whisper, then she repeated it louder each time. "Yes, yes, yes, I will marry you." They shared another kiss as the entire restaurant cheered and applauded his proposal and her acceptance. Even the couples on the dance floor had stopped to look on. Tony placed the ring on her finger and kissed her as the tears streamed down her face. They embraced each other as Tara and Terry congratulated them. "Tara, will you be my maid of honor?" Serena asked, still crying.

"Of course I will. I wouldn't have it any other way."

Tony then turned to Terry and extended his hand and said, "Best man?"

"You got it," Terry said, smiling widely and shaking Tony's hand and hugging him at the same time. The band, as if on cue, started playing "When We Get Married" by Larry Graham; and the two of them shared their final dance of the evening.

By the time they cleared the restaurant, it was seven fifty; and the limo was waiting for them to appear. The driver pulled around as the couples stepped out on the sidewalk. As they headed for the coliseum, Serena was still in a daze. She had not let go of Tony's hand since before he'd proposed to her. She looked at the ring and kept saying it's so beautiful. "Tony, this is unbelievable."

"I'm glad you like it," he said, smiling as they shared another kiss. He actually knew it was the perfect ring for her the moment he saw it. There was only one like it, and he knew it would be perfect for his future wife. He smiled at the thought of that. Tara and Terry were happy for their friends. "Serena, I guess this means we'll really be sisters now."

"Ah, that's right. Now I *will* have someone to call sister. That couldn't make me happier." The girls shared a hug, and Tara found herself crying. She knew Tony and Serena were meant to be together, and she felt partly responsible for their union. They were the perfect couple, and she knew they loved each other from the moment they met. Terry listened to Tony talking to Serena and was proud of his friend. He had pursued Serena because he knew she was special. He was patient and knew just what to say to her. He knew that the man sitting before him was no longer the boy who had multiple girlfriends at the same time and who was in and out of relationships like they meant nothing. Tony had grown up and was handling his business. *They say, "There is someone for everyone."* Terry smiled at this thought as he looked at Tara. He too knew Tony and Serena loved each other from the moment he saw them together at the mall. It was a chaotic day for him, but the bond between him and Serena was so obvious even during his time of turmoil. He admired what they shared.

The concert was great; and Earth, Wind & Fire blew the audience away. Carmen had gotten Tara backstage passes since she'd been working in the entertainment business. Carmen and Tara put the incident with Sheila behind them, and both vowed to remain friends. Not only did the group get pictures with EW&F, but they also received autographed pictures. One of the members recognized Terry right away, and Terry reciprocated by signing a few autographs of his own. It was indeed a memorable night, and Tony only wanted to make it complete by making love to his new fiancée, but the opportunity never presented itself. He knew they would have all the time in the world in Savannah. The limo dropped the girls off at Tara's parents. Serena didn't want to leave Tony but knew tomorrow would be a full and busy day. They were leaving for Savannah at noon. It was four hours away, which would still give them plenty of daylight to enjoy the beach.

Tony was up at six o'clock, getting the meat prepared to go on the grill. Terry joined him at nine o'clock to help him finish up so they could eat lunch at eleven o'clock and leave on time. Tony and Serena had been on the phone most of the night and decided to get some sleep at four o'clock. Tony only got two hours of sleep and was really grateful to Terry for helping out. The family started showing up around ten o'clock, and Mr. Danston brought his ingredients for his famous barbecued baked beans. Mrs. Danston was there to fix the green salad and potato salad. Tara and Serena were setting the table and pouring ice over the drinks. Tonya worked on the music and was glad she'd brought her AC adapter since the batteries were dead from the picnic. Tara and Serena rode with Mr. Danston in his truck so they wouldn't have to leave Serena's car unattended at Tara's grandmother's house. Tony and Terry had the grills going. One contained pork and the other beef. When Serena saw Tony standing over the grill in his apron, she smiled, remembering when he cooked lunch for them at his house. She smiled as she walked up to him and planted a warm, juicy kiss on his full, inviting lips. No one seemed to notice, and she was glad. Tony looked down at her finger and was relieved to see her still wearing her ring. He wanted to make sure she hadn't had a change of heart. He wanted to announce to everyone there that they were getting married but wanted Serena to meet his mom first. He wanted his mom to be the first person he told. He smiled as he kissed Serena again before she went inside to help his dad and stepmom.

Tony was on the phone with his mom while Serena sat next to him. Tara and Terry were in the backseat asleep. Serena looked back and laughed, wondering if they were up all night too chatting on the phone. Serena thought back to the lunch shared with Tara and Tony's family. Mr. Danston noticed the ring and looked at her and Tony but said nothing. She'd hoped he wasn't upset. When they departed, he hugged her the same way he always did, and this let her know that he wasn't upset. After all, she'd considered asking Tara if her father could escort her down the aisle and hand her off to her dad. Serena's father was disabled and knew walking her down the aisle would be a difficult task to carry out. She wondered if Tony had told anyone else that he and Melissa had ended their relationship. Probably not since he'd only told her after she'd asked. *What if everyone there thought he was still seeing her?* She began to feel sick when Tony looked over and ended his conversation, noticing her uneasiness. "What's troubling you, lady?" he asked as he took her hand. She immediately smiled as her heart warmed hearing him call her lady. This man knew he could read her mind. "I was just thinking how badly things might have looked today. Almost two months ago, you were in Atlanta with Melissa. Now here I am showing up again, and we appear to be a couple. What will your family think of me?" she asked, looking troubled, and placed her head in her hands.

"Serena, I've never told my family my every move. They're used to me and my way of living. Believe me, my dad absolutely adores you." Serena's face lightened up. "Do you really think so?" Tony laughed. "Yeah, I know so. We've discussed you on more than one occasion. Do you know my dad watched us from the kitchen window at his house when you were here before?"

"What!" Serena exclaimed. "What do you mean?"

"He saw the bond that we shared but didn't think too much about it until he saw us saying good morning before breakfast."

"Oh my god, I can't believe he noticed it. I'm really embarrassed now."

"No, don't be, he was once our age too. It's okay. I know he will be pleased once he hears of our engagement." Serena looked shocked. "I'll give them the good news when we return on Sunday." *Wow, he really is just as excited as I am,* she thought to herself as she looked out the window.

After being dropped off last night, Serena could hardly wait to get to her cell phone. She told Tara she'd be in shortly, which actually turned out to be an hour later. She called her mom and surprised her with the news. Her mom and dad were both happy and couldn't wait to meet Tony. After receiving advice about not rushing into anything and make sure he's got good credit and a savings account, Serena was able to get them off the phone before they started talking about a prenuptial agreement. She smiled as she remembered the conversation.

Terry and Tara woke up as Tony and Serena slowed down and drove through downtown Savannah. There were people everywhere, and it was a beautiful site and so full of history. Tony called his mom again to let her know that they would be there in fifteen minutes. She lived in a condo on Tybee Island. Her name was Tamela, and she was going to be away tonight celebrating Independence Day.

She was going to hang around to chat with them for a few hours but would be picked up by her date at five thirty.

Downtown Savannah was absolutely stunning, and you couldn't ask for better weather. Serena hoped they'd be able to walk on the on the beach and maybe take a trolley ride to see all the sights. Tybee Island was separated from Savannah by a bridge but was relatively close. The homes were gorgeous, and the water looked so blue and so inviting. When they pulled into Sunshine Acres, she grew more and more excited. Tony's mom lived in a gated community right on the beach. "How perfect," Serena said in amazement as Tony stopped to punch in the security code. Terry and Tara were really impressed and were anxious to get out on the beach, and they did just that. Tony was thankful for the time alone with his mother and his fiancée without any distractions.

Once inside the beautiful three-bedroom condo, Serena felt totally comfortable. She was sitting across from Tony's twin. His mother was an absolutely gorgeous woman in her early fifties, and it was evident she took care of herself quite well. Her hair was curled; her nails were done in a classy deep red polish. She was dressed in all white with a red, white, and blue pendant on her lapel. She wore two rings, one on each ring finger, and no more. Her makeup was very conservative. After all, her beauty was natural, so she didn't require a lot of makeup. Serena watched Tony greet his mom when they entered the foyer. Tony kissed his mom and hugged her as Serena realized the two were very close and had what appeared to be a very strong relationship. That's another thing her mother had warned her about—the relationship between mother and son. "It could tell you a lot about him, and the way he treats his mother is the same way he will treat you," she could hear her mom say. Well, that's another test he just passed. She knew his credit was remarkable because they actually compared points. He had a savings account, but she wasn't sure how much he had saved up, which didn't concern her. What she did want to do was open a joint account for them as soon as possible. She'd already mentioned it to Tony, and he agreed without hesitation. They both had something to bring into the marriage. They both had investments, homes, secure jobs, and a savings account. Her parents would be proud to have Tony as their son-in-law.

When Tony introduced Tamela to Serena, Serena shook her warm hand and was very happy Tony wanted her to meet his mother. When

Tony finished introducing her as his fiancée, his mom screamed, "Oh my god, my baby's getting married!" Tamela dropped Serena's hand and pulled her in for a warm, motherly hug. She reached for Tony as she was hugging Serena. "Congratulations, baby. This makes me so happy, congratulations to you both. Welcome to the family, Serena," she said as she flashed her million-dollar smile, and Serena knew immediately where Tony had gotten his winning smile from. "Tony, I am so proud of you," she said as she hugged him again. Tony was pleased his mother accepted the union and said, "Mom, I knew you would love her."

"Of course, son, as long as she makes you happy, I'm happy too." They took a seat on the couch. "It's about time you find a special lady to spend the rest of your life with." Serena heard that word again and knew it was an honorable title. They chatted for a while, and Serena showed Tamela her ring at her request. She was glad Tony spared no expense when selecting this precious gift to his fiancée. Serena told Tamela about her life in Texas and that she was in the military. She didn't seem alarmed at all that they'd only known each other for two months. She was a firm believer in going after what you want in life. "Life is too short to let it pass you by." She knew her son was in love when he talked nonstop about Serena whom he'd met during the Memorial Day weekend. She kept her thoughts to herself because at that time, her son himself didn't know he was falling in love. "Well, I'm glad this has turned out so well. I'm glad I was able to meet you and get to know you before the big day. Speaking of big day, have you two set a date yet?" she inquired.

"Well, because of a few obstacles, we're not able to choose an exact date because we both have jobs, and one of us would have to make a sacrifice and relocate, but we're thinking sometime around May."

"Well, I'm sure it'll work itself out. I would like to help you with the planning process, Serena, if you're okay with that." Serena was speechless at the suggestion. She was just introduced to her, and already she'd accepted her into the family and wanted to help make their day become a reality. She broke out into a huge smile and said, "Of course, I wouldn't have it any other way. Thank you."

"No need to thank me, that's what I'm here for. Tony, make sure you give Serena my contact information. I gotta feeling we're going to be talking quite a bit. I'm so excited," she said, returning the smile.

There was a knock at the door, and Tony opened it to find Tara and Terry standing there. "Perfect timing, come on in," he said as he stepped aside and allowed them to walk into the foyer. Tamela appeared and greeted Tara with a hug. "It is so good to see you again," she told Tara. "Likewise," said Tara. It had been several years since they'd seen each other. The two had a good relationship and enjoyed each other's company. Terry walked in behind Tara and stood towering over her. "Hi, Ms. Walker, long time no see," Terry said as he leaned down and planted a kiss on her cheek. "Terry Jones, my, you have really grown. The last time I saw you, you were much smaller and thinner. You look great, and you're all grown up," Tamela said with a laugh as she hugged him.

Ms. Walker had made her homemade chilli-cheese nachos on the stove top with her special blend of tomato sauce. Tony had told her what time they were arriving, and she offered to make a snack. On the table, she'd placed two boxes of pralines, one regular and one chocolate. It had been years since Serena had had pralines, and she felt like a kid in a candy store.

Ms. Walker had left for her party and said she'd be back by noon tomorrow to see them off. "Make yourselves at home," she called over her shoulder as she walked out the door. They'd made plans to go down to the waterfront to watch the fireworks. Terry and Tara were getting their overnight bags out of the truck while Tony and Serena sat out on the deck enjoying the sun.

It was five forty-five, and Tony and Serena knew they couldn't wait another minute to start their own fireworks. They'd been together two whole days, and still they'd not ventured past kissing. As if reading Serena's mind, Tony led her into the bedroom they would be sharing. Serena washed up while Tony went down to grab their bags from the truck. He was back in less than five minutes. Terry and Tara decided to eat while Tony headed for Serena. Before she could step out of the bathroom, Tony met her at the door and began ravishing her with his hot, steamy kisses all over. His sexual appetite turned Serena on and she gave into him. Tony quickly and recklessly unbuttoned her blouse and revealed the fullness of her breasts peeking over the peach lace bra. He kept telling himself to slow down, but it was almost as if he was starving, and Serena had just what he needed to satisfy his hunger. Serena was so beautifully created he just wanted to taste her and kiss her from head to toe. He began to moan loudly once he knew she was about to lose control. Serena went to the floor and began squirming under Tony's touch. She pulled his shirt over his head and exposed his beautiful smooth brown skin. He was more muscular than she remembered, and this turned her on even more. When they heard the music coming from the living room, Serena laughed to herself and figured they were getting too loud. Tony was so preoccupied he didn't seem to notice. Serena knew he was a man on a mission, so she let him have his way. He kept telling her how beautiful she was over and over as he admired her body. They both had been hungry for each other and couldn't wait for the incredible release. Soon they were both exhausted and lay there holding each other, replaying the powerful session over again in their minds. After a brief intermission, Serena rolled Tony over and straddled him while she leaned down and kissed his neck, nipples, and chest; and before she could go any farther, Tony was ready again. The second encounter was slower and deeper, and Serena knew the difference between having sex and making love with Tony. What they'd just shared said far more to each other than any words could express. They held hands as the second release approached, and this time they were past exhaustion as they began to drift off to sleep holding each other. Serena lay down on Tony's chest and whispered, "I love you, Tony." *It sounded so seductive coming from her lips*, Tony thought. It was like music to his ears. Tony was startled by her confession and pulled her up to him where their faces were even. "And I love you, Serena," he said sincerely as he looked into her eyes, wanting her to know it was true. They shared a kiss that seemed to seal their love and commitment to one another. They would spend the rest of their lives together as husband and wife.

Melissa had to work overtime and was not able to get on the road until ten o'clock. She was furious. Not only was she going to arrive later but also had to travel on the holiday, which meant she had to constantly be on the lookout for cops. She had been working on her story. It had been a month since she had been intimate with Tony, but that was enough time for her to conceive. Although Tony used a condom, accidents happen. The condom could have had a hole in it causing a leakage, which could be just enough sperm to fertilize an egg.

When Melissa passed by Tony's grandmother's house, she didn't see his truck or any cars bearing Texas plates. She did however see Terry's car and knew they all must've been together. There were a few other cars bearing plates from Mississippi, Louisiana, and North Carolina. Terry must've been spending time with Tara while Tony wined and dined Serena. It was Saturday evening when she made her first visit. Her second visit was at seven thirty that evening and still no sign of them.

It was eight o'clock when they decided to head downtown. They brought the picnic blanket with them just in case there was nowhere to sit. They were right; the place was packed. They enjoyed the boardwalk and being out in the sizzling night air. The firework display was completely breathtaking as the crowd oohed and aahed. The four of them shared a blanket as they sipped on the fruit-flavored drinks. Serena had been sneaking peeks at her beautiful ring since last night. She'd hoped she wasn't too obvious, but it was an extremely beautiful ring. She couldn't wait to show it to her parents.

When Serena woke up to find Tony next to her, she smiled to herself. She wanted more mornings like this; but for now, she'd take them whenever she could get them. She held her hand up again and admired her ring and thanked God for sending this incredible man into her life.

Tony stood on the balcony talking to his mom before walking back inside to join the others. As they said their good-byes to Tamela, she hugged Serena again and told her to call as much as she wanted to. They were headed back to Atlanta, and Serena was on cloud nine. She and Tony had drifted off to sleep in the backseat. This time it didn't take much convincing for Tara to drive her brother's truck; after all, he'd not had much sleep since Serena was in town. He and Serena had obviously been up all night, and both were moving slowly this morning. Tara and Terry laughed as they teased the two lovebirds in the backseat while they slept peacefully. It was a four-hour trip, and they actually woke up about thirty minutes from Atlanta claiming they were starving. Tara pulled over at a Pizza Hut right off the highway, and they went in and ordered two pies. Serena and Tara went over to the jukebox to get the music going while the guys chatted at the table and waited for the pizza to be brought out.

It was now nine o'clock Sunday morning and still no sign of Tony or his truck. Melissa was glad she was able to crash at Elva's house after the firework show last night. Tony would have to be back today since he had to work on Monday morning. She was getting more and more irritated by the second. Now she had a foolproof plan since all she had was time on her hands. She reached into her purse and pulled out an envelope addressed to her from the Columbus OB Clinic. This envelope contained her pregnancy test results. The letter should be enough proof for Tony. She would only use this secret weapon if she couldn't convince him otherwise. *I just need to get him away from Serena long enough to make him fall in love with the idea of having a baby together and eventually fall in love with me again,* she thought to herself as she headed into town, checking the local restaurants and hotels for Tony's truck.

"So what's going on?" Tara asked anxiously as she reminded Serena of a kid in a candy store.

"What do you mean?"

"You know what I mean. Have you two set a date yet?" Serena started laughing, enjoying hearing her friend refer to their wedding date. "Not yet, but it's going to definitely be after next summer. We're not sure who's moving, him or me. I may try to PCS to Benning next year, or he may be coming to Texas."

"What? Are you serious? This is great. I can't believe it. So he's open to moving away from Columbus and leave his house behind?" Tara asked, surprised.

"Well, we've not gotten that far. If he were to come to Texas, I'm not sure if he'd rent his house or sell it or just leave it vacant. I don't want to push him one way or the other on that. I'm sure we'll have to make several compromises. If I PCS to Georgia, I'll probably have one of my close friends monitor my house while I rent it out," she said smiling, letting Tara know she was speaking of her.

"Serena, you know I would do anything for you, so that's the least of your worries. So what you're saying is that everything depends on your status? That actually means we could still have a fall wedding." After processing what Tara was suggesting, she said, "You are absolutely right; we could have a fall wedding."

"Well, we have plenty of time to plan," Tara said. Serena's mind was already racing ahead to next year, beginning the planning process.

"Hey, Tony, are you okay man?" Terry asked. Tony smiled and said, "Yeah, I'm fine. I am the luckiest man in the world to have found Serena and convinced her to marry me."

"Man, you don't waste any time. I knew it was serious between you two when I first met her in May. Some things are just meant to be, and this one, my brother, is crystal clear, and I'm happy for you. So have you set a date yet?"

"No, not yet," Tony said, sounding surprised. "We have some things to work out first before we can proceed with setting a date. You know she wants to make a career out of the army, and I have to wait until next year to find out if she can come to Georgia or if she's staying in Texas."

"So what are you hoping for?"

Tony was quiet for a while and said, "You know, this girl is almost too good to be true, and I feel blessed to have found her. So I am willing to do whatever it takes to be together." Terry sat back, surprised to hear his friend speak of Serena with such endearment. He knew Tony was truly in love, and he was happy for him. "Well, just let me know what you need me to do for the two of you. I'm only a phone call away."

The girls returned to the table, and they enjoyed their favorite pizza with breadsticks. They were headed to Atlanta when Tony decided to check his phone. There was a call from his grandmother, but no message was left. He called back but got no answer and wondered what the call was about. "What's wrong?" Serena asked. "I'm not sure; Big Mama called but didn't leave a message."

"Do you think something's wrong?" Serena asked with concern in her voice.

"No, she would've left a message if something was wrong. We'll be there in ten minutes. I'm sure she's okay."

On her last trip, Melissa decided to wait at the house rather than burn her gas. She hoped Tony's grandmother would be able to shed some light on his whereabouts. *Tony should be back now,* she thought as she pulled into the driveway and got out of the car. Terry's car was still there in the same place it was parked on yesterday. *They must've gone out of town for the weekend,* she thought. *Where could they have gone?* she wondered as her thoughts ran wild. She knocked on the door and waited for his grandmother to open the door. She got no answer but remembered where she kept the extra key. Melissa walked around to the back of the house, reached up over the door, and pulled down the spare key. She let herself in the house and went into the bedroom Tony normally slept in and found only a few of his clothes on the dresser. After searching the room, she came up empty handed. She walked to the front door and took a seat on the porch. She was getting desperate and wanted to talk to Tony. She reached for her cell phone and started to dial Tony. She stopped in the middle of entering his number. *He'll never answer the phone if he knows it's me, especially if he's with Serena.* Melissa walked back in the house and picked up the phone in the kitchen. She dialed Tony's cell number, but her call went directly to voice mail. She definitely did not want to leave a message, so she hung up.

It was five thirty when they pulled into their grandmother's yard. The girls were getting on the road at seven o'clock to head back to Texas. They would be back in San Antonio between 10:00 and 12:00 depending on how many stops they made along the way. Terry was not flying out until the morning for Miami. Tony had decided to leave after the girls left. He had to work Monday morning and should be arriving in Columbus around 10:00 that night. They'd picked up the golden oldie station after leaving Pizza Hut and sang all the way home. They were working on Debarge's "I Like It" when Tony stopped singing and stared at the red convertible sitting in the driveway, bringing the truck to an abrupt halt. "What the hell is she doing here?" he asked as if it was meant to be a thought only. He pulled into the driveway and wondered what could have brought Melissa all this way knowing she wasn't invited. They'd not spoken in a couple of weeks after the big fight, and he couldn't think of anything that wouldn't wait until he got back home. He wondered what conversation she'd engaged in with his grandmother. Serena stopped singing too and looked at the angry expression Tony's face had changed into. She then looked at Tara, wondering what was going on. They all got out of the truck as Tony headed for the house ahead of them. The three of them unloaded the truck and went into the house after Tony. Just as they hit the porch, they heard Tony and Melissa arguing. Tara dropped her bags and ran inside to mediate and to keep them quiet, not wanting to disturb her grandmother. As she made a quick search of the house and the bedroom, she discovered her grandmother wasn't home; and she ran back into the living room where they were getting louder and louder. Terry and Serena put the bags into Terry's car, not really wanting to be involved in the altercation. As they decided to enter the house, Tara was standing between Tony and Melissa trying to keep Tony back, which was harder than Tara would have liked to admit. Terry ran over to assist in keeping Tony away from Melissa. "What is going on?" Tara screamed, looking at Melissa who was clearly shaken. She had been crying and was holding a letter up in the air. Serena wondered if she'd found one of the letters she'd written to Tony shortly after they left Columbus, confirming they had been together. "Ask your brother," Melissa spat in Tara's direction. "He is part the blame too, because it takes two." Just then Tony lunged for her, and Terry had to run to get in front of him while Melissa backed up to the dining room. It was obvious their grandmother wasn't in the house. No one could sleep through this. "Tony, what is going on?" Serena asked calmly, not sure if she was ready to hear the answer. Before he could respond, Melissa was spilling her guts. "Well, Ms. Serena, if you must know, I am carrying Tony's baby; and I do not plan on having an abortion if that's what he thinks." Serena looked at Tony with a look of complete despair and disappointment as she tried to wrap her mind around what Melissa had just told her. "What do you mean? Tony, what is she talking about? How could this be?" Terry was still restraining Tony as he tried to break free. "She is lying, Serena, please don't believe her," he pleaded with her as he screamed, "She's is just trying to keep us apart."

"I am not lying, Tony, and you know it. We've been together since Serena left, and don't you dare try to deny it. I missed my period three weeks ago, and I went in for a pregnancy test, and I have my results right here." Tara was speechless. She reached over and took the letter from Melissa, who was now gaining strength and going after Serena. "It looks like I'm going to have little Tony and there's nothing you can do or say at this point. I am going to love this baby with all my heart even if his daddy doesn't want to be a part of his life." Melissa turned to Tony and said, "I do expect you to do your part and pay half of the hospital bills, and it's up to you if you want to be there for the delivery next May. Oh, just know that I will be seeking child support once the baby is born." This time Tara looked at Serena and saw that her world was coming to an end as she sat down in the floor, remembering all the promises they'd made to each other the night before. Now she wondered if they even had a future. Tara escorted Melissa out onto the porch and read the letter from the OB Clinic in Columbus. Well, it was true; Melissa was definitely pregnant and going to have a baby. Tara wished she could believe it was someone else's baby. She knew what this would do to Serena; she thought about the sight of her sitting on the floor. She looked at Melissa as if to warn her about not coming in the house, and she ran inside to Serena and shut the door. Her friend was still sitting in the same place on the floor with Tony sitting on the floor beside her, repeating "I'm sorry" over and over again. Serena's pain was indescribable, and she shook all over.

The man of her dreams had proposed to her, and she had accepted. They were making plans to marry. He told her he and Melissa were over, but they had to be together intimately recently for her to be a few weeks' pregnant. What was she supposed to do now? Accept this child and become a stepmom before she even become a mom? What kind of life would they have together? It was obvious Melissa wasn't going anywhere and would always have a place in Tony's life, as would her child, which would be a constant reminder of this painful time.

Serena didn't break in front of Melissa and refused to break in Tony's presence. A tear rolled down her cheek as she looked away from Tony while he was still holding her. Terry had taken a seat in the living room, and Tara joined him. "Serena, please talk to me," Tony said as he saw the tear roll down her face. He reached up and wiped her tear away, but she still wasn't responding. "Serena, please listen to what I have to say." Tony looked at Tara as if asking for help to get through to her. Tara joined them on the floor. "Serena, please talk to me. We all care about you, and we are here for you." Tony got up to read the letter Tara had brought inside. He was even angrier after reading the letter, and he couldn't believe he had impregnated Melissa. If it was true, she had to have done something to sabotage the condom he used with her. He was livid as he stormed out the front door and headed for Melissa who was already in the car just waiting for something else to happen. Terry went after him.

"What can I do for you?" Tara asked Serena. "Tell me, I'll do anything." Serena looked at her friend with a distant look on her face. "Get me out of here," she whispered as if afraid someone else might overhear them. Tara looked stunned. "What? You want to leave?" Tara repeated. Serena nodded. Tara remembered they'd been dropped off yesterday by her mom and dad. They would have to get a ride from either Tony or Terry.

As Tony caught up to Melissa's car, she rolled up the windows and locked the door and stared at him. She'd never seen him this angry before. There was no turning back. She'd already announced to the world that she was pregnant with his child, and she had proof. Proof, where is the letter? Oh no, Tara took the letter from her, and now

Tony had it. *I need to get that letter back,* she thought as she panicked. From the look on Tony's face, there was no way she would be able to reason with him. He ran up to her door and tried to open it; realizing it was locked, he struck the front windshield with his fist. "Why are you doing this to me?" he yelled. Melissa started the car and backed up with Tony following the car out to the end of the road. "Why are you doing this?" he asked again. Melissa couldn't look into his cold eyes anymore. If there was ever any hope of them reuniting, after today, it would never happen. She knew Tony would hate her for coming between him and Serena; and when he found out she lied and orchestrated this whole thing, he could actually press charges. Melissa pulled away with all of this on her mind. She knew she'd gone too far but couldn't take it back now. She reached inside her purse and cursed Tony for buying that hussy an engagement ring. After she'd conducted her search of the bedroom, she'd found the receipt from Zales on the bathroom floor. He spent $2,300.00 for an engagement ring, and he's only known her for two months. Melissa was livid. She'd been dating Tony for over a year, and they never talked about marriage. She would fix him, she thought to herself as she headed for Columbus.

Tara and Serena walked out onto the porch and headed for Tony's truck. Tony walked up to the truck after they'd gotten in and almost looked defeated still holding the paper. Terry was right beside him, trying to calm him down. When Tony saw the girls in the truck, he heard Tara start the truck. He walked over to the passenger's side and opened the door and looked at Serena's despondent face. "Serena, I love you." She sat there quietly. "Let me know when you're ready to talk to me. I need to explain some things to you. I'm going to get to the bottom of this, I promise." She reached down and was trying to pull the engagement ring he'd just given her off. "Wait, what are you doing? Are you saying you no longer want to marry me?" Tony's voice wavered as he felt his heart sink. "Serena, please don't do this to me, to us. I love *you,* and I want you to be my wife." He placed the ring back on her finger and bent down to kiss her. Even in the midst of all the confusion and uncertainty, she believed he still loved her. She didn't respond to his kiss, and Tony noticed. He was now even more determined to get to the bottom of Melissa's scheme. He closed the door and went over to talk to Tara. "What time are you leaving?" It was six fifteen, and they'd planned to be on the road by seven o'clock.

"We're planning to leave at seven," Tara said as he stepped away from the truck, allowing Terry to speak with her. Tony stood on the porch as he and Serena focused on one another. It was more like a staring contest as Terry and Tara said their good-byes. "Don't worry about Tony; I'll drop him over to get his truck," he reassured Tara. As the girls backed out of the driveway, Tony and Serena were still focused on each other; but neither said anything or made a move.

The girls were driving down the highway when they spotted Melissa's car at the gas station. She was walking back to her car when the girls passed by. Melissa looked up just in time to see Serena sitting in the front seat of Tony's truck. She wondered if she'd done all of her lying in vain. She was pissed that he would have the nerve to be riding her around in his truck knowing *she* was carrying his child.

Tony sat on the porch not able to believe what had just happened. How did Melissa get in the house, and where was his grandmother? Melissa acted as if she knew about the engagement, because she wanted a reaction, and she definitely got one. How could she have known? Before he could finish his thought, he jumped up and ran into the bathroom. He remembered placing the receipt on the shelf over the toilet when it fell out of his pocket as he changed clothes. He remembered it all too well. He had just left Goodwill and stopped by the mall in search of a ring for Serena. He placed the bag with the ring in it in his glove compartment and locked it but brought the receipt and warranty information inside to read over it. He left it in the bathroom, but now it was nowhere to be found. He walked into the bedroom and found it on the bed. He didn't remember bringing it out of the bathroom and figured if Melissa had time to search the house, she had time to find his receipt. He walked to the back door to see if she pried the door open, but he remembered she too knew where his grandmother kept the extra key. That must've been how she got into the house. He grabbed his belongings from the bedroom and locked up the house as Terry was waiting for him.

As the girls pulled in the driveway, they immediately put their bags in Serena's car. They had packed for their trip home before they left for Savannah. Serena was still quiet, and Tara decided not to push. As they checked Tony's truck for any of their things, Serena looked down at her ring again. She was tempted to leave it behind in his truck but agreed they needed to talk before making any decisions, only now she was not ready for it. She decided she would remove it if she became uncomfortable in the presence of Tony's family, but for now she'd wear the ring Tony had proposed to her with. She didn't want to be faced with any questions that were too painful to answer. She said a prayer to herself before heading into the house.

Tony and Terry headed to his dad's house hoping to catch the girls before they left. It was only six forty-five. Surely they'd still be there. Tony's mind was racing. He needed to see Serena one last time before she left for Texas. They'd talked about seeing each other again before Labor Day, which was two months away. Neither of them thought they could live without each other that long. Tony smiled at the thought of him and Serena both agreeing two months was too long to be apart. They wanted to see each other once a month until they decided what they were going to do about a wedding date.

When Tara and Serena entered the house, Tonya had her bags packed and by the door. Both the girls laughed when they saw this. "My baby sis says she is ready to roll, huh, Tonya," Tara teased, doubling over in laughter. Serena joined her in laughter. "Tonya said she was ready, and here she is," Tara teased. After the girls finished laughing at Tonya, Tara's expression turned serious. "Hey, Tonya, I didn't see mom's car in the driveway; where are they?" Tara asked.

"Oh, Big Mama's cousin fell and hurt her hip, so she asked Daddy to take her to the hospital to visit her. Mom knew Daddy had been drinking and agreed to drive them. They said to apologize to you and Serena because they figured they wouldn't be back in time to see you off." Serena drifted off and had one thing to be thankful about: she didn't have to worry about trying to hide her feelings from Tara's parents. Laughing at Tonya definitely made Serena feel better. She just wished the last hour and a half had been a nightmare; but as she glanced down at her finger, she knew it was real. Tara had disappeared into the back and came back and yelled, "All clear." Serena knew that meant they'd left nothing behind. Serena laughed a little beginning to feel empty inside again, not knowing where she and Tony stood. There was also something nagging at her, but she couldn't figure out what was eating at her. Serena jumped to her feet. "All right, let's get Ms. Tonya packed up and hit the road," she said with her best attempt at a normal smile. "We're a few minutes ahead of schedule." Serena smiled at Tara when they got in the car, but her mind was elsewhere. Serena was about to pull off when suddenly she figured out what was bugging her. She looked in the rearview mirror and saw Tonya with her earphones on and looked at Tara. "Tara, if your grandmother has been gone since this morning, how did Melissa get into her house?" she asked, almost in shock. Tara stopped digging in her bag and looked at Serena and immediately turned to Tonya. "Tonya." She waved to get her attention. "What time did Mom and Dad leave?" she asked with concern.

"They left right before noon, and they had to drive to Birmingham."

"Oh, okay," Tara said, trying to remain calm and not wanting to alert Tonya. She turned around with a frown on her face and said, "I know that psycho did not break into my grandmother's house. That was her on the phone calling Tony." Tara's mind was racing. She turned to her friend. "Serena, whatever you do, don't give up on Tony yet. I'm beginning to think like him. He's told me on several occasions some of the weird things Melissa's done in the past, and you remember the stunt she pulled with the phone the last time we were here." Serena looked at Tara, beginning to feel hopeful. "Yeah, you're right, but if she's making this up to drive a wedge between me and Tony—" Tara cut her off, "Then she wins. I believe that now more than anything, she's got to be lying, and I'm going to get to the bottom of this." Serena felt like half the load had been lifted as she pulled out onto the highway.

"Tara, I would like to apologize for pulling you away from Terry earlier the way I did," Serena said sincerely. "I wasn't thinking clearly, and I know you didn't get a chance to tell him good-bye."

"No, Serena, you needed me; and he understood. That's what friends are for. It's okay." Serena felt better and let her favorite jazz station do the rest.

Terry was driving over the speed limit when he headed down the stretch to Tara's. "We'll make it just in the nick of time," he said, trying to give hope to his friend who'd slumped down in the seat next to him and covered his face with his hand. Tony tried to put the incident out of his mind because he kept running into roadblocks as he attempted to piece this very complicated puzzle together. He hadn't said a word since they'd been in the car. When they pulled into the driveway and found Serena's car gone, Tony's heart sank. He immediately felt sick. He felt like Serena had left him, and he would never see her again. He finally broke the silence. "They're gone," he said with so much despair. "They're gone; how could they be gone?

How could she leave me? I've got to find her, to see her, to tell her that I love her, and to make sure she still loves me," he said to Terry without looking at him. Without hesitation, Terry turned the car around and headed toward I-20. This time he had his emergency lights on, and Tony sat up on alert and began to search for Serena's black Maxima.

Terry glanced over at his distraught friend. He felt completely helpless as he watched Tony falling apart. He remembered how Tony was there for him when he was going through the recent drama with Tara and Sheila. Tony offered his friendship without hesitation after all these years to support him, and for that he was grateful. He was now back with Tara, and he felt as if he owed Tony. Tony was going through hell, and there wasn't a thing Terry could do about it. He couldn't imagine going through anything so devastating. Terry vowed to help Tony get the much-needed answers, and he knew just where to begin.

The girls had been on I-20 about five minutes when Serena saw a lot of commotion in the rearview mirror. "What the heck . . ." she said, looking up at the traffic behind her, causing Tara to look in her mirror too. Tara noticed Tonya was already asleep. *She must've been up all night anticipating this trip,* she thought as she smiled to herself. Looking at the traffic behind them, Tara said, "It's probably an emergency vehicle."

"Oh, you're probably right," Serena said, going back to her jazz station. When Serena looked up again, she noticed the car getting closer; so she moved to the inside lane to allow it to pass. The car switched lanes as she switched lanes, and this concerned Serena. "Tara, what is up with that car? It's almost like it's following us," she said. When she heard Tara say, "That looks like Terry's car," Serena slowed down and looked again. It was Terry's car; as she realized, her heart was beating so fast. There was a rest area coming up, and Serena pulled off the highway. Tara jumped out of the car to see Terry while Tonya napped in the back. Serena wasn't sure of her next move as she turned the engine off. When she looked up in the rearview mirror again, she was startled to see Tony walking up to her door. She wondered if she felt as bad as he looked. Tony watched her before he made an attempt to open the car door. The door was unlocked. He wanted nothing more than to beg for forgiveness, but he didn't want to scare her off. He reached for her hand, beckoning for her to come out of the car. He'd seen Tonya in the backseat and wanted some privacy. He led her over to the picnic tables in the opposite direction of Tara and Terry. As he escorted Serena to a seat at one of the tables, he contemplated what he could say safely. Once they were seated, Tony stared into Serena's face. "Serena, I don't blame you for being angry with me after everything that's happened. I cannot explain to you why this has happened, but I have a sneaky suspicion that everything is not as it seems. Please know that I've not lied to you. I promised to always tell you the truth whether it's good or bad, and I have kept my promise. I have no reason to lie to you now." Realizing that Serena was listening, he continued, hoping she'd keep an open mind. "When you asked me if Melissa and I were still together, I said no, and that was the truth. In my heart, Melissa and I have been over for quite some time; but the moment I met you, I knew I couldn't ever love her because I had fallen in love with you. So we drifted apart after your visit and eventually broke it off. Melissa was pissed about her not being able to come to Atlanta with me, and I think that was the beginning of my trouble. I should have broken it off with her a long time ago, but I guess I was keeping her around for convenience. There is no way I could have gotten her pregnant," Tony said, trying to spare her the intimate details. For the first time, he'd said something that Serena had reacted to. He no longer felt he was talking in vain. Serena wasn't sure whether it was something Tony said or the way he said it, but she was beginning to believe him.

Terry and Tara cuddled as they were happy to see each other again to say good-bye the right way. They watched Tony and Serena and hoped they could work things out. "What do you think about all this?" Tara asked.

"I don't know Melissa at all, but it seems like she is putting on this whole show to get Tony's attention."

Tara interrupted, "Do you know that was Melissa calling from Big Mama's house earlier on Tony's cell?"

"What?" Terry said, surprised. "I think Tony figured out how she got into the house, but he's not mentioned the phone call. He's been pretty preoccupied."

"We should have her arrested," Tara said. "She entered that house well aware that she was not invited, and no one was home. That can't be legal." Tara continued.

"No, I wouldn't think so, but she had prior knowledge of where the key was hidden. I don't think that would carry much weight if you're looking to press charges. We need to come up with a way to help Tony figure this whole thing out, and I know just what to do."

Serena was still quiet as Tony continued talking. "When I discovered your car missing, I panicked and felt like I'd lost you forever. I just needed to see you again. I needed to know that you still loved me and that you were on my side. I promise you I will get to the bottom of this, but I need to know you're with me." He looked at Serena with a serious look on his face. Serena wasn't sure how to respond, but she knew without a doubt that she still loved Tony and hoped he could find out what was really behind Melissa's story. "Serena, please say something, anything. Do you still love me?" he asked, coming even with her face as he held his breath and waited for her to answer. After a brief pause, "Yes, I still love you," Serena said almost in a whisper. Tony could see the pain in her eyes as she answered him, and he reached out to embrace her. This time she embraced him too. That was all he needed to further ignite his fire to figure this whole mess out. As long as he knew the woman he loved and wanted to spend the rest of his life with was on his side, he could do anything.

This time when they separated, Serena searched her CD changer for her favorite song by Najee. Listening to Najee brought a smile to her face and Serena could breathe a little easier as she and Tony went their separate ways. Serena and Tara waved good-bye to the guys as they got back on the interstate. Tony was glad he'd had another chance to see Serena. They didn't talk about the next time they'd see each other because neither of them were sure how this was going to turn out, but at least now there was hope.

PREOCCUPIED

As Tony and Terry headed back toward Atlanta, Tony's heart was light; and he was now more determined to get some answers so that he and Serena could possibly put their lives back on track. Terry pulled into the Danstons' driveway and saw Big Mama getting out of the car with the Danstons. Tony looked confused and began to wonder how long Big Mama had been with his dad but said nothing. Terry, reading his expression, said, "Tonya said her parents took Big Mama to the hospital to visit her cousin earlier today, as in before we left Savannah." Tony now knew that his grandmother never called him on his cell phone. It had been Melissa calling from her house. He grew furious at her deceit and wondered where it would end. "Tony, I know you probably have everything all planned out, but let me help you figure this one out." Tony looked up as his frown disappeared, and he began to process what his friend was offering. "I owe you one, but more importantly you and Serena belong together. I don't know Melissa from Jane, but her whole story seems weak, and I just want you to know that I'm here for you." Tony was speechless as he felt somewhat energized now hearing someone else voice their doubt about Melissa's story. Tony said nothing. "I will be back for Labor Day, but I can come sooner if you need me to." Tony finally spoke after taking everything in. "Man, I appreciate your wanting to help, but I don't know how much you can do. I pray that this whole mess is a scheme created by Melissa to keep Serena and me apart. If she really is pregnant by me, I can kiss my future with Serena good-bye," Tony said as the reality of what he'd just said hit him like a boulder. What if Melissa was carrying his child? What would become of the relationship he'd started with Serena? He couldn't bear the thought of losing her. Was Melissa expecting him to marry her? Tony's heart sank as he imagined the worst. Terry saw the sour expression on Tony's face. "We'll figure it out. Give me a call tomorrow evening, and we'll come up with a course of action." Tony snapped out of his thoughts and gave Terry the brotherly handshake and hug.

They headed for the house as Terry said his good-byes to the family while Tony headed inside at the request of his father. Mr. Danston said good-bye to Terry and followed his son inside. His father instantly knew something was troubling his son watching the drastic change in his demeanor. He poured two cups of coffee. "Do you want to tell me about it?" he asked, full of concern. Tony sipped his coffee and said nothing. Mr. Danston knew his son was as stubborn and proud as he was when he was his age, so he gave him some time. "So when's the big day?" he continued. Tony almost choked on his coffee wondering if they were thinking of the same "big day." Tony didn't have the heart to make the announcement to his family about the engagement. Although he'd shared the news with his mother, he was unsure of his future with Serena. He was so embarrassed and hurt that he decided to wait until things were sorted out before he announced anything. This broke the silence as Tony said, "Dad, what are you talking about?" He looked at his son and laughed. "Boy, I knew you'd fallen in love with Serena long before you'd figured it out." After observing them from the window that morning, Mr. Danston knew there was something special happening between Tony and Serena. A later conversation with Tony confirmed he had feelings for her. "I'm assuming you've broken things off with Melissa since you and Serena went away for the weekend. What could possibly be wrong?" he asked again. Tony took a deep breath and let out a long sigh. "Nothing," he said in a frustrated voice, "everything is falling apart, and I can't fix it." Mr. Danston sat staring in disbelief, wondering what could have gone wrong since yesterday but didn't want to pry. He knew Tony had a habit of keeping things bottled up inside until he could sort things out himself. Realizing Tony wasn't ready to talk, Mr. Danston said, "Well, son, let me know if there's anything I can do to help you." He stood up and patted his son on the shoulder.

Tony told everyone good-bye and decided he needed to get on the road. Sitting in Atlanta sulking wasn't getting him any closer to a solution or Columbus. He could think better when he was alone on the road. After all, he could do a whole lot of thinking in two hours as his thoughts led him to the interstate.

As Melissa raced down the highway, she was trying to figure out a way to get the letter back from Tony. Melissa pulled into the driveway and gathered herself as she walked up to Kayla's door. She knew Kayla would be furious, but she was panicking and needed her help. After knocking several times, she looked at her watch realizing it was after ten o'clock. *What could I have been thinking?* she thought as she remembered Kayla and her daughter were probably asleep. She knew Kayla had to work tomorrow, and the day care center opened at five thirty. Melissa kicked herself as she turned and headed back to her car. *I'll call her tomorrow at work and fix this before it becomes a problem.* She had promised not to show anyone the letter from the clinic. She knew Tony would take her word for it since she had a medical background. She began to replay the confrontation over in her head as she tried to determine when her plan fell apart and what possessed her to present the letter to the entire audience. Not only had she shown the letter to Tony but she'd let Tara take it away from her, and now Tony had it. It was only supposed to be used as a last resort. Melissa had everything planned except for the scene where she had to enter Tony's grandmother's house with the spare key when she wasn't home. After she told Tony she was pregnant with his child, he was supposed to come to her and tell her how happy and proud she'd made him, and he'd forget about pursuing Serena. What man wouldn't want a son? They had been together for over a year, and he knew she came from a good family and wealthy background. Why wouldn't he want a future with her and their child? Melissa had to snap out of her fantasy as she remembered she wasn't pregnant, nor did she have the proof of her pregnancy. Kayla would be livid. She had to find a way to get the letter back from Tony and fast. He hadn't made it home yet, and he'd banned her from coming to his house since the last incident. Melissa tossed and turned all night wondering what story she could tell Tony to get her hands on that letter again.

Tony woke up at five thirty after only five hours of sleep and immediately wondered how far the girls had made it. He wanted to call but knew Serena needed some time away from him. He'd picked up the phone to call several times last night while driving home but decided against it. He knew Tara would call him as soon as they made it to San Antonio. As Tony pulled into the parking lot at work, he got out of his truck hoping for an uneventful day. It was Monday morning after the Fourth of July; he was sure things had calmed down since the weekend's activities. He knew from years of experience as a fireman there were hundreds of accidental fires during the Fourth of July weekend. Most of them would start with someone not knowing how to operate their new grill or from someone claiming to have stepped away from the grill for just a minute or long enough for things to get out of hand. He closed his eyes and said a prayer before he walked into the station. It was six twenty, and formation was at six thirty. As he stood in front of his locker putting his bag away, he noticed the letter from the clinic sticking out of the bag's side pocket. He remembered putting it there last night when he made it home. He didn't bother to look at it but folded it and placed it in his shirt pocket.

The girls arrived in San Antonio at eleven o'clock and decided to order pizza and wings for lunch. Tara placed their bags in her car as it sat in Serena's garage. Serena took her bags inside as Tara and Tonya followed her onto the deck. She grabbed the cordless phone to check her voice mails. There was only one message, and that was from her mom wondering why she hadn't called. Serena knew that was a conversation she wasn't prepared to have—not for a while anyway. Serena would call her after she knew she'd left for work. Serena knew her dad went into the office every morning at seven o'clock so she wouldn't have to worry about him picking up the phone when she called to leave a message. The girls enjoyed each other's company so much so they steered away from the subject of Tony and Melissa most of the way home. Chatting with Tonya kept them preoccupied. What Tara had ascertained from their brief conversation about Tony was that Serena's feelings for him had not changed. She did not want to ruin his chance of starting a family and raising his son or daughter. Her grandmother had told her long ago that if you really love someone, love him enough to let him go; and if he comes back to you, then you'll know it was really love. Serena applied the old adage to her current situation. She was also a firm believer that everything happened for a reason.

After saying good-bye to Tara and Tonya, she pulled her hooptie into the garage and checked her mailbox. She decided it was time to call her mom to let her know she was okay. She hung up after leaving a message, relieved that no one picked up. She would be in a relaxed mode for the rest of the day and Monday, prepping for work on Tuesday. She unpacked her bags and ran a hot bubble bath in her garden tub. Her heart still ached for Tony as she tuned in to the jazz station. After deciding she was in for the day, she headed for the kitchen for a glass of wine, which she took into the bathroom with her. She lit her scented candles as she slipped into the hot sea of bubbles and longed for Tony. Just as she began to relax, the phone rang. Serena scolded herself for not remembering to bring the phone into the bathroom with her. Whoever it was would have to wait. She was long overdue for this pampering session and didn't want to ruin it, so she let the phone ring.

Tara had just pulled out of Serena's driveway when she reached for her cell phone to call Tony. He answered on the first ring. "I was just about to call you. Did you make it back okay?" he asked, concerned. "Yeah, we've been back for a while. We decided to have lunch at Serena's. I'm just leaving her house now. How are you doing?" Tara asked her brother, not sure what the answer would be.

"I'm doing okay right now, but I'm not sure how long that's going to last."

"Why, did you find something out?" she asked anxiously.

"No, not yet, but Melissa's on her way over here to get that letter she had yesterday. She said she would need it when she went in for her checkup tomorrow." Tara was quiet as the wheels began to turn. *Now why would Melissa need the letter for an appointment,* she thought to herself. Tara and Serena were both in the medical field, so this sent up a red flag. "So what are you going to do?"

"What, about the baby?" Tony asked, shocked.

"No, about giving her the letter."

"Well, I'm going to give it to her. She's on her way over as we speak."

"What? She's coming to your house?" Tara asked, alarmed.

"No, I'm at work. I don't want her back at my house."

"Okay, do you have a copier there?"

"Yeah, we have a copier."

"What about a fax machine?"

"Yes, Tara, what's up?" Tony asked impatiently.

"Two things bro: I want you to make a copy of that letter and please don't do anything to cause Melissa to be suspicious. Just give her the original back and don't let on that you've made a copy. Second, I want you to fax a copy to me at work. Do you have time to do that before she shows up?"

"Yeah, I'm in the back office. She's going to meet me out front in five minutes."

"Okay. Well, go and do what you have to and call me back once she leaves." Tony pulled the letter from his shirt pocket and did as Tara had asked. He wasn't sure what she had in mind, but she was on the case.

When Tony walked outside the fire station, he saw that Melissa was waiting outside her car. Seeing her again angered him immediately. He was glad they were meeting in a neutral zone. As he walked toward the car, he noticed she was on her cell phone. *This should be an easy transaction,* he thought as he approached her. He reached in his pocket and handed her the letter. She took the phone away from her ear long enough to say thank you. She opened the letter and smiled as she tossed it into the car as Tony turned on his heels without saying a word. He was thankful for the calm exchange. By the time he'd entered the building, Melissa had driven off. After he finished talking to Tara, he decided to try Serena. He knew she needed some time, but he hoped she'd be ready to talk. It was almost two o'clock when he decided to call her. The phone rang four times before the answering machine picked up. He left her a message and hoped she'd call back.

Melissa let the top down on her car and let the wind take her away. She was so relieved that she'd gotten the letter back from Tony. Now she just hoped Kayla didn't find out she'd dropped by last night. She smiled to herself realizing everything was back on track. She figured Tony wouldn't ask about her appointment. It was not like he was going to accompany her.

When Terry called Tony, they three-wayed Tara in on their conversation. Tara agreed to take the lead and make a few phone calls to see if she could get any information on Melissa's pregnancy. Terry offered to help in any way, and Tony was going to do some snooping of his own.

When Serena climbed out of the tub, she grabbed the phone on her way to the kitchen. She had a new message, and she hoped it wasn't her mother. She was almost afraid to listen to the voice on the other end but was completely overjoyed and relieved to hear the voice belonged to Tony. She was so happy that he'd made contact she almost cried. He wanted her to know that he was thinking about her and that he loved her. She called back but got his voice mail and decided not to leave a message.

ON A MISSION

Three weeks had passed, and Tony was growing more impatient. He wasn't sure what was going on with Serena. They had been playing phone tag for weeks, and he was beginning to think she was avoiding him. Tony had decided to show up for Melissa's doctor's appointment at the clinic. She had been calling every three or four days with updates. Tony was beginning to lose hope of this being a hoax. *Who could think of such an elaborate scheme?* he thought as he shook his head in disgust. He didn't have the heart to tell Serena, and maybe in a way he was avoiding her too. Melissa said her next appointment was on Thursday at ten o'clock. Tony was getting off at nine o'clock and decided to drive by the clinic. He parked and waited for her to show up. There were several people entering the clinic, and Tony thought he recognized one of the ladies in scrubs but was too far away to know for sure. He hadn't seen Melissa since that day at the station and wasn't sure if she'd be showing by now or not. It was ten o'clock and no sign of Melissa. Tony drove off and headed for home.

Tara had run into dead ends as she tried to dig up information on Melissa. The people on the other end of the phone kept saying they couldn't release any information without the mother's consent. Tara didn't feel the questions she was asking were violating the Privacy Act, but she kept calling hoping to get a different person each time. After three weeks of obstacles, Tara remembered Terry's cousin, Karen, who worked for Quest. Quest performed lab tests, and it was the biggest laboratory in Georgia. Maybe she could have Terry contact Karen to see if she could give them more information than they had, which was very little after three weeks of digging. Terry was traveling with the basketball team, but she was able to leave a message. It took him a few days to respond; but when he did, he mentioned that Karen was out of the country on business but would be back next Thursday. Tara was disappointed but felt hopeful that Karen could get answers she could not. She talked to Tony every week, but she didn't tell him about the progress she was making. She didn't want him to get his hopes up for nothing. He'd mentioned that he'd not spoken to Serena in a while, but Tara assured him that she was fine.

When Melissa called Tony again, he asked how her appointment went on Thursday. "Oh, everything was normal," she answered hesitantly. She wondered why Tony was concerned with her appointment all of a sudden. "The doctor said I was progressing normally to be eight weeks pregnant." Tony got quiet as he processed what Melissa had just said. He was not ready to hear that admission. He began to feel trapped, so he soon hung up. He needed to know who her doctor was and when her next appointment was. He would have to save that for the next conversation. He decided to go for a swim as he sat out on the deck. He remembered Serena's visit to Columbus, and he longed to hear her voice and her laughter. He wondered if she was still wearing the ring. Tony made a few laps in the pool and scrambled out of the water when he heard the phone ringing. It was Tara, sounding overly excited on the other end. "Tony, are you busy?" she asked anxiously.

"No, I'm just sitting outside on the deck; what's up? Is something wrong with Serena?" he asked as he held his breath, not sure of what to expect.

"No silly, Serena is fine. Do you know the name of the doctor Melissa is seeing?"

"No, I've not gotten that far yet; why, what's going on?"

"Well, you remember Terry's cousin, Karen. You know she works at Quest."

"Yeah, go on."

"Well, her lab does all the blood work for city of Columbus."

"Go on," Tony said as he was beginning to get excited too.

"Well, she called me today and told me that she didn't have any record of Melissa getting a pregnancy test within the last ninety days."

"What, Tara, what are you saying?"

"I'm saying there's no record of the Columbus OB Clinic submitting blood work for a Melissa Stanley." Tony felt dizzy as he stood on his deck and decided to take a seat. Tony was speechless. *Could this mean that this whole thing was a hoax?* he thought to himself. "So if you can get the name of her doctor, we can check all the blood work he or she has submitted in the last ninety days and go from there." Tony wanted to call Melissa right away, but he knew he had to play it cool and wait for her to call him, or she would become suspicious.

When Tony got off work on Monday, he drove by the clinic again. This time he went inside the clinic to take a look around. He had just taken a seat in the waiting room when Melissa called him on his cell phone. He was cordial to her, remembering he needed information from her. She offered him the information on her next appointment. It was scheduled for August 30. "What doctor are you seeing?" he asked her. Melissa hesitated longer than she should have but blurted out, "The appointment's with Dr. Spencer." She had heard Kayla talk about Dr. Spencer several times before and knew it would be okay to use his name since Kayla worked for him. "Okay, well I'm in the middle of something. Did you need anything?"

"No, I was just calling to let you know that we're doing fine." Tony quickly got off the phone and walked up to the receptionist. "Yes, I need to confirm an appointment for the thirtieth," he said.

"Okay, sir, is this appointment for you or your spouse?" Tony quickly corrected her, reluctantly, "It's for my friend." The receptionist looked confused. "My, uh, girlfriend," Tony offered, not wanting to give Melissa that title again. "What doctor is she assigned to?" the receptionist asked while she logged on to the computer. "She's a patient of Dr. Spencer's." Her reaction or her lack of surprise let Tony know that there indeed was a Dr. Spencer working at that clinic, and he felt his heart sink. He hoped Melissa was making this story up. After pulling up Dr. Spencer's calendar and looking at August 30, she didn't have a record of Melissa Stanley having an appointment. Just then the girl Tony had seen the other day walking toward the clinic in scrubs walked in. The receptionist turned to her and said, "Kayla, this gentleman is here to confirm an appointment with Dr. Spencer for the thirtieth." Not looking in his direction, she said, "Okay, I'll be right there." As she said it, Tony realized this was someone he'd seen with Melissa last year when they first started dating. It was Kayla Turner, and she and Melissa had gone to medical school together. When she approached the receptionist, she looked up at Tony for the first time and showed a hint of recognition. He was shocked to see the receptionist speaking to Kayla and nodding in his direction. "Sir, who is the appointment for?" she asked as she logged on to the computer without looking at him. "It's for Melissa Stanley," Tony said, paying close attention to her fingers on the keyboard. As soon as she'd heard Melissa's name, she stopped typing and seemed uncomfortable. "And you are?" she said to Tony. "I'm her, uh, boyfriend, and I wanted to accompany her on her next visit," he said convincingly. Realizing she wanted more, he told her he was Antonio Walker.

"Oh, hi, Tony, how are you? It's been a while."

"Yeah, I guess so" was all Tony could muster up. The receptionist looked on; and from her expression, she thought Kayla was acting weird. The phone rang, and the receptionist excused herself to answer it. "Oh," Kayla said, "that's right, Melissa just scheduled this on Friday, and I forgot to put it in the system." She reached in her scrub pocket and said, "Here it is right here. I cannot believe I forgot to put it on his schedule; Friday was a hectic day for me," she tried to sound convincing. After Tony left, Kayla remembered when Melissa introduced her to Tony when they first started dating. He seemed like the perfect gentleman. She always liked Tony and envied the way he treated Melissa. Now she wondered if she ever deserved him.

As soon as Tony left the clinic, Kayla picked up the phone to call Melissa. "Melissa, what is going on? Why is your man here checking up on your appointment?" she said, sounding irritated. Melissa was at work but soon made her way outside to talk in private. "What do you mean he was there?"

"I mean he just left the clinic trying to confirm your appointment with Dr. Spencer on the thirtieth."

"What? You've got to be joking. He could care less about going to an appointment with me." Suddenly, she thought maybe he's changed his mind about becoming a father as she smiled to herself. "Melissa, Melissa," she could hear Kayla's frightened voice coming through on the receiver, "how does he know what clinic you're being seen at?" Melissa thought long and hard about her question and began to wonder the same thing. She'd never told Tony when suddenly she remembered the letter he'd gotten from her. She knew he must've read the letterhead, but she couldn't tell Kayla that. "Never mind that," Kayla snapped.

"How did he know to ask for Dr. Spencer, Melissa?" Kayla was furious that she'd gotten dragged into this mess further than she would have liked.

"He asked me, so I had to tell him."

"Okay fine, but why didn't you tell me?" she said through clenched teeth.

"I just told him this morning," Melissa said. "I was making my rounds and was going to call you on my break." Not having paid attention to the initial part of Kayla's conversation, Melissa asked, "Who did he ask for when he called?"

"What do you mean called, he was here in person." Now Kayla was almost screaming because she had to repeat the events leading up to his visit. Melissa almost dropped her phone. "Tony was there in the clinic?"

"Yeah, that's what I'm trying to tell you. Look, I don't know what's going on, but you'd better put him in check because I'm not losing my job over this." And she hung up the phone. Melissa felt sick. What could Tony possibly be up to?

Tony called Tara as soon as he got in the car and three-wayed Terry too, hoping he had made it back to Miami. When he answered, it was obvious he was at practice, so Tara got right to the point. "Terry, Melissa's doctor's name is Spencer. Please call Karen right away and have her run his name."

"Okay." Terry said his good-byes to both and went back to practice. Tara had promised Tony she wouldn't mention any of this to Serena until they knew for sure what they were dealing with.

It was Wednesday before they heard anything from Terry. "Well, guys, looks like your suspicions were right all along. There is no record of Melissa having any tests done or ordered by Dr. Spencer. Karen even went a step further to make sure no doctors from the clinic ordered a pregnancy test for Melissa, and she came up with nothing." Tony screamed, "I knew it! I knew it! She's been lying all along. How is that possible when she had the letter from the clinic?"

"She couldn't have made that up," Tara said.

"Well, I didn't tell you this before, but I ran into an acquaintance at the clinic when I went there the other morning. She may be able to help me, and guess who she works for?"

"Dr. Spencer," Tara and Terry said in unison.

"Thank you two so much; now I just need to go by the clinic one more time and find out how this letter came into existence." He was getting stronger because he'd caught Melissa in a lie, and he wasn't going to make things easy for her after all the hell she'd put him and Serena through.

He picked up the phone to call Serena. He wanted to hear her voice, and he hoped this time she would pick up. She picked up on the second ring. "Hey, baby," she said, answering the phone. He was surprised to hear her voice and even more surprised by her welcomed greeting. "Hey, lady, how are you?"

"I'm good." After talking for a few minutes, Tony told Serena that he missed her and hoped she still wanted to be with him. He couldn't bring himself to ask her if she was still wearing the ring. He had an incoming call. The name on the caller ID showed the call was coming from Quest Laboratory. He was shocked to see this and ended his conversation with Serena, promising to call again soon. When he clicked over, he heard Karen's voice on the other end of the phone. "Tony?" she asked. "Yes, this is Tony." He waited for her to introduce herself; and when she did, he knew it had to be important for her to be calling him at home. She got right down to business. "Do you still have the letter that your former girlfriend showed you that stated she was pregnant?"

"Yeah, I have a copy of it."

"I need you to bring it down to my building. I'll meet you outside. How soon can you be here?" Tony wondered what was going on; but whatever it was, he was grateful for her help. He closed his eyes and thanked Tara for advising him to make a copy before turning it back over to Melissa. "I'll be there in thirty minutes," he said, jumping in the shower. He had been out in the yard and couldn't possibly go anywhere looking or smelling the way he did.

Melissa was beginning to get anxious about the whole story. Kayla was already upset with her for letting Tony see the letter and telling her that Dr. Spencer was her doctor. Kayla found herself in over her head. All she'd agreed to do in the beginning was produce the letter for Melissa because she wanted to get back at her ex-boyfriend. Kayla was a single parent who couldn't afford to lose her job. She knew they were running out of time.

Tony pulled into the parking lot and walked toward the picnic area where Karen told him she'd meet him. He wouldn't have felt comfortable going inside and was glad they were meeting outside. As soon as he took a seat, he saw Karen approaching with a white lab coat on. Tara was right, she hadn't changed a bit. They shook hands when she finally reached him. Tony produced the letter, and Karen jotted down the patient ID number and scanned over the content. It was a letter she'd seen before from the clinic, but she was beginning to have a bad feeling about this. She promised Tony she'd call once she got any news. He thanked her and headed for his truck. As he drove off, he saw Karen wave before she entered the building.

Tony had always wanted a child since he could remember. He knew he would make a great father, but he wasn't ready to have a child with Melissa. Not that she wouldn't make a good mother, but because he didn't love her. He loved Serena and wanted to marry her.

As Tony pulled away from Quest, he was on cloud nine. No one had been able to prove Melissa even had a blood test done. It was beginning to sound more and more like some elaborate plan created by Melissa. He three-wayed Tara and Terry and gave them the news. Tara was so happy to hear the news. "So what does this mean?" she screamed into the phone. "Well," Tony said calmly, not wanting to get too excited, "it's looking like Melissa made this whole thing up, but we have one more thing to check, and that's the authenticity of that letter." Tara knew immediately when Tony told her Melissa's reason for wanting the letter back from him that there was something fishy going on. It sent up a red flag when Tara mentioned it to Serena too. "Well," he continued, "Karen's tracking that down, and I think I'm going to pay Kayla a visit."

"Who is Kayla?" Terry asked. Tony completely forgot to tell them about Kayla. "She's the acquaintance I mentioned before. Kayla's Melissa's friend and she works at the clinic." Tara was now yelling into the phone, not believing her ears. "What are you saying? Melissa and this Kayla girl are friends?"

"Yeah, they've been friends for a while and were friends when I met her." Before Tony could finish, Tara blurted out, "Oh, so now Melissa's got her friend involved in this mess too?" Tony was stunned at Tara's summary. He was beginning to put the pieces together, but maybe Tara and her infinite female wisdom had just completed the puzzle for him. "Bro, it looks like this nightmare is about to come to an end for you and Serena," she continued. Just the sound of that was like music to his ears. "I sure hope so; although the bond we have is remarkable, I could never put her through anything remotely close to this again. I wouldn't put myself in that position." Before the three of them ended the conversation, Tony said, "Tara, can you find out if Serena's got any major plans next Saturday? I have four days off and thought about surprising her."

"What do you mean, you're coming to Texas?" Tara asked, bursting with joy.

"Well, yeah, if this saga ends before then, and I'm hoping it will, I would like to tell Serena in person."

"Consider it done. I'll tell you as soon as I find out."

Tony was beginning to feel like himself again, like there was no black cloud hanging over his head. *What if this was a hoax? That says a lot about Melissa. She must really hate me and what Serena and I share to put us through this.*

Melissa decided to check in with Kayla to make sure things were going as planned. Kayla was so upset with Melissa because now she was receiving phone calls about Melissa's pregnancy test. She'd just gotten in from lunch and had a message from Karen. She knew Melissa was keeping something from her. The message even referenced the letter that Kayla had created for Melissa. She was fuming when she found out that not only had Melissa produced the letter to someone other than Tony, but now the lab was calling with questions about its validity. She knew that's what it was; and to make things worse, her friend, Karen, was the person leaving the message. Kayla never planned for Melissa to take this story as far as she did. She had hoped she'd tell Tony the truth by now. After all, they'd broken up and weren't on good terms. If she thought Tony disliked her before, it would really be easy for him to hate her after this. Kayla knew she would be relieved once Dr. Spencer found out what she'd done, and Melissa would go unpunished while Kayla would have to find employment quickly because she had bills to pay, not to mention care for her three-year-old. She was beginning to feel sick with worry. Now, as if things couldn't get any worse, the lab was calling about Melissa's case. She knew it was Karen's voice on the voice mail. Not only would she lose her job, but she'd lose her friendship with Karen as well. They had been friends for six years, and she'd even asked Kayla and her daughter to be in her wedding in September. What would she think of her now? She heard Melissa pleading on the other end of the phone to keep their secret. Melissa knew Tony would definitely hate her if he ever found out. As long as Kayla kept her end of the bargain, they would be okay. Melissa knew she had to buy some time. She had to find a way to get in good graces with Tony to see if she could get pregnant with his child. She would simply tell him she was late and that she probably got her dates mixed up once she delivered the baby later than May. She got off the phone with Kayla after convincing her that nothing would go wrong as long as they stuck to their stories. Melissa was working on a foolproof plan that would keep them both out of trouble.

Tony tried reaching Serena but only got her voice mail. So he left a message, which was how they'd been communicating lately. He knew Serena was busy and sometimes would return his call the next day, but that was okay with him. When she left messages for him, he'd always call her as soon as he got them. He knew she was scared of the outcome, and so was he, but he was still hopeful of a happy ending. It had been a month since he'd seen her, and he longed for her. He hadn't heard from Karen again and figured it would take some time to dig up the information. As soon as he hung up, Melissa called. "Tony, I need some help moving my bedroom furniture around, and my mom and dad are out of town. Do you think you can come over to help?" Tony almost asked her why she needed help, but he figured she'd say because of the baby she was not allowed to move heavy objects. He didn't say anything at first, but after thinking about it, this might work in his favor, so he agreed.

Melissa was excited because Tony had agreed to come over. It had been two months since she'd been alone with him. She had been shopping for baby furniture and decided if nothing else convinced Tony that she was expecting, this would. She then hoped he would stop nosing around. She'd assembled the furniture for the baby with ease. She couldn't very well ask for help from her family since they knew nothing of her pregnancy to begin with. She'd also stopped by the library and checked out some parenting books and placed them around the house. She'd gone as far as purchasing a small tummy pad, which most women used as protective wear. Melissa decided to use it to add a little bulge to her midsection. She had everything in place as she eagerly anticipated Tony's arrival. She decided to take a quick shower and slip on something provocative. When she answered the door, Tony looked as handsome as ever. He had a fresh haircut, and she detected a faint hint of his cologne. Once he stepped inside, Melissa offered him something to drink. He refused and asked her what she needed help with. She led him into the bedroom and headed for the bassinet. Tony was shocked to see all the baby furniture Melissa had set up in her room. He was speechless as he took it all in. Melissa stood by the bassinet and asked Tony to move it into the sitting room. As he watched her lift her arm pointing in the direction of the sitting room, he realized she was showing. Her face looked the same, but her stomach was noticeably larger. He snapped out of the shock of seeing her with all the baby furniture and realized he was staring. He lifted the bassinet and placed it on the Sesame Street rug she'd placed in the middle of the floor. He then moved the dresser and changing table into their positions. He even put together a Sesame Street Mobile over the bassinet. The last thing to move was the rocking chair Melissa had purchased for herself. Tony was working so diligently to set up the baby's room he didn't bother to check his cell phone when it rang. He'd taken it off when he began lifting the furniture. He didn't know how late it was when he discovered he suddenly felt hungry. He looked at his watch realizing it was after nine o'clock. He'd been at Melissa's for three hours. There were still a few things left to do before the room was complete. Melissa said she'd get her mom to hang the drapes and put up the wallpaper border when she returned from her trip. She made Tony pizza and hot wings knowing he wouldn't refuse it. When she walked out of the kitchen, she opened a beer for him without asking and placed it beside his food. He sat in front of the television and enjoyed the meal. Once he'd eaten, he felt energized enough to hang the drapes and put up the border without Melissa having to ask. By the time Tony finished decorating, he had drank four beers and knew he'd had one too many. Melissa knew Tony wasn't a big drinker, but she also knew Corona was his favorite beer. She stopped at the ABC Store after talking to Kayla and got him a six-pack. She wore a black lace chemise that flattered her shape. Melissa knew Tony would not be able to resist looking at her breasts while they moved around the house together. As Tony felt the beer take control of him, he flopped on the couch and leaned back into the soft plush pillows. He knew he was high and would not be able to drive home for a few hours. Melissa took the remote and turned on the CD player. She'd been listening to Jagged Edge and thought how appropriate the music was as she turned the lights down low. She rested on the seat next to Tony hoping he'd take the bait. She eased over closer to him and began to rub his chest. Tony was dozing off when he realized Melissa was coming on to him. He grabbed her hand and removed it. He told her he wasn't ready to go back down memory lane with her. She was obviously upset but still determined. She leaned over and kissed Tony's soft lips. He didn't open his eyes; but he told Melissa, "No, that's not why I'm here. I'm here for the baby." Tony didn't realize what he'd said as he dozed off, but Melissa heard and knew her scheme was working.

Tony drifted off to sleep and thought of his last night with Serena as he did every night. He could almost feel her. It seemed so real as he reached out to touch her soft, supple skin lying on top of him. Tony knew he wasn't at home, but he had to clear his head and remember exactly where he was. As he caressed her, he looked around the pitch-black room and realized his pants were down and he was aroused. His pants were around his knees, and she was planting kisses on his thighs and working her way up. He looked around the room again trying to clear his head. He knew he was in a familiar place when suddenly he remembered where he was. He was at Melissa's, and she was kissing him uncontrollably as he tensed up, trying to get a handle on his emotions. Tony hadn't been with anyone since Serena over a month ago and never had the urge to until now. He tried to sit up; but Melissa was even more determined when she felt Tony resist. She knew he was turned on by his response as she worked harder. She needed to be with him one more time. Tony still found Melissa attractive, but this was the last thing he wanted. Melissa sat on top of him trying to gain total control of the situation. Tony knew what Melissa was trying to do, and he was turned on enough to give her what she wanted. He was trying to stand again when he began to remember all the drama and mess she'd started. This time when he went to stand, he was able to get his feet on the floor. Melissa held on to Tony as she curled her legs around him and held on to his neck. To her surprise, Tony reached around his neck and pried her arms from around him. Melissa reluctantly stood in front of Tony, knowing he wasn't going to give in. He put some distance between the two of them as he pulled his pants up and reached for his cell phone and keys and told Melissa he had to go. As he was walking toward the door, he turned to Melissa, realizing his timing was perfect. "Melissa, I don't know what's going to happen between us, but I do plan to be there for our child. I will take you to your next appointment. It's time I start acting like a dad," he said as he walked out her front door.

Serena wondered why Tony hadn't called back. She had begun to worry and thought maybe he'd gotten called in to work. She'd left a message hours ago but felt like Tony needed her, so she reached for the phone to call him again at ten thirty.

Tony walked into his house at eleven fifteen and longed for Serena. He went to the bathroom and took a cold shower when he remembered his phone rang earlier while he was at Melissa's. He wrapped himself in a towel and rested on the bed to check his voice mail. It was Serena. He smiled as his heart skipped a beat. It was eight o'clock when she called, and he felt bad for not checking his cell to see who was calling. It was eleven thirty now, and he was embarrassed about what just took place at Melissa's. He knew it was too late to call Serena back, so he lay in bed and turned on the television. He felt like he was finally getting somewhere with his investigation. He'd done what he'd gone to Melissa's to do. He wanted her to know that he would be there at Dr. Spencer's office with her for her next appointment. It was too dark to see the reaction he was looking for, but her stillness and silence gave him satisfaction. When the commercial went off, *The Five Heartbeats* came on. Tony immediately started laughing as he remembered the last time he'd tried to watch this movie he was with Serena. He decided to call her anyway even if it meant leaving another message because he wanted to hear her voice. He dialed her number and heard her sweet, sultry voice say, "Hey, baby." He sat up, surprised she picked up on the first ring as if she were waiting for him to call. He was even more surprised to hear the greeting. He missed her terribly and was hoping she missed him as much. "Hey, lady, what are you doing up answering the phone this late?" he said jokingly.

"I actually had the phone in my hand to call you back," Serena laughed.

"Sorry, I didn't call you sooner; how have you been?"

"I'm okay, I just find myself missing you and thinking about us more and more each day I'm away from you. I miss you, and I can't wait until this storm blows over."

"I know what you mean. I think we're finally making some progress, and I'm hopeful this will be all over soon, and we'll get the answers we've been looking for. I miss you, Serena, more than you know. I think about you every night before I close my eyes. It's so good to hear your voice."

"Yours too," Serena said, smiling into the phone as if Tony could see her. They talked for an hour, which was the most they'd talked since she left Atlanta, and for this he was thankful.

Melissa was still embarrassed about last night. She hadn't been with Tony in two months and longed to be intimate with him again. She was being selfish, and she knew it. She had accomplished her mission of the evening, which was to convince Tony of her pregnancy so he would stop snooping. Anything else would have been extra. She wanted it all, but for now she was content.

Tara and Serena had lunch together the next day. Serena had been busying herself with different projects away from the house to keep her sanity. She was a patient person, but this situation was getting the best of her. Talking to Tony last night had given her hope again. When she'd finished talking to Tony, she got on her knees, as she did every night, and prayed to God for peace, strength, and guidance. Tara was getting a refill on her soda when she returned to find Serena with a somber expression. "Hey, penny for your thoughts," Tara said as the girls joined together in laughter. Tara knew exactly what Serena had been thinking about and wished she could update her friend, but she didn't want to give her false hope. She kept quiet as they talked about the upcoming weekend. "Hey, I forgot to tell you the Miami Heat are playing the Spurs Saturday night. Do you want to go?" Tara asked excitedly. Serena was dying to see Terry play, and this would be the perfect outing for her. "Are you serious? That would be awesome," she shrieked as they gave each other high fives. "Okay, consider it done. We have a date next Saturday night. I'll talk to Terry tonight to see if he's still good for the tickets." Serena and Tara laughed. She knew her friend better than that. Tara probably already had the tickets at home and had a big to-do planned for that evening. That was just her style. Tara enjoyed making her friend laugh again. She'd already made arrangements for the three of them to attend the game next weekend. They would meet Terry after the game to celebrate. *Tony couldn't have chosen a better weekend to surprise Serena with a visit,* Tara thought as she smiled to herself. Now that she was certain Serena would be around, she could relay that info on to Tony.

Tonya had really hit if off with one of Tara's co-worker's children. Bailey and Tonya attended the basketball camp together and had become really good friends. Of course Tonya wanted to return to

Texas next summer. Saturday's game would be their last summer outing together and Tonya was really looking forward to it. Tara had already arranged to let Tonya fly back to Georgia with Tony. This flight would be a first for her so she was overjoyed to hear her big brother would be accompanying her on her trip home.

Tony had worked three consecutive days at the fire station. He and Shawn switched duties again. Shawn had gone on a cruise with his girlfriend, so Tony agreed to work his two-day shift for him if he'd reciprocate the next weekend. Tony was really looking forward to flying to Texas. He'd never been to San Antonio before but had heard some wonderful things about its history and the River Walk. Serena had no idea he was planning to surprise her. He'd bought his ticket flying out on Friday morning and returning Monday afternoon. He was going to check out the local fire stations too while he was there. He knew he could get a glowing letter of recommendation from his boss, no problem. This was another secret he'd kept from Serena just in case she couldn't get transferred to Georgia when it was time to renew her contract. Tony knew once he got off work on Monday morning he was going to pay Kayla a visit at the office. He'd not heard from Karen, but he needed answers, and he wanted them before he left to see Serena.

Tara dialed Terry's number but decided not to three-way Tony. She needed to talk to Terry one-on-one before speaking with Tony. "Hey, Tara, how's it going?" he said when he picked up.

"I guess things are status quo, but I'm getting a little concerned. It's been over a week since Karen got the letter from Tony. Have you spoken with her lately? Do you know what's going on?" Tara asked impatiently.

"I spoke with her two days ago, and she said her contact at the clinic hadn't returned her call and that if she didn't hear from her by the end of the week, she was going to place a second call first thing Monday morning."

"Okay, well, please keep me posted," she said, trying to remain calm.

"Honey, I wouldn't have it any other way," he said, hanging up.

Tonight Serena and Tara were going to go out to dinner and maybe catch a movie. Tonya invited Bailey to go with them and spend the night at Tara's. Serena went to the bedroom and picked up her engagement ring and tried it on to make sure it still fit. She

196

decided not to wear it until she and Tony had resolved their issues. She didn't want to have to explain to everyone why things were on again and off again. So to make life simpler, she decided to leave it at home. She'd spoken to her parents a couple of times since she'd returned, and they were still the proud and overjoyed in-laws to be. She didn't have the heart to mention what had been going on. Maybe things would work out for her and Tony, and she wouldn't have to tell them at all.

Melissa called Kayla at home. She'd decided not to call her at the clinic again until things cooled off. Kayla was getting ready to take Lauren to a birthday party at the recreation center, so she didn't talk long. "Let's do lunch next week," Melissa said, "you choose the place."

"Sounds good, I'll give you a call to let you know what day is good for me."

"Okay, have fun at the party." When Melissa hung up, she started working on her plan B. If she couldn't get Tony in bed within the next week, she would have to use drastic measures. Two options came to mind. The first was to sabotage the condom if they make it that far. The second option made her shudder as she asked herself how far she was willing to go to win Tony over.

It was Sunday night, and Tony had just returned from a house fire. A child was trapped in the bedroom as it burned, and Tony's team was the first to arrive. The mother who saved two younger children was not able to get to her six-year-old son. She was devastated as were the firemen. As they somberly returned to the station, Tony realized he was crying as he got off the truck. He hit the shower and knew he needed to talk to Serena. She was the only thing in his life that could ease the pain. As he listened to the phone ringing, he quickly grew disappointed when she didn't pick up, so he left a brief message. He went to his bunk and searched the channels for *In Living Color*. He knew this show would give him something to smile about. It was his favorite comedy show. As soon as he relaxed, his cell phone started ringing. He figured it was one of the guys, so he picked it up without looking at the caller ID. "Tony, what's wrong?" Serena asked, full of concern. He turned the TV off. "Hey, baby, what makes you think something's wrong?" he asked, trying to downplay the message he'd left and the tragedy he'd witnessed earlier. "Tony, I know you better than you think, and I'm concerned about you," she said, this time a bit more anxiously. His reluctance to answer made her heart sink. She immediately thought it had to deal with Melissa and the baby. *Oh my god.* She began to panic. *What if he'd found out it was true, and she was pregnant with his child?* Serena felt sick as she plopped on the bed and braced herself for the worse. Tony finally spoke. "We lost a child tonight," he said, barely audible. "What?" Serena was alarmed as the only words she could make out was "lost child." Her thoughts began to race uncontrollably. *Did Melissa lose her baby?* she thought to herself and began to feel sad. "We lost a little boy in a house fire tonight," Tony said, this time clearer. "Oh no," Serena said instantly. "I'm so sorry. Are you okay?" She knew by the sound of his voice he was devastated but felt the need to ask anyway. "Yeah, I'm coping, and I am much better now that I'm talking to you," he said as Serena's heart melted. Tony was glad; this was one of the few times Serena decided to return his call right away. The station had a grief counselor on call, and he would be arriving soon to address Tony's team. The two of them laughed and talked for a few minutes before he headed to formation for the counseling.

When he awoke, it was six forty-five. Roll call was at seven thirty, so he had just enough time to grab a bite to eat. The next shift would be there shortly, and he would be able to go home for the first time in four days. After last night, he was more than ready to be in the comfort of his own home. He said a prayer for the little boy and his family before he fell asleep that night.

Kayla arrived to work at eight thirty. The clinic opened in thirty minutes, which meant she had enough time to prep and restock the exam rooms before the first patient. Dr. Spencer was out of the office today, so she'd help Gwen at the front desk as much as she needed. Dr. Spencer was out of the office again on Wednesday afternoon. She figured that would be the perfect day to have lunch with Melissa.

It was nine twenty when Tony pulled into the parking lot. He looked around to make sure Melissa was nowhere in sight. When he entered the waiting area, he asked Gwen if he could speak with Kayla. "Oh, she's in the back. She'll be right out." Gwen recognized Tony from his last visit. He took a seat in the waiting room and watched the Weather Channel. He paid close attention to what the weather in San Antonio was going to be for the weekend. He heard the door down the hallway close and saw Kayla coming toward the front. She looked troubled, and he wondered if that was her reaction to seeing him or if something else was going on. He watched her while she spoke with Gwen. "Oh, Kayla, you have a message," Gwen said as she handed her the message she'd taken earlier. "She says it's the second time she's called," Gwen said as Kayla reluctantly unfolded the paper and saw the message was from Karen at Quest. Kayla knew this game was about to be over. Not only was Karen calling again, but now she's calling the main clinic number and not her direct line as she'd done before. Kayla knew it would only be a matter of time before she asked someone else for assistance. She hated avoiding her friend, but she couldn't lose her job. She placed the note in her pocket as Gwen informed her that Tony was waiting to speak with her. *Oh no, when it rains it pours,* she thought. Two people inquiring about Melissa's pregnancy on the same day only minutes apart. She felt trapped as she tried to anticipate Tony's questions but didn't have enough time to think things through clearly. She could put off returning Karen's call until the end of the day, but Tony was here now. Thinking quickly, she grabbed her purse and asked Gwen if she wanted a coffee from Starbucks. As she approached Tony, he rose to his feet and extended his hand thinking about Tara's take on the whole situation believing Kayla was somehow connected to Melissa's scheme. He wanted to be her ally. After all, she had something he needed, and he wasn't about to mess it up, so he was cordial to her. Before he could say a word, Kayla said, "Would you like to take a walk?" Tony thought this was a strange gesture but decided to go along with it. "Sure," he said as they walked out of the clinic door together. They were silent until they reached Starbucks when she asked if he wanted a coffee. Tony thanked her but said no, he just needed to ask her some questions. While they were waiting in line, Tony said, "I really need your help." Kayla was quiet until she'd gotten her coffee, and they took a seat at a table in the rear of the establishment. "What can I do for you, Tony?" she said with a strained smile and looking down at the table. Tony started speaking slowly, "I am racking my brain trying to figure out how I got myself in this predicament." Kayla didn't ask what he was talking about because she knew he suspected her. Tony went on. "I have some very strong suspicions about Melissa's pregnancy. Kayla, if Melissa is really pregnant, I would take care of my child without hesitation; but Melissa's not been herself since we split. I just need to know if she's out to get me for moving on with someone else or if this thing is real," he said sincerely. Kayla looked up from the table and into his eyes for the first time since they'd arrived at the coffee shop. She knew what this was doing to him, and Melissa had no right to play with anyone's life like that. "I just need to know for sure. Now I have to admit she's doing and saying all the right things, but too many things just don't add up." Tony didn't want to show his hand, so he stopped with that. Kayla swallowed hard and knew she wouldn't be able to continue this charade for Melissa. Tony saw her shift in her seat as she grew very uncomfortable. "Look, you don't have to tell me everything, but a yes or no would be nice." He smiled, and this caused her to relax too. "I know Melissa is your friend, but look at what she's doing to me and to you. With Melissa, life is all about Melissa." Kayla finally spoke, "Did you bother to ask Melissa what you're asking me?" This shocked Tony as he thought about what she was asking and had to be honest with her. He'd never once asked Melissa whether or not she was really pregnant. "No, but I don't feel I can get an honest answer out of her. I can't trust her anymore; and since you work at the clinic, it would be impossible for me to believe you didn't know the truth." Kayla shook her head and said, "I'm sorry, Tony, I can't do this. Please don't show up at my job again unannounced." She stood up and walked away from the table. Tony was stunned by her demeanor and her directness. He had tried to do this the easy way and protect her at the same time, but it didn't go so well. The longer he sat there, the more irritated he became. *Since she's not willing to talk to me out of the office, maybe she'll be more willing to talk to me when I show up on Wednesday when Dr. Spencer returns.* He'd overheard Gwen tell a patient that the good doctor would be in the office on Wednesday at eight thirty, and so would Tony. When Kayla got back to the office with the coffee, Melissa had called. She went in the break room to call her back. "Hey, girl, what's up?" Melissa said.

"Oh, not too much. What can I do for you?" Kayla asked, getting straight to the point.

"I need you to do me another favor." But before she could finish her statement, Kayla had gotten upset after realizing Melissa was trying to take advantage of her. Melissa was putting her family and her job at risk asking for these ridiculous favors. Kayla was upset that Melissa continued the charade and seemed to have no regrets. Melissa wanted her to mail a confirmation of pregnancy with a progress report to Tony's house. No one would have to know. "The letter would go directly to Tony," Melissa insisted. "I need to buy some time."

"I don't know if I can do that," Kayla cut her off.

Melissa continued as if she hadn't noticed the irritation in her friend's voice. "Okay, well, think about it. You can let me know over lunch. When can you get away?" she asked.

"Wednesday at eleven o'clock is good for me. I'll let you know where later," Kayla said. Melissa had gotten under Kayla's skin from the moment she opened her mouth to ask for another favor that she forgot to tell her about Tony. Now all she wanted to do was get her off the phone. When she hung up, she wondered how many more favors Melissa could possibly ask for without feeling the least bit guilty. She couldn't afford to get implicated in this scheme and needed to find a way to keep her name in the clear. She knew Melissa was running out of rope, and sooner or later she would hang herself, and Kayla needed to put some distance between the two.

Before Kayla got off that day, she knew exactly what she needed to do. She called information for Tony's number and told herself she was doing the right thing as she dialed his number. He was surprised to hear from her after their earlier conversation, but he was glad she called. They spoke briefly, and she asked Tony to be in position NLT eleven o'clock on Wednesday. Kayla got off the phone suddenly having the urge for Chinese food.

Tony was practically walking on air after his conversation with Kayla. After their initial conversation that morning, he knew she wouldn't be willing to divulge anything to him. Maybe playing the "good guy" role worked after all. He had a new sense of respect for Kayla. It took some courage to make that call. Now he finally felt he was one step closer to getting closure. He didn't bother calling Tara or Terry and didn't want to involve them again until this whole thing was over. They'd already done so much for him. He had to work Wednesday and Thursday before he got his four days off. He was already getting excited about his trip. He felt that he and Serena had been apart long enough. He turned the radio up loud and began cleaning up the house. He danced over to the desk and pulled out his tape recorder. "You never know when this might come in handy," he said to himself as he placed it in his overnight bag he took to the station every day. He wanted to make sure he had the proof he needed to clear his name.

He got up early the next morning to mow the yard and clean the pool. He knew four days was a long time to be away from his house. He called Brian and asked him to check on the house while he was away.

CONFIRMATION

It was ten thirty on Wednesday. Tony told his lieutenant he had a very important appointment at ten forty-five that he couldn't miss. Once he cleared it with his boss, he asked Mario to borrow his car. He didn't want to take any chance on his truck being spotted. When he showed up at Peking Duck in uniform, he immediately wanted to be incognito. He changed shirts in Mario's car so as not to attract any unnecessary attention. When he walked in, he had the tape recorder in his jacket pocket. He scanned the dining area and found the perfect booth and took a seat with his back to the front entrance. He sat with his back to another booth, which was where Melissa and Kayla would be sitting. Tony had already coordinated with his waitress to keep that table open. The booths had high backs and were separated by wooden walls with plants arranged on top for privacy. Tony checked the tape to make sure it was rewound. He pressed the record button before positioning the tape recorder under the greenery on the wall. He knew Melissa would be sitting with her back against the wall. It was ten after eleven when the girls showed up, and Tony was getting nervous. When he saw Melissa coming toward him, he slid over to the corner so as to be concealed, to keep out of her view. As the girls went to get their food, he made eye contact with Kayla as she allowed Melissa to walk ahead and glanced back in Tony's direction. Kayla looked completely comfortable with the arrangement while Melissa talked nonstop as she always did. When they returned, they sat and ate in silence for a while. Tony was beginning to wonder if Kayla had warned Melissa of what was going on. Finally, Melissa spoke, "So, Kayla, what do you think about the favor I asked you about?"

"Melissa, I told you I couldn't do that again. I'm risking my job and the ability to care for my family."

"It's only a letter, and no one has to know," Melissa whined. Hearing this from Melissa caused Tony to sit up straight, realizing he'd heard part of the confession he came to hear. She continued, "I told you it would be completely safe, Kayla."

"Yeah, that's the same thing you said about the first letter," Kayla said, wanting Tony to hear everything.

"Girl, you are too paranoid. I told you to leave Tony to me—just do your part, and he won't be any trouble." Tony had to laugh at Melissa's calmness and assuredness that he could be handled as if he was so easily convinced. He laughed to keep from standing up and confronting her. Kayla kept the conversation going. "So if you can handle him so well, why did he show up at my office?"

"Don't worry about that. You took care of it and handled it like a pro."

"Well, Melissa, that's the problem. I shouldn't have to handle anything. This is your scheme, and I don't want to play anymore. You said it wouldn't come to this, but I feel myself getting in deeper and deeper. My advice to you is to cut your losses and tell Tony the truth." Melissa let out a hearty laugh and said, "You can't be serious. I could never tell Tony what I've done—he'd kill me."

"No, you can tell him you lost the baby," Kayla urged, "and I can vouch for you." Kayla knew Melissa would never go for this version, but she didn't want to see her friend hurt either. "Look, if you continue this dangerous game, someone's going to get hurt."

"Hey, maybe you didn't hear me," Melissa said angrily. "I need to have Tony's baby. That's the only way he's going to stay with me. I love him too much to let him go. I will not consider deviating from my original plan, and that's final," Melissa snapped at Kayla. Tony was sitting there in total shock. He couldn't believe Melissa would go to such grave lengths to ruin his life. She claimed she loved him, but how could she continue lying to him especially when he no longer loved her? He wasn't sure if he ever loved her. Kayla stood up and tossed some money on the table. "Sorry, Mel, you're in for a rude awakening." She walked away from the table not looking back. Melissa was so pissed she didn't bother going after her. "She is out of her mind, and I am going to make this work," Melissa said quietly at the table. Once Tony saw Kayla walk out the exit door, he stood up and placed the tape recorder back in his jacket pocket. He walked around the wall to look at Melissa. She was sipping on her drink when she looked up into Tony's face, and she choked on her drink as Tony towered over her. She instantly felt sick not knowing how much he'd heard. As she tried to regain her composure, she asked, "What are you doing here?"

"I was sitting here enjoying my lunch until I overheard you talking about me and the imaginary child you're carrying." Melissa spilled her iced tea over the food left on her plate as she stood up to reach out to Tony. She could've died right there in the middle of the restaurant. As he turned to leave, she begged, "No, Tony wait, let me explain. I—" He cut her off in midsentence. "No, Melissa, I don't want to hear any more of your lies. I've heard all that I need to hear, and to think that we were ever a couple makes me sick," he spat.

"Tony, wait." She rushed from the table. "I love you more than you could ever imagine, and I know deep down you still love me too. Don't walk away from me like this. Please give me another chance," she said as she began to get louder.

"Melissa, your greed and deceit is going to be the death of you." Tony realized where they were as the lunch crowd began to fill up the dining area. "I never want to see you again," Tony said, surprisingly calm. "We have nothing else to discuss," he said through clenched teeth and jerked his arm from her grasp. As he got into the car and headed back to the station, he realized he felt sorry for Melissa. He was angry and relieved at the same time. He could have easily fallen for her story had he not cared enough about Serena to deliver the truth to her. He thanked God for the guidance as he made his way into traffic. He pumped up the volume as he realized the last month of hell he'd been through was over, and he was "free" again.

It was finally over, and he and Serena could go on with their lives as planned. Once back at the station, he replayed the tape and was pleased that he clearly got every word of their conversation. He three-wayed Tara and Terry and gave them the good news. They were thrilled for Tony and were relieved the nightmare was finally over. He didn't give them any details other than he had a confrontation with Melissa and that she'd admitted to everything. There would be plenty of time for that later. Right now, he had another important phone call to make, and this time it was to Karen. After reaching Karen at the lab, he told her that he'd gotten his answer and thanked her for her help. She agreed to shred the letter and told Tony she was out of it but to let her know if he ever needed anything in the future.

Tony's third phone call was to Kayla. She picked up on the first ring. "Kayla, I know what you did for me wasn't easy. Thank you for being the bigger person. I really appreciate your helping me get to the bottom of this mess. Everything's been taken care of with Karen, and she's agreed to shred the letter and forget about it." Kayla let out a loud sigh and said, "Thank you, thank you for allowing me a way out, Tony. I knew it was bad business, but I was trying to help out a friend that I cared a lot about but then discovered she didn't care about me or my well-being enough to call this whole thing off. I felt trapped and didn't know how to undo the damage I'd done."

"It's okay," Tony reassured her, knowing that he very well could still be searching for answers had she not come forward. "We've all done some terrible things in the past that we regret, but the most important thing is that you learn from it and make sure you don't make the same mistake again. Look, Melissa doesn't know that we were working on this together, so don't feel guilty about doing what you did. If you are willing to forgive her and should the two of you become friends again, you don't have to worry about me mentioning our collaboration." Kayla was floored. She had done something to ruin this man's life, and not only did he save her job but he was willing to spare her friendship with Melissa too. He was a very remarkable man, and she knew without a doubt why Melissa was so desperate to hold on to him.

SURPRISE GUEST

Serena was looking forward to spending time with Tara and Terry. She had already scheduled their appointments at the spa. Tonya wasn't into getting her nails manicured yet, but she agreed to a shampoo and style. Normally on Friday's, Tara and Serena were released early, so Serena scheduled the appointments for four o'clock to be on the safe side. It was two o'clock, and Tara was heading to her car. "Hey, Tara, where are you going?" Serena called out. "Oh, I have to run an errand," Tara said as she opened her car door. "I'll see you at the salon," she said and waved as she got into her car and drove away. Terry was already in town and had checked into his room. Tara saw him long enough to say hi before leaving for the airport. When Tara pulled up to the airport, she searched for Delta Air Lines logo. She spotted Tony standing outside with his bags. She was so excited about her brother coming to Texas. He saw her Honda Civic pull over to the curb and started toward her. She jumped out of the car and raised the trunk as Tony approached her. He could barely get his bags in the trunk before his sister grabbed him and hugged him tightly. He hugged her back, feeling the excitement rubbing off on him. "Congratulations, Tony, congratulations," she said.

"Thank you, sis," Tony said as he remembered all the drama Melissa had put him through. "I'm just glad this whole thing is over. Now I've got to get to Serena. I haven't spoken with her since Wednesday after I found out, but I didn't tell her. I wanted to wait until I was here," he said, thinking of how happy Serena was going to be that it was finally over. He could not wait to see her face. "I couldn't have done this without the help and support you and Terry provided. That means a lot to me." They pulled up to Terry's hotel, and Tara was hanging up with Terry when she pulled up to the main entrance. "Terry will be right down. Tell him I'll be back around eight o'clock to get you two."

Tara tooted her horn as she pulled out into the traffic. It was four o'clock and knew Serena was always punctual and probably at the salon looking at her watch.

The girls sat side by side getting their feet massaged and pampered. Tonya was already under the dryer. She was spending the night with Bailey so the girls could go out. Tara suggested she, Serena, and Terry go to dinner tonight at Pappadeaux Seafood Kitchen. They had the best seafood in Texas. It didn't take much to convince Serena to eat good seafood. It was her favorite, and Tara knew that. "Why not, I'm already dolled up with nowhere to go and nothing to do." The girls parted and went home to shower and change. It was seven forty-five when Tara pulled into the hotel's parking lot. She saw some of the Miami Heat players down in the lobby as she waited for Terry and Tony to come down. When they stepped off the elevator, Tara lit up. Terry was wearing a sports coat and jeans and looked like he was going to a photo shoot. Tony looked just as handsome as they approached her. His teammates turned to look at Tara when Terry greeted her with a kiss on the cheek, not wanting to mess up her makeup. They started teasing him about it. He turned to say, "Tara, this is everyone," as he looked around the lobby. "Everyone, this is my girlfriend, Tara." Tara was beaming from the attention and the introduction as they said good night and headed for her car.

Serena slipped on her floral-print sundress and tan sandals as she prepared herself for a night out with good friends. She began to miss Tony. After all, whenever she and Tara were with Terry, Tony was there too. This would be different, but she knew she would feel closer to Tony just by hanging out with them. She walked over to her jewelry box and looked at her engagement ring, which she did every day, and hoped that one day she would be able to wear this ring proudly and not have to worry about someone stealing her happiness away. She placed the ring on her finger, and this time she decided that was where it belonged. It was eight twelve, and Tara would be there in three minutes. She picked up the phone and dialed Tony. His voice mail picked up, so she left a message. "Hey, baby, I just wanted you to know I miss you like crazy. Call me soon." Before she hung up, she said, "I wish you were here." Serena was still smiling to herself about the message she'd left as she heard a car pull up to the house. She went to the bathroom to check her hair and lipstick before she walked out. Thinking Tara should have rung the doorbell by now, Serena hung up the phone and headed to the front door. She swung the door open and stared at the familiar man standing there. She knew who it was but couldn't force herself to believe Tony was standing on her doorstep. Serena looked down at the shoes then the way he wore those jeans. She noticed he had on a nice sports coat and a white shirt underneath. She finally mustered up enough courage to look up at his face and immediately started screaming as she looked into Tony's eyes. She threw her arms around him, and he did the same. They completely blocked out everything that was taking place around them as they hugged, kissed, and cried right there on Serena's front porch.

They made it to Pappadeaux Seafood Kitchen around nine o'clock and didn't have to wait long for a seat, but the four of them were starving. Tony told them what happened at the table. Tony had told Serena it was finally over as they stood on her porch, but now she heard the details. They were all amazed at Melissa's deceit but were relieved the whole thing was a hoax. They enjoyed their meal as Tony looked at Serena's finger, realizing how good it made him feel to see her still willing to marry him. Serena saw him looking down at her hand and thanked God she decided to wear the ring again. Tony turned to Serena and said, "Serena, I am so sorry for putting you through this hell. Now we can put this whole nightmare behind us and get on with our plans. Thank you for sticking by me and for believing in me. You have made me a happy man, and I love you."

"I love you too."

EPILOGUE

It was their first week back since their honeymoon. Serena rolled over to turn off the alarm clock. There was nothing like an afternoon nap, which newlyweds often took advantage of. She stared at her husband's peaceful and handsome face and set the second alarm for him. She kissed him as she got out of the bed. It was the first day of summer, and summers in Texas were nothing to play with. She eased the door shut behind her as she walked out to the mailbox. She opened a familiar envelope as she tried to figure out what it was and who sent it. She ripped it open as her enthusiasm grew, and she laughed with excitement when she discovered it was a wedding invitation to Tara and Terry's wedding next August. She looked down and rubbed her stomach and said, "Looks like Aunt Tara's getting married, TJ." Tony was putting on his uniform when she went back into the bedroom to give him the news. She figured he'd be up early today. After all, it was his first day at work at the San Antonio Fire Department.